THINGS IMPROBABLE

EDITED BY ATLIN MERRICK

Improbable
PRESS

First published by Improbable Press in 2023

Improbable Press is an imprint of:
Clan Destine Press
www.clandestinepress.com.au
PO Box 121, Bittern Victoria 3918 Australia

National Library of Australia Cataloguing-In-Publication data:

Improbable Press
Things Improbable

978-1-922904-26-3 (hb)
978-1-922904-23-2 (pb)
978-1-922904-24-9 (eb)

Cover artwork by © Holly Humphries
Layout & Typesetting by Dimitra Stathopoulos

Improbable Press
improbablepress.com

For all of you who create and dream,
please keep going

*

And for Joseph Carey Merrick
always and forever

CONTENTS

EVERY DAY IMPROBABLE

There's a pretty blue planet somewhere far out there where it's said to rain glass.

There are several species of chicken with bones that are black.

Yours, mine, every single human's tongue print is unique.

And there are more viruses on earth than there are stars in the entire universe.

Our world is full of so very many improbable things, and yet even with all that wonder, isn't there a shivery delight in imagining even more, stranger still?

Yes?

Good, because in *Things Improbable* nearly three dozen writers bring us things more peculiar, like the day when shadows come down from the trees to at last share our terra firma. Like the gentlest of ways to keep demons at bay. Like a place where impossible limbs kind of…grow.

Distant worlds are all well and good, but there's a special frisson to stories that take place in a nearby neighborhood or lake, in the suburb beside *this* one, and the orchard behind *that*. Improbable things appear in the back garden, happen during a walk in the woods, or live inside your house right now. Though do go careful, for here you'll find themes of profound loss and struggle, too.

Now, kindly budge over and make room for monsters and bugs and golems, for strange, stranger, and very strangest still.

Atlin Merrick
Winter 2023

INSTRUMENT OF DESTRUCTION
Dominick Cancilla

"Is this delay unavoidable? I'm going to be late for my flight."

"You'll be fine. I just need to ask your friend here a few questions. Sir, if you could—"

"It won't answer you."

"Excuse me?"

"It can't talk."

"Do you mean he can't speak English?"

"It can't talk. It has no lungs."

"Let's step aside so we're not holding up the security line. If you could both follow me?"

"This seems unnecessary."

"It will only take a minute."

"The fool wouldn't accept my tickets. They are completely aboveboard and paid for. I have my valid passport."

"The officer was doing his job, ma'am."

"Doctor."

"Doctor. I'm sure we can get this sorted out in no time."

"I have no time. I am on urgent business."

"Your flight doesn't leave for over an hour. Even if you hurry, you'll have to wait anyway."

"Harumph."

"Now that we're out of traffic, there are a few things that need clarifying so you can be on your way. Are you in a position to answer questions for your friend since—"

"Not my friend."

"Well, for your companion?"

"Not my companion."

"Partner?"

"Not my partner."

"But you are traveling together, right? He—"

"It."

"Sorry, it's carrying both of your suitcases. That seems like you're together."

"We are not traveling together any more than my pocketbook and I are traveling together. It is my possession."

"Hey, your personal relationship isn't any of my business – no need to go there. Let's concentrate on straightening out the issue with your tickets."

"There is no issue with my tickets."

"I'm afraid there is. You have two tickets."

"I do. First class, non-stop to Düsseldorf."

"The problem is that there are two of you—"

"There are not."

"Well, for the airline's purposes there are two of you."

"There should not be."

"—but both of your tickets are in your name."

"That is perfectly sensible. I am traveling alone but need extra room for my possessions."

"Are you trying to argue that this is some kind of support animal?"

"It's not an animal."

"Because we only allow service animals, not support animals, and it has to be a dog. We don't even allow miniature horses anymore."

"Not a dog. Not a horse. Not an animal. In service. This has become tedious. Do you not have terrorists and smugglers on whom to spend your time?"

"This is for your benefit, but you're right — this is probably taking longer than it has to. Let's see if we can handle it another way. Can you please ask — what's his name?"

"Its name, and I will not tell you its name because that would give you power over it."

"This is going to get confusing if I can't call it something."

"Fine. Esther."

"Esther?"

"Yes. I had a great-aunt named Esther. She taught me to play the sumponyah."

"All right. Can you please ask Esther to take off its helmet?"

"It's not wearing a helmet."

"Then can you ask it to remove its mask?"

"It's not wearing a mask."

"Look, I'm trying to move you along here and we keep tangling up in vocabulary. What I want is for Esther to remove whatever it is that Esther has over its head so that I can see what Esther looks like."

"Then you will be disappointed. This is a solid piece of iron, cast into this shape from molten metal of absolute purity. There are no seams, flaws, or openings."

"Then how did Esther get in there?"

"There is no 'in there.' Do you have in mind that Esther is some kind of suit?"

"I thought you were coming from a comic book convention or something."

"We are coming from a cave in which I prayed upon the names of God for forty days and nights before inscribing a glyph of TRUTH upon my creation in a manner passed down through the ancient writings of my spiritual predecessors."

"It does look like a suit."

"It is not. In a technical sense, Esther is naked."

"The appearance of clothing is remarkable."

"Thank you. I fashioned it myself."

"Then it's a robot."

"It's not a robot."

"You mean it's an android, then?"

"It is not a robot of any sort, it is a golem."

"A what?"

"A golem. Are you having trouble understanding me? Should we speak in another language?"

"I don't think that would help."

"Because I am conversant in fourteen languages and read fluently thirty-six others."

"English is fine."

"We could have this conversation in Covenantal Paleo-Hebrew, which I can speak, read, and write with perfect clarity, and which might be appropriate for the subject. Although now that I think about it, the word I'd probably use for 'robot' in Covenantal Paleo-Hebrew is the same word I'd use for 'golem,' which would be ironic and ambiguous."

"That's a kind of machine, though?"

"Was your education neglected? It is not a machine."

"But there's gears or actuators or something inside to make it move."

"Esther is hollow, completely empty aside from incidental air, the force of my will, and an invocation of the Divine."

"But it can walk."

"Obviously."

"And it's not a machine."

"We have covered this."

"But you bought a plane ticket for it."

"How else was I supposed to get it on the plane?"

"That makes me think you're playing games, this is a suit, and there's someone in there without a passport that you're trying to escort to Germany."

"There is nobody in there."

"Am I correct that Esther doesn't have a passport?"

"The history of Celtic grammar I brought to read on the plane also doesn't have a passport."

"If this isn't a person, why didn't you check it as luggage?"

"I tried. Esther is too heavy to be checked as luggage."

"Too heavy?"

"Six hundred pounds."

"Seriously?"

"Have I been anything but serious? They suggested that it be shipped as cargo, but then there would be issues with customs."

"And you can't ship living things as cargo."

"Esther is not living."

"Maybe a casket? They do ship caskets."

"Esther is also not dead. Can we get to the point of your interrupting my trip?"

"Well, to be perfectly honest, I'm not sure how we can let Esther here on the plane under regulations. It acts and – if you ignore its hair and clothing being a solid mass – mainly looks like a person, but it doesn't have a passport. You say it isn't a person, but you're treating it as one."

"I am not."

"You bought it a ticket."

"I bought myself two tickets."

"What about your luggage, then? You are allowed one carry-on piece and one personal item, but Esther here is carrying two suitcases. If you have two suitcases as carry-ons, it implies two people."

"It does not. The rule is one carry-on per ticket, not per person. I have two tickets and two carry-ons."

"But if Esther isn't a person, then it's luggage, which means you have three."

"Esther isn't a carry-on; it's my personal item."

"It doesn't work that way."

"Then can we agree it should and I will be on my way?"

"I can't do that. Look, I'm sure we can find a way to fix this, but you'll need to work with me. All right?"

"If it will move things along."

"Let's take this from the top. What is your purpose of traveling to Düsseldorf?"

"My purpose is not to travel to Düsseldorf. My purpose is to travel to Langweiligestadt."

"For business?"

"There I will rain punishment upon all for the insults with which I was battered in childhood. None will be spared, from the spark not yet born to the ancestor turned to dust in the grave, all will suffer."

"Sounds serious."

"As a divine judgment."

"You must have significant issues with those people."

"They made fun of my reading our traditional tales and said I played the sumponyah like a drunken duck."

"Got it. And this town's near Düsseldorf?"

"No. There's a gem and mineral show in Krefeld where I will be purchasing three gems unearthed in the diaspora that, when placed in the sockets in Esther's temple, will allow it to shine rays of colored light to illuminate, dazzle, confound, raze, or slay as desired. I'll be taking a chartered flight to the airstrip below Langweiligestadt after that."

"So, part business, part – family issues?"

"How is this your airport's business?"

"It's really not. I'm just trying to get a big picture so I can find a solution we can all live with."

"This is foolishness."

"I don't make the rules. Speaking of which, can I assume you won't have any trouble getting the suitcases through x-ray?"

"All prohibited materials have been abandoned or destroyed. There's a ritualistically prepared century-old goat head in the green bag, but I have an import/export permit and it's not preserved in liquid."

"Good. Esther won't fit in the x-ray. Any problem with it being patted down by hand?"

"It will not attack without a command."

"What I meant was, it's not delicate? Doesn't have any breakable parts?"

"Esther is indestructible. Should you run into it with a tank, have a care for the tank."

"That's good. I can make an argument about treating it like a person to help it pass security checks, but that doesn't help us with the plane ticket. And whatever solution we come up with needs to work both here and when you go through customs in Germany."

"Are you proposing a disguise?"

"I can't imagine how we'd disguise someone–"

"Something."

"–something over six feet tall with a complexion like a cast-iron stove. Besides, I'm not willing to break regs, but I don't mind assisting you in bending them a bit. You seem like a nice person and I don't want you to miss your rock party."

"Mineral show."

"Right. Besides, growing up in Ranchview, Iowa, I got teased for playing the trumpet. I never really felt a sense of community until I joined the Marines. You get some sympathy points from me for that."

"I don't ask for your sympathy. The people of Langweiligestadt get none of mine."

"Like I said, ex-marine. I get it. The trumpet, though – that gives me an idea. Is it okay if I give Esther a little knock on the chest?"

"As you wish."

"Let's see. Interesting."

"You can hear it is hollow, as I said."

"Huh. Can you get it to knock on its own chest? Lightly, like I just did?"

"She will obey my commands without question. Creation, knock upon your chest as this officer has done."

"Whoa – you hear that?"

"I must admit that was surprising."

"Like a bell. Now ask it to do it again, but more of a slap and with its mouth open a little."

"Creation, do as the officer has described."

"Damn!"

"My word."

"I'm no expert, but I'd swear that was a pure note."

"Does this mean something to you?"

"Maybe. Do you know what hamboning is?"

"I am a vegetarian."

"No, not ham bones – hamboning. Doing the hambone. It's a way to make music by slapping your body."

"I am not familiar with this."

"It's something my granddad used to do, but I never had a talent for it myself. Let me think for a second how to show you."

"That may not be necessary. Are you proposing this is something Esther could do?"

"That's what I was thinking."

"And there is a reason beyond your own entertainment?"

"Definitely."

"Then all I need do is command it. By its nature, Esther understands all language, so if 'hamboning' is a word, Esther knows the meaning even if I do not. What would you request?"

"I can't think of any of the songs Granddad used to do. Could it do The Marine Corps Hymn in hambone?"

"I am vaguely familiar with that piece, but my knowledge is no boundary here. Esther, do as the officer requests."

"___"

"___"

"I–"

"Oh, my."

"That's – it's–"

"Esther, enough."

"___"

"Officer?"

"___"

"Officer, are you crying?"

"It's – I'm okay. Sorry. That was so – it was beautiful. It was – I can't even describe it."

"We have drawn attention."

"Holy – listen to that applause! I've never heard anything like it before. Not in the airport."

"This was an impressive performance and revealed a use for the golem I had not contemplated, but I don't see what it earns us."

"Hang on a second. Wave and smile to people. Nod appreciatively, as if their reaction is what you expected."

"I am not accustomed to this kind of attention. It feels unnatural."

"But it's nice though, right?"

"I suppose."

"Then I think we have the solution to our problem."

"How so?"

"There's no exception for giving a seat to oversized baggage or non-living people or things that look like robots, but you can definitely arrange to purchase an extra seat for a musical instrument."

"Certainly not a piano."

"No, not a piano. But a bass fiddle, a tuba, a valuable violin – sure. I'd only have to make a little adjustment on the computer, Esther becomes a musical instrument, and you are good to go."

"That would be welcome."

"Glad to hear it. And now that you know Esther can hambone, any thoughts?"

"How do you mean?"

"Well, look at the reaction you got."

"Americans idolize military songs."

"It's more than that. The tone was incredible. I've never heard anything like it."

"Nor have I. I expect rarified energies of the Divine vibrate well with musical performance."

"Then what about taking it on the road? Go on stage. Fill a concert hall."

"Perhaps after the rightful obliteration of Langweiligestadt."

"After? Why not before? Think of the fame! The money!"

"I have no use for either."

"Then think of the envy. Think of the jealousy. Think of the sorrow in the hearts of every single person who deeply regrets mistreating you when you were growing up now that you are famous and renowned beyond anything they could have dreamed."

"Keep talking."

"Think about Esther up there on the stage, giving a light show with those gems, performing music like nobody has ever heard before."

"Maybe with accompaniment on a sumponyah?"

"Sure! Why not?"

"It would be nice not to have to hide from international accusations of genocide."

"Yes, that."

"I will take your suggestion under advisement. You can now make the change to our ticket?"

"It'll be done before you get your bags through the checkpoint. You can be on your way."

"Thank you, officer. Your assistance is greatly appreciated."

"Glad to help."

"If it should come to pass that there is a performance in Iowa, perhaps we can stop by Ranchview and Esther can teach select individuals a lesson about properly appreciating the trumpet."

"I would like that."

"Then we will be on our way. Creation, Stars and Stripes Forever, if you please."

FL☺WER
Sarah Tollok

Had someone ever called out and asked the name of the large, lone figure moving soundlessly through the trees – and they actually understood the low, rumbling yet melodic response – then that someone would know the figure called themselves Flower.

However, the rare moments when Flower or their kind have been seen, no one has ever thought to ask them their name. They have thought to take a picture, or even raise a shotgun, dreams of tabloid fame running through their minds. Some run screaming in the other direction, yelling, "Sásq'ec" or, later, "Bigfoot!" Mostly, though – more than one would think – eyes glide right over Flower and their kin despite their large and imposing stature. After all, they are never in one place for very long. Or it may be more precise to say they are never on one plane of existence for very long.

Flower has wandered these parts for as long as they can remember, though it is many different versions of the same forested mountain range. Sometimes, as frequently as every few steps, Flower shifts. The shift tickles and tingles Flower's surface, all of their individual strands of fur standing on end, dancing. Then the air itself ripples. For a moment, there is a dizzying rush of duality. Then, the shift settles, and there is a different reality than there was the step before.

Mostly, the forests are beautiful and verdant. But sometimes, they are stripped clean of all life, a rolling nothingness as far as the eye can see. Some versions are underwater, tall tree stumps holding fast against currents and acting as young reefs. Some have taller, rougher mountains, with a liquid heat flowing not far under Flower's impressively large but tender and agile feet.

Flower tries to avoid shifting into the existences that are harsh or uninhabitable for them, but they have had a few scares in their long lifetime. There is a short window, as the shift is subsiding, when one can change one's mind about fully settling in, can continue the journey until a kinder destination presents itself.

Flower loves this field on the edge of this particular forest. It's filled with their namesake with so many different faces. As they settle in, Flower and the little flowers of the field are one and Flower feels the flow of nutrients coming up from the roots. They feel the new leaves and petals unfurling in the sun. They feel the flowers' placid yet persistent hope for the vibrations that mean bees are visiting and making their efforts worthwhile.

On the edge of this field, within some existences, there is a little girl. She lives across a strip of long flat black rock, at the far end of a field of strangely uniform tall grass that her family harvests and tills and replants and harvests and tills. The flowers of their field cower and turn away from the sickness the girl's people spray upon the grass, so the girl walks into Flowers' field. She doesn't appear to like to look upon her house. She sways in the breeze that stirs Flower's fur and the many blooms, and she breathes and breathes. Flower finds themself breathing with her, and lingering longer. The sun is warm and bright. It glints off the drops that run down the girl's cheeks. Flower flexes their toes into the soil, then takes one quiet step, then another, out of the shadow of the trees. The girl finally turns her head towards Flower. For the very first time, with this little girl, Flower is seen. The girl doesn't waver. She regards Flower, then faintly begins to smile.

Being seen and not feared is a new sensation for Flower. They take another step towards the girl. The girl's fingers lift, flutter, she starts to raise her hand, to reach. But a sound on the breeze cuts through the peace of the moment. The girl spins in recognition and clutches her thin arms around herself. The sound comes again, a voice, laced with rage and sharp edges like the loud thing with blades that cuts down their grass.

The girl whispers something to Flower. But even if Flower understood her language, the wind sweeps the words away, and the girl returns to her home without looking back.

Flower watches until they can no longer see the girl, then takes a step, shifts.

Flower goes back to their wanderings, but finds themself waiting at the edge of the little girl's meadow even more than before, even in the seasons and realities where there are no flowers in bloom. Even when there is no house, Flower still looks for the girl.

Then, after so very many shifts, there she is. She is bigger now. She is still thin as a sapling, still sways in the wind, but there is a strength there too. There is a weight to her that cannot be seen with eyes alone. Flower can't be sure that it is the same plane where they met the girl before. It doesn't matter, though. The girl turns to Flower, as if expecting to see them. And there is the smile, smaller than before, and filled with the tentative but brave anticipation that Flower senses in the meadow blooms when they come up early, pushing through the last of the snow, impatient and insistent despite the threat of a killing frost.

Over many seasons, and many more shifts, Flower sees and nears the girl, but she is always called away before they can meet properly. The girl becomes a woman. The woman swells with a child. Later it is the cries of the child that call the woman away from the meadow. The woman grows gray, her limbs hard, and over the years she sometimes wears dark bruises just under the edges of her old dress.

But the woman always turns to see Flower, always smiles, and her hand reaches for Flower, if only the briefest twitch, the smallest hint of movement.

Flower sees many things change over time and across the many realities they shift through. The worlds where everything is in ruin become more plentiful, harder to avoid. The blossoms of the meadow become harder to find. Flower has scars from being buffeted by fast moving machines they were not able to dodge quickly enough, and panic and pain make shifting harder. The shifts feel more and more like running away through a thickening, clinging fog, rather than the light and curious exploration they used to be.

Flower shifts with nearly every step now, settling only when they are very weary.

They try to stop looking for the girl, the woman, the old woman. They try to save themself from the inevitable truth that the woman will someday no longer exist by thinking she is already gone. Flower hopes she found the peace she had always been looking for in the meadow.

Flower is tired.

They sit on the edge of the meadow, one that is nearly intact. There are even some bees; they are getting harder to find as well. Flower allows themself to just be in this moment, sucking on honeysuckle. For one so big, it takes very little to sustain them. Flower is patiently holding out some of the delicate yellow flowers, hoping for a bee, when they see the woman.

She is very gray, more bent than before, but still walks with sure steps on bare feet. She holds her head up to the sky, facing the wind. Then she reaches out, but not for Flower.

Flower feels it, the barest resonant ripple in the thin curtain that hangs between planes. And it isn't Flower who's doing it.

The woman isn't just reaching with her arms, she is *reaching*. She is trying to shift.

But she's trying too hard. The fabric between realities cannot be ripped open or pushed aside with force. It will resist those efforts. But the old woman can't help it. The hope that she carries in her from when she was a little girl has evolved from shy, to sure, to strong, to desperate. The woman is reaching with all of herself. She can feel it isn't working and this hinders her efforts, making her push that much harder, and making the curtain resist that much more.

There comes a voice calling from the house, sounding more annoyed than worried.

This time, the woman doesn't turn back. Instead she looks for Flower, and she takes a step towards them.

Flower walks to the woman, placing more of their large footsteps in one reality than they have in a very long time. As Flower nears, the woman's expression fills with relief, and her reaching becomes less frantic. The curtain calms and thins.

Flower finally takes the woman's hand. The woman smiles like Flower has never seen her smile before, and Flower finds themself smiling as well. A loneliness that Flower didn't realize they had been carrying, heavier with every step for so very long, melts away like ice clinging to blades of grass in the spring. The two new and yet long-time friends beam so bright at one another that the blooms around them feel it and start to turn in their incremental way towards the warmth of their joy.

The calling voice grows nearer. Flower can feel eyes upon them, and the voice changes to fear and violence. But Flower feels no fear, and neither does the woman.

The woman's hairs all stand on end and ebb with the flow of the stream of realities that open for them. She giggles like a little girl, and rubs her thumb back and forth through the fur on the back of Flower's hand. It feels like gentle sparks, snowflakes, and the footsteps of bees.

Together, they take a step.

ODDNOQ

Iris Black

My name is Oddnoq, and I am a Figment employed by Bump in the Night (BitN), a subsidiary of the LLC, Them, Inc. Yup, I'm the Monster that lives under the bed. Not to be confused with the Thing that lives in the closet. That's a whole different division, and I try to avoid those guys. They can be a little weird; I think it's prolonged exposure to mothballs or something. And they tend to drool. A lot.

I've been around for as long as humans have been curious about what's out there in the dark. The first time a kid was freaked by what was outside the circle of light thrown by the cook fire, or what was hiding in the tall grass outside the cave, my kind was born.

At the beginning of my employment, I didn't have a name, just a designation: BitN 2731. I got the name Oddnoq from a father who was telling his nervous little girl that the sounds she was hearing were just the "Odd knocks that an old house makes when it settles down for nighttime." After that she started to say "Goodnight Oddnock," before she went to sleep. I'd give a little quiet knock in response. I liked the name and made a little change to the spelling

– the letter 'Q' is my favorite, it's the little tail.

BitNs aren't here to scare kids though, that's a huge misconception. I think it comes from parents always telling their kids, "Oh, that's nothing to be frightened of." With kids, saying something like that can conjure a fear that wasn't there to begin with. Sometimes saying nothing would be better. BitN has always been a special task force to protect kids from the actual scary shit that's out there. And believe me, there is a lot of scary shit out there.

In my time I've seen kids go through all sorts of stuff. Bullying at school – both as the bullied and the bully – scared of the dark, bad dreams, poor grades, fear of swimming, riding a bike, and clowns. The clown thing I can totally get behind, I mean, you've seen one right? They're awful. Some kids get so worried about stuff they stop eating or talking. Others are afraid to tell their family they are gay, or they want to ask a parent to stop drinking. Everybody is scared about something in their lifetime. If they tell you differently, tell them to come talk to me. I know better.

I keep the bad away. Most of the bad is just garden variety, happens-to-everyone bad. Sometimes it's not.

For example, one time I was assigned to a kid whose mother's boyfriend tried to molest him. This piece of walking garbage crept into the kid's room one night, stinking of cheap beer, and pulled the covers off the bed. I could feel the dread coming off the kid in cold waves that let me know there was trouble brewing. The kid made kind of a gaspy-startled noise, and the boyfriend clapped his hand over the kid's mouth and said, in a slurry drawl, "Shhhh, it's our secret."

Oh, yeah, did I mention that BitNs can shape-shift? We can, and it's really kinda cool. I made an on-the-spot decision to reveal myself to a grown-up. We can do that if the situation calls for it, and this situation definitely called for it.

At the boyfriend's slurred comment, I reached out my hand and gripped the dude's calf. I made sure my hand was cold, and scaly, and that the fingers were tipped with 3 inch talons. Using my grip on his leg as leverage, I dragged myself out from under the bed and pulled myself to standing by using his scrawny frame as a ladder. By this time the rest of me looked like a combination of a snake (people, I've found, really don't like snakes) and a tattered, rotting corpse.

I looked him square in his bulging eyes, and told him to leave the kid alone. That it would be "our secret," and then let my bottom jaw fall off. He pissed himself and fled. I shifted back to something less gross (in this case the Los Angeles Dodgers current second baseman, Steve Sax), winked at the kid and took my place back under the bed. The boyfriend never came back and I was assigned to another kid.

Once in a while, the kids catch on and figure out that I'm there – maybe I get sloppy and manifest somewhere other than under the bed. One kid caught me reading his algebra textbook. I just had to see why it made his mother swear so much. I had shifted my appearance to look just like him, so when he saw me sitting at his desk, I just told him he was having a dream, and to go back to sleep and not worry about it.

Another one saw me standing in their pantry, eating dry Super-Choco-Sugar-Bombs right out of the box. He crossed his arms and said, "I knew it! Mom!" I dropped the box, vanished, and put in for an immediate reassignment. I'd been sneaking the cereal for months, and the kid got blamed for it. But the cereal was just so tasty. I feel sorta bad about that.

My assignment this time – Raymond – was four and had just started to wonder what's out there in the dark. But Ray, he was pretty sharp, so he wasn't scared, but ravenously curious. "Dad, how far does space go?" "Dad, could ants get as big as cars?" "Mom, if I bite my fingernails and swallow them, will a hand grow in my stomach?" "Do you think that grandpa can hear us from heaven?" Questions all day long, his poor parents were exhausted by bedtime.

At the beginning, I had no idea why I was there. No creepy nanny, no night terrors, no trouble potty training. He even ate his vegetables without much of a fuss. This kid had a mom and dad who loved him and would go to the ends of the earth to make sure he was safe. Ray's big sister was a pain in the ass, but can't all big sisters be kind of like that?

About two years into the job I got lazy, and Raymond found out I was there. He caught me in the middle of the night playing with his little toy cars. I couldn't help myself, I just love all the little details. Anyway, he was getting up to use the bathroom, so I froze, one car in each hand. We made eye contact, just for a second or two, and then he kept going.

The next morning at the breakfast table he told his mom that, "Grover was playing with my toys last night." I have no idea which Grover he meant. It could have been the blue shaggy puppet thing or Grover Cleveland for all I knew. I had been assigned to the 24th president of the United States when he was a kid, so maybe? I wasn't concentrating too hard on my appearance, so it could have been either one.

"That's a funny kind of a dream," his mom said. "God, you're so weird," big sister Sally said.

So, I just hung around there under the bed, minding my business, and kept an eye out for trouble – I even put one up on a bookshelf so it could have a good view of the whole room.

We'd cross paths now and then, with him always thinking I was a dream. Then, when he was 8 or 9, one night he leaned down over the edge of his bed and asked who I was. I was reading one of his comic books, and was caught so off guard that I answered.

"Uh, I'm Oddnoq, I live under the bed?" It came out as a question.

"Duh, I know you live under the bed."

"Uh, yeah. So. You don't need to be afraid of me." Smooth, Oddnoq, real smooth.

Cool as you please, Ray says, "I know, I'm not afraid. I've kinda known you've been down there for a while now. It's cool, I won't rat you out." He smiled at me and stuck out his hand to shake on it.

I made sure my hand was human looking (BitNs are basically bipedal humanoid in shape, but we're, well, sort of blank when we aren't trying to look like anything specific), and shook his hand. "Okay, thanks Ray. Go to sleep, math quiz tomorrow."

"Ugh, I know." Ray sat up and flopped down onto his bed, making the frame squeak. "G'night Oddnoq." He was out like a light in five minutes.

We got on pretty well after that. Ray got bigger and started middle school, made good grades, made some good friends. His sister got to be less of a pain in the ass. Sometimes his friends would come over to play video games or have a sleepover. I like sleepovers because sometimes the other kids' BitN would tag along for the night; we could catch up and trade stories.

Things carried on pretty smoothly until eighth grade. Thirteen years old, that horrid age when kids start to get grumpy about most everything and start to smell. They are unintentionally rude, and think the dumbest shit is hilarious. I've seen it before, during my time under the bed.

But Ray got sad. He went quiet, and if his mom or dad asked what was up, he'd give the patented teenage answer of, "I'm fine."

Ray wasn't fine, I could tell. I'd been around him for long enough to know that there was something not right. There was something going on that only he knew about. His mother had gotten him a journal as a birthday gift, and he wrote in it for hours. It was like he was trying to write the trouble out of his head; get it all out on the page, so he could get back to what 'fine' was.

I didn't read the diary, because even though I'm a Figment, that shit's just not cool, you know?

Finally, I couldn't stand the silence and decided it was time to ask him what was up. Maybe he could tell me what he thought he couldn't say to anyone else.

"Ray, what's going on?" Ray had just climbed into bed for the night. "You can tell me whatever it is. And before you say 'I'm fine,' I know that you're not. I've been under here since you were four, so I know a bit about you and being 'fine.'"

More silence.

"You know you can tell me anything, right? It's not like I'm going to tell anybody – I can't. You're the only one who can see me."

The silence above me continued, but Ray shifted and dangled a hand over the edge. I reached out and brushed it with mine. "Whenever you're ready then."

Weeks passed and Ray continued to answer his parents with "I'm fine," and, "It's nothing Mom."

One night I decided to spend the night under his parent's bed, to maybe get some information on what else was going on in the house. I popped over to their room, listened at the door for a few seconds – I didn't want to slide in on them doing that naked wrestling thing that you folks find so entertaining – and slipped into the space under the door.

"I'm sure he'll tell us when he's ready," Ray's dad was sitting on the edge of the bed, taking off his watch.

Mom was already under the covers and said, "But it's already been months. Years, really. I think I've always known. I know my kid."

So, they knew what was going on, but were letting Ray come around to tell them in his own time. I wondered what it could be.

"Why can't we just ask him then?" Dad toed off his socks and swung his legs up onto the mattress. "Is he afraid we'll be angry at him?"

"That's probably part of it, although I don't know why. You and I have never said anything negative about it." Mom rolled onto her side to face Dad. "Let's wait a little longer, 'kay?"

"All right. He's a good kid, but I worry he's stressing himself out over nothing." Dad rolled to face Mom.

"Well, it's not nothing to Ray." Mom kissed dad and I made my retreat. No naked wrestling for me please and thank you.

Back under Rays' bed, I tapped the frame and whispered his name.

"Ray?" Tap tap. "Hey, Ray, you awake?"

"Yeah, Oddnoq, I'm up."

"Can I come up there with you?" I poked my head out from under the bed.

"Sure, come on out."

I crawled out from under and sat at the foot of his bed. He was propped up at his end with a pillow behind him.

"I was just in your parent's room, and they were talking about you." His eyes got big, so I continued, "Hold on, hold on. Nothing to freak out about. Actually, this could be really good."

Ray readjusted the pillow and said, cautiously, "Yeah, how's that?'

"Well, nobody knows you like your mom, right? I've been around moms and kids for centuries and try as they might, kids can never fool mom. Like, ever. So, yeah, she knows about that time the peas got flushed down the toilet."

Ray threw an eye roll at me. "So, what does she think she knows now?"

"Well, that's the thing. I have no idea, because neither your mom or dad said what it was. They were talking about being worried about you – and before you get started – that is their job, okay? They worry about you, it's built into the parent contract." He was still looking skeptical.

"I don't know what they're worried about because you haven't ever said, not to your friends when they are here, not to your sister, not even out loud while you're alone in here with me. You write in that journal your mom got you, but you don't talk. Not even in your sleep."

Ray shifted around some more, looked down at his hands, which were having a private little war in his lap, and then, back up at me. "You can't tell, right? If I tell you, you can't say anything, right?"

"Not a word, I'm a Figment, who'd believe me? And besides, it's not my place to tell."

He took a deep breath, and paused. He seemed to be gathering his thoughts. Or his courage. He let the breath out in a rush that carried a garbled sentence with it. "I-don't-feel-like-a-boy-I'm-really-a-girl-I-don't-know-what-to-do-I-feel-like-I'm-faking-my-life."

Oh, Ooooh. He's a she. Sure. No problem.

"So, you are a girl, inside, yeah? And all the sad, quiet, 'I'm fine' stuff is because when you see yourself, the way the outside looks doesn't match up with how the inside feels. Right?"

Ray winced. "Yeah, that's kind of a simple way to say it, but yeah. Transgender is the word for it."

"You know this isn't something new, right? I mean, transgender folks have been around since, well, since people have been. Always and forever."

I got up off the bed, stepped to the middle of his room and proceeded to give him a visual history lesson of all the different ways a person could be a person. Shape-shifting can come in really handy.

There were the Mahu of Hawaii, the Sekreta of Madagascar, the aboriginal sistergirls and brotherboys of Australia, the Ninauposkitzipxpe of the Blackfoot tribe in North America. I showed him the Metis of Nepal, the Bakla of the Philippines, the Mashoga of Kenya.

There were so many ways to be a person; I needed to show him that. I was sent to protect him from the scary stuff, and this was his scary stuff. He was afraid to be his true self. Excuse me, *her* true self.

"So, you see, there are so many cultures where male and female aren't the only way people are made. You're not wrong in the way you feel." I settled back into my usual blank shape and sat back down on the bed. "You're fine. By the way, what should I call you?"

Ray had watched my whole presentation with wide eyes. When I asked what her name was, her face kind of crumpled up, and her lips started to tremble. Fat tears slipped from her eyes and rolled down her cheeks. Oh, damnit, I've made her cry.

Then her whole expression changed. A smile that was so big it looked painful lit up her face.

"Ray, you all right?"

"Call me Rachel. I'm Rachel." At that, Rachel flung her arms around my shoulders and gave me a hug. It was my first hug. It was nice.

"Thank you, Oddnoq. I feel so much better, lighter. Brighter." And she did seem like she had been transformed.

"How do I tell mom and dad? I can't just spring something like this on them over dinner. 'Mom, Dad, I'm actually a girl, can I have more green beans please?'" Rachel was swiping at her nose with a tissue. "Do I just tell mom and let her tell dad? What about Sally? God, she'll be such an ass."

"I don't know. But from what I overheard tonight, they seem pretty sure they know what's up already. Your mom does, anyway. And they love you, never forget that. I've watched them with you for nine years. I don't think there is anything you could tell them that would upset them or disappoint them."

I stood back up and got off the bed to crawl back to my usual spot. "Start with your mom, that's what I would do anyway. She's cool. But for now, get some sleep. See you tomorrow night, Rachel."

The next week, Rachel brought her mother into her bedroom and explained her gender identity, and how long she'd been sure of the fact that she was a girl.

For a precarious few moments, her mother was silent. Then she whooped with joy. "Oh, honey! I'm so happy you finally felt comfortable enough to say something! I'm sorry you felt like you had to keep the secret for so long though." Mom drew her daughter into a tight hug.

"You're not mad. Disappointed? What about dad? Or Sally?"

"God's balls no! How could I be mad or disappointed that you are my perfect, brave, beautiful kid? I do have a question though." Mom brushed Rachel's hair out of her face. "What's your name?"

"Rachel."

Mom kissed her girl's forehead, "I think that's lovely. We'll tell dad whenever you're ready, okay? And don't worry about Sally, your sister will be fine."

I smiled to myself. My assignment was over.

PREGNANT
Eli Hayden Loft

My name is Eleanora. I'm 42 and pregnant.

But I shouldn't be.

My hand is shaking, letter crumpling between clumsy fingers. My request for an abortion, denied. Just like my request for sterilization. Just like my request for contraception. With the complications from my last pregnancy and the danger of dying during this one, I really believed they would grant me permission.

I was so naïve.

It's worse now. It's not just me suffering. My baby is formed wrong; she won't live more than a few minutes. Her brief life will be filled with pain.

"It's part of His plan."

"Everything happens for a reason."

Those were the excuses doctors gave instead of risking their reputations by recommending termination. But what reason could there be for letting this baby suffer? My well-being didn't matter because I had to 'serve my purpose' and now, tiny and beyond saving, so must she. For the peace of mind of the men who get to make the decisions, for the salvation of the doctors' souls.

Maybe it's a blessing that she didn't grow right. Her pain will be brief, and she won't understand it. She won't grow up knowing her weak body is maintained only for procreation. Her pain will be shorter than it is and will be for my other daughters. She won't live like the three of us, forced to churn out as many children as we can before the effort kills us.

My name is Eleanora. I'm 42, and I won't live to see 43.

TĀNIWHĀ
Thomas Badlan

Rawiri stood on the Piopiotahi docks and watched thirty feet of wave rush up the fiord toward him. Tourists and boat crews were running for their lives, but Rawiri's feet felt heavier than the world.

"Wiri! Run!" someone shouted.

A hand was suddenly wrapped around his wrist and Aihe was at his side. The spell was broken. They ran together, the water roaring behind as it rushed between the steep mountainsides of Milford Sound. They left the docks and hopped over the metal railing next to the gravel picnic area, sprinting toward the parking lot. Tourists were shoving each other while trying to get onto their coaches. Horns blared while cars crashed together and scraped through any possible gap. Rawiri saw Lacy from the ticket desk collide with a pākehā and both went sprawling. He wanted to stop and help but Aihe had eyes only on what was up ahead.

The roar of water was getting closer, a force of nature that wanted to swallow them without thought or mercy. They passed the information center and café, its staff and customers spilling out onto the street. A car missed them by inches as it sped up SH94, halting their progress. Rawiri glanced back at the bay and saw one of the cruise boats catch the crest of the wave and rise like a child's toy in the bath. A crewman fell into the water and the boat followed, capsizing.

"Keep going, Wiri!"

To their right Milford Sound's little airport was in the path of the wave. One of the tour helicopters took off, rising quickly into the sky. Rawiri felt a spike of jealousy as it pulled away.

The wave struck the headland. A wall of gray water slammed into the shoreline and then kept going. He saw the airport crews fleeing, tiny figures he knew were already dead.

"This way!" Aihe called.

His arm was aching, feet throbbing. There was no pain in it. Nothing but the terror. Aihe was taking them toward the backpacker's hotel. If they got inside, up to the roof, they might be safe. Instead, she pulled him onward. Up in the windows Rawiri saw a series of terrified faces peering down.

"Where are we going?" he panted.

"Up!"

At the next carpark they peeled off onto one of the footpaths into the rainforest. They passed a family carrying their young children and a pair of booted backpackers with panicked American accents. Rawiri peered back down into the valley through the rimu trees as the water swept against the stranded cars and began to carry them away.

There was something else as well. A dark shape, moving among the debris. For a moment he saw something glittering among the brown sludge, moving fast. There was a flash of emerald green as a long, thin tail surfaced and flicked. A sound followed, guttural, turning plaintive.

Aihe yanked him on.

"*Tō tero!* You want to die?"

Rawiri ran even faster, muscles burning. They left the trail, scrambling up a loose shale rise, where they finally stopped. A hundred feet below, the valley, their home, had been swallowed by water.

Rawiri sat down and tried to catch his breath.

"This isn't happening," Aihe breathed, leaning on her knees.

She pulled her cell out of her shorts pocket and started tapping, then held it up in search of signal. The jungle around them was silent. Even the tui birds had stopped singing.

"Agh! Dad's not answering."

Dad. Rawiri felt his stomach clench. He'd been too terrified to even think about dad. Or their cousins, Ruru and Tipene. All of them worked in Piopiotahi. It was about then that he vomited all over his shoes.

"We go south," Aihe said eventually.

It was starting to get dark and the waters weren't receding. They followed a trail that Aihe promised would lead them back home. They didn't see another living soul. Rawiri kept tripping on tree roots because he couldn't take his eyes off the flood.

"Watch where you're going! I'm not carrying you!" Aihe snapped.

The sun began to set, casting the clouds aflame, the forest darkening. Rawiri began to recognize the sweep of the tooth-like mountains on either side of them. The path led downward through fallen mānuka trees and deep pools of water, shining with an iridescent slickness.

"Is this…oil?" Rawiri asked.

"Maybe the tsunami did something to that new drill they set up offshore?"

Rawiri remembered the protests over the last few years, the petitions and debates in parliament. Dad had been a key organizer, as a local business owner and member of the Ngāi Tahu. It seemed like they'd been right. Oil exploration off Fiordland was a bad idea.

"What if dad isn't at home?" Rawiri asked after a long silence.

"He will be."

Rawiri felt sick. Home in the summer months was a trailer park among the trees just off the highway. He loved it, it was where they escaped the city, where dad had started his kayaking business and where he'd made his last memories of mum. He didn't want to see it a ruin. It was more than just a place; it was where they belonged.

Aihe spotted the trailer first through the debris. It was still standing, but the walls were no longer white, and all the windows were gone.

"Dad?" Aihe called.

Nothing. Just more quiet. She searched their trailer for any signs of life. She came out looking defeated. She checked the other trailers as well, including the one owned by Ruru and Tipene. Tipene's old truck was parked on a small rise next to the trailer and had narrowly escaped the flood. Aihe returned, shaking her head. Everyone was either evacuated or missing.

Aihe looked deflated but then took a moment and stood a little taller.

"Come on," she said, "let's go and pack some clothes."

The front door was hanging off its hinges and the interior was completely sodden. Some of the furniture had tipped over. Rawiri went to his bedroom, took a breath, and pushed open the door. His room was on the east side and had been spared the full force of the wave. Over his shoulder he heard Aihe's sigh. Her window was gone, branches entangling her bedcovers, the walls mud splattered.

"It's okay. Grab your stuff," she said and squeezed inside.

Half the items on his shelves had fallen onto the floor, but otherwise it wasn't much worse than the usual teenage neglect. The carpet squelched but otherwise he'd gotten off lightly. He packed fast, trying to think about what he really needed, while also grabbing his All-Blacks shirt and Nintendo Switch. As he was heading out the door, he spotted his mother's pounamu necklace on the floor where it had fallen. It was shaped like a curving fishhook, made of deep green jade. He pulled the necklace on and pressed a hand down so that it settled over his chest.

Outside he waited for Aihe.

"How was it?"

"Trashed," she shrugged.

"Sorry, Aihe."

She forced a smiled.

"It's a good day's hike to Te Anau. Can't sleep in there and it'll be dark soon. I reckon the loft space might have stayed dry. Camping gear might be okay. You get the tent and sleeping bags and I'll find us food. We can camp on the hill. I'll leave dad a note."

She sounded so confident that he did as she said. As he went to find the camping gear, Rawiri realized he was holding tightly onto the pounamu around his neck.

It was getting late by the time they reached the hill, a wide-open space beneath Mount Talbot. The sounds of the forest had remerged. A few kea parrots were hoping around in the undergrowth, playing and chattering.

"Like the good old days, eh?" Aihe said.

She began to put up the tent, while Rawiri set up the camping stove and started heating a tin of soup. They had come out here camping a lot, usually with dad, but sometimes just the two of them, at least until Aihe had her growth spurt and stopped wanting to do anything fun. As they ate, the moon emerged from behind the clouds and lit up the hillside. Down the incline, a shimmering mirror emerged, nestled in a scar in the land. The trees there had either been demolished or drowned.

"That's new," Rawiri said.

The new lake, about the size of an oval rugby pitch, had been abandoned by the wider floodwaters as they receded. A series of small waterfalls ran downhill, suggesting it too would eventually drain away.

"We'll be okay. We'll find dad and get out of here," Aihe said and for the first time in ages, reached over and pulled him into a hug.

They settled down soon after. As Rawiri climbed into the tent, he heard something grumble in the dark, a long and low sound, almost mournful. Aihe was rummaging around for a flashlight and didn't seem to hear. Rawiri listened carefully but didn't hear it again. Shivering, he zipped up the tent and shut out the night.

He dreamed of Maui. Maui, skinny and weak, standing on the waka's edge, his fishing line taut. His brothers were lying in the boat, terrified. The line was pulling them across a vast churning ocean, spray soaking them with every crested wave. They had laughed at Maui, not wanted him to come along at all. Now they were begging for him to cut the line, but Maui refused. He was not going to let some fish beat him. Faster and faster they went, until the line threatened to pull them all under the waves. Maui grit his teeth and slowly, long hours later, he wrestled the beast under control. The monster surrendered, ending its thrashing battle and surfaced. It towered over their little boat and never again would the brothers deny Maui a place in their waka.

Maui named the fish Hāhau-whenua but his brothers were too busy hacking up the prize to congratulate him. In the dream, Rawiri watched as the cuts in the fish's flesh deepened and widened, becoming valleys and hills. The running blood ran till it cleared and became waterfalls and rivers. Slowly, but surely, the fish was transformed, becoming Aotearoa.

He woke in the dark, the dream still heart-poundingly vivid. One of Aunt Whina's stories, fresh from sheer repetition. He lay in the dark and listened to his sister's soft breathing. Deep down he knew what caused tsunamis, but deeper still he believed that Hāhau-whenua had given one last dying thrash of their tail.

He needed to pee. Moving carefully, Rawiri unzipped the tent and crept across the grass towards the trees. He shivered as the chilled dew soaked his calves. Relieving himself against the closest nikau palm, he looked out over the new lake. When he was done, he crept closer, feeling like he was still in the dream.

At the edge he stood in the mud and peered across the flat plane of water. The night was still, the water reflecting the broad sweep of stars above. A wave lapped over his splattered toes. Then another. Oil coated his skin with its stinking sliminess, a cloying, acrid smell.

The stillness was suddenly broken. Ripples were chasing each other across the water toward him. Rawiri squinted, trying to find the source. Something was moving quickly closer, bobbing up and down. Rawiri's breath caught as he realized the size of it. He tried to turn and run, but once again, his feet disobeyed.

Just before it hit the shore the shape veered left, a wave washing against Rawiri's legs. He followed the shape as it glided through the shallows, and suddenly dived out of sight. The ground began to shake so violently he almost lost his footing. Then the vibrations lessened, but the trees further along the lake shore shook instead. Soil erupted among them and something lumbered into the open.

Rawiri didn't know what to do. His mind was screaming conflicting ideas at him; run and hide, freeze and hope. The only thing he knew was that whatever he did, it would be away from the tent, where Aihe still slept.

Before he could decide, it emerged from the darkness. A long, sleek body about a size of a bull, covered with shining scales. A wide, flat face turned in his direction and exposed a jaw with rows of sharkish teeth. Two oval eyes rolled and focused; pupils flecked with orange. The creature offered a strange guttural roar and lumbered forward. Rawiri raised his hands, a placating surrender he knew would do nothing to stop this monster from tearing him apart.

In that moment, he thought of Maui.

"Kia kaha!" he called.

The creature kept coming but let out a quick shrill call that echoed around him.

"Kia māia!"

It slowed. Feet skidding in the mud.

"Kia Manawanui!"

It stopped right in front of him. The creature lowered its head, hiding the maw of teeth.

"Kia hora, te marino, kia whakapa pounami te moana. Kia whakaute tatou tetahi ki tetahi."

Without thinking, Rawiri reached up and put his palm flat against the creature's blue green scales. They were smooth as glass. Rawiri could feel the creature's hot breath on his face. Locking eyes, Rawiri saw understanding there. The creature sniffed at pounamu around his neck with slit nostrils.

"Wiri!"

Aihe's voice rang across the clearing.

Rawiri felt his insides twist.

The creature turned, its eyes sharp and focused on Aihe, teeth bared. It leaned back to leap and suddenly Rawiri's feet could move. He stepped between them, arms raised.

"No!"

The creature looked from him to Aihe, confusion clear on its face. It calmed, a long row of thin spines along its back flattened. Rawiri put his hand back on the creature's head and tried to keep his voice soothing.

"It's okay. We're not going to hurt you."

"Wiri…" Aihe called, her voice full of barely suppressed panic, "get away!"

"I think it's okay. I think they're friendly."

"Friendly?"

"It knows *te reo*!" he said.

She looked at him like he'd lost his mind.

The creature sat down on their haunches, looking remarkably like some gargantuan lizard dog, a long thin tail swaying across the mud. Rawiri saw a discolored patch of scales on their chest, a spreading pattern of gray among the blue and greens.

Aihe inched her way closer, eyes wide in the dark. She reached up a shaking hand and placed it next to his. She laughed, sounding a bit unhinged. The creature only sat there, chest rumbling with a feline purr. Rawiri no longer felt afraid, only a strange sort of calm.

"I think it's a kiakiataki!" Rawiri said.

"Those are just Aunt Whina's stories, bro," Aihe said, not taking her eyes off the creature.

Rawiri shook his head in astonishment and gestured to the massive beast sat beside them.

"It's just some undiscovered creature, dredged up by the tsunami."

"Whatever you say, Aihe."

The creature stood up abruptly and turned back towards the

lake. It crouched and leapt, surprisingly high, sliding gracefully into the water. Rawiri and Aihe stood watching the shape as it moved into deeper water.

"Can we keep them?" Rawiri asked.

There was no sleeping after that. They sat by the lake and waited for the sun to rise. In the water the creature circled for hours, looking trapped. It eventually abandoned swimming, climbing laboriously up onto a small boulder at the water's edge.

"They're a kiakiataki," he said again, "the guardian of Piopiotahi."

"Even so, we can't stay here, Wiri," Aihe said.

He knew. Somewhere out there, their dad was looking for them.

"Are we walking to Te Anau?" Rawiri asked.

"Yeah, it's a long way though."

"Maybe we should go back to Piopiotahi? That's where they'll look for survivors."

Up on a rock, the creature let out a long, mournful cry that echoed around them. To Rawiri it sounded sad and lonely, trapped so far from the sea. Already the water was lower than it had been the night before. The creature had legs; could they move back to the sea by themself?

"Maybe we take the kiakiataki back to Piopiotahi!" he suggested.

"Are you mad?"

"We can't leave a guardian spirit here!"

"It's just an animal, Wiri."

"That understands te reo!"

"It doesn't understand *teo reo*! It doesn't understand anything!"

Rawiri huffed loudly.

"We should at least try to help them."

"We're out in the bush, our home is flooded and we don't know where our family is. Can we focus on what matters here?"

"This matters too!" he shouted.

Aihe's face darkened, but Rawiri stood his ground.

"What do you want me to do? Put a leash on it?"

"What's dad always saying? That we are connected to the land.

The Māori were here long before the pākehā. We have to protect them. Look at all the oil in the water, Aihe. Look at the state of the kiakiataki. We have to try to get them back to the water, so that they can protect this place."

Aihe sighed.

"How do you know it'll even follow us?" she asked.

Rawiri stood up and stepped to the edge of the water.

"*Taniwha!*" he shouted.

The creature's head shot up. They stood and leapt off the rock, slicing neatly into the water and surfacing close to the shore. The guardian lumbered up onto dry land, water falling away in rivulets. They walked right up to Rawiri and dropped their head. Rawiri put his hand there and looked back at his sister with a wide grin.

"Show off," she said.

They set off before the midday heat. Aihe went first, picking them a path through the bush, back towards town. The guardian padded along beside him, breathing loud, chest rising and falling. The creature's once bright scales were now growing dull, a few flaking away across their chest.

"It's okay," he told them, putting his hand on their flank, "we're taking you home."

The kiakiataki grumbled but kept moving.

The path Aihe took led them back into the valley, where the waters had mostly receded. There were still lots of deep pools they had to skirt around, which the creature slid gratefully into, wallowing in the mud for a moment before having to be coaxed out. Aihe was starting to show less hesitancy around the guardian, though seemed content to leading the way.

They passed their trailer park and then followed the access track up toward the road. Aihe stepped out first, wading through deep water and up onto the tarmac. The road had been partially cleared, at least enough to get vehicles through. Waterlogged cars and telegraph poles littered the verges. Rescue workers already hard at work, though no one was currently in sight.

"Maybe we can wait here, flag down the next people who pass?"

"What about the guardian?" Rawiri asked.

"Maybe they'll help us?"

"What do you think they'll do when they see the kiakiataki?"

Aihe seemed to consider this.

"We're in the *wops*, Wiri. We're just kids. We need help."

"They'll take them away for study. They'll die, Aihe. We're the only ones who'll help."

Aihe sighed and closed her eyes.

Rawiri smiled broadly, knowing for the moment, he'd won. That smile faded when he saw the creature, crouched in the shallow water. Their scales were falling away, a gray sickness spreading. The guardian let out a low grumble as Rawiri approached. He could feel their power waning.

"We need to hurry, they're dying."

Aihe came to his side, her brow furrowed.

"We need a truck or…" she said and turned back toward the forest.

Tipene had bought his truck at nineteen. It was now a beat-up old thing, its wheel arches rusting, its breaks what he called 'temperamental.' And it was their only option. Though only sixteen, Aihe had occasionally driven it up the access track and even a few miles down the highway with dad supervising.

"Tipene's going to kill us," she muttered leaving Rawiri to babysit the kiakiataki, while she went to find Tipene's keys. Rawiri prayed the truck could make it through the waters.

The guardian seemed content to lie in the mud.

"I'm sorry this is happened to you," Rawiri said, "I promise we'll get you home."

Aihe returned half an hour later, the truck protesting as it pushed its way through the flood, tires spinning. It pulled itself up onto the tarmac, engine rattling painfully.

"You did it! You're brilliant!" Rawiri called.

The guardian rolled over and buried themselves deeper.

Rawiri knelt down in the water. "This is how we get you home!" he said, stroking scales, "don't give up now!"

He felt tears rolling down his cheeks and squeezed his eyes shut. Rawiri heard the creature rise, breathing ragged, lumbering footsteps slow. He went with the guardian, leading them toward the truck.

"It doesn't look so good," Aihe said.

They helped the creature one leg at a time, pushing and pulling until the guardian was able to crawl up. The truck's suspension creaked painfully with their full weight.

"Oh, Tipene's really going to kill us," Aihe moaned.

"You okay to drive?"

Aihe smiled. "What other option is there? You, shorty?"

He hugged her. "Thanks for believing me," he said.

"We're family, Wiri, you egg."

Aihe got up into the cab and turned on the engine. With the guardian in the back the water almost reached the top of the wheel arches. Rawiri climbed up and perched next to the creature. Then they were off, driving slowly along the road back to Piopiotahi.

"This is our valley. We live back there," Rawiri told the kiakiataki. "We work through the summer, but usually we live in Christchurch. I prefer it out here though. I feel like the land is ours again. It used to be ours before the pākehā arrived. Aotearoa we call it. I think you know all that though. I think you guard Piopiotahi. Did we force you out with the oil rigs and ships and people? I think you might have caused this tsunami, or we caused the tsunami and forced you out. Either way, it wasn't your fault."

They drove around a cluster of cars strewn at various angles.

"I don't think you want to hurt anyone. Maybe we were hurting you with all we do?"

The kiakiataki let out a low sound that started guttural then turned shrill.

"I'm sorry," Rawiri said and patted their side.

It was a beautiful day, bright sun reflecting off the flood water, the rainforest around them vivid and lush. Birds flew across the valley in rainbow colors. If you ignored the odd floating car or uprooted tree, they might just have been on a pleasant river cruise.

As they rounded the next bend in the road, Rawiri's mood darkened. A string of emergency vehicles and police cars were parked across the highway. Florescent men were working hard, blocking their progress.

"Oh, shit," Rawiri heard Aihe say.

His heart sank quickly. They were cut off from the sea. The kiakiataki let out a low, mournful howl, as though understanding exactly what was happening. It was over. The guardian would die, claimed by the pākehā, dissected in some lab.

Rawiri felt immediately fury.

"Drive," he said, almost inaudibly.

A couple of police officers had got out of their cars and were wading slowly forward, arms raised. They didn't seem to have noticed the truck's cargo.

"Drive!" Rawiri shouted.

The kaikiataki whooped loudly.

"Drive, drive, *drive!*"

Aihe swore again and put the car in gear. It lurched forward, water spraying. The two officers hesitated and then began to retreat before diving out of the way. Aihe aimed them at the small gap between two parked cop cars and screamed in preparation for impact. Rawiri braced.

Suddenly the guardian was leaping up and overhead, their shadow tearing over the truck as the truck bed lurched up and down, almost throwing Rawiri clear. The kiakiataki dove straight into the floodwater, a geyser of water and tarmac rising between them and the blockade. The truck plummeted downward, into darkness. Rawiri blinked and held on tighter as the truck bucked beneath him. Through the windshield he could see the guardian as it tunneled downward, legs thrashing. The truck followed. Around them the earth shook, dirt and road surface falling around them.

"Go, go, go, go!" Rawiri screamed, knowing Aihe couldn't hear him.

The truck sped up and followed the guardian as they plunged deeper. Rocks and soil crashed against the truck and Rawiri tucked himself as tight as he could against the cabin. They were leveling out though, the tunnel behind closing, collapsing in on itself, flood waters rushing in to fill the void. All he could do was watch with wide eyed terror as they sped through the roaring dark.

Ahead sunlight blossomed and the kiakiataki leapt into open air, amidst a spray of water and soil. The truck was free, suddenly airborne. Wheels spun and the engine raged. They landed with a lurch that sent Rawiri falling into the truck bed among wet soil and churned tarmac. Above the sky was blue and full of fat drifting clouds. A shadow fell and the kiakiataki was there, looking down at him with bright eyes.

Rawiri scrambled aside, groaning in pain, as the guardian pulled itself back into the truck and collapsed with a screech of metal. Their shine was gone, long tail dragging limply through the water. Aihe was looking back at him, eyes wide, knuckles white against the door.

"Let's go," he said.

They drove the rest of the way into town without obstacle beyond what the flood had left behind. About half a mile from Milford Sound they had to abandon the truck and continue by foot. The kaikaitaki had regained a little strength but didn't look well. Their spines were drooping and they were limping, struggling over even the smaller chunks of debris.

The sun was setting, a dazzling beauty falling over Piopiotahi.

"Nearly there," he told the guardian, helping to lead them over obstacles.

Further along the river Rawiri could see rescue workers and a helicopter hovering overhead. They were close to the former edge of the land, the water getting deeper. The guardian had collapsed against the hull of an upturned boat. Just a day ago he had watched the wave approach from this very spot.

"You're here! It's right there. You can make it!"

The kaikaitaki looked out across the bay, along the steep sided mountains and out to the ocean beyond. The water was dazzling.

"You are the guardian of this place," Rawiri said, putting his hand on the creature's scales.

He could feel the rumbling within. The raw power. The magic.

"We'll do our best to look after it as well," he promised.

The kiakiataki lifted their head. Then a foot. They pushed themselves slowly up and slid over the boat into the water. Rawiri and Aihe climbed up after them. The guardian kept moving, swimming into deeper water. As they moved further away, their shine seemed to return, twilight sunlight glinting off their scales until they were shining. For a little while the kiakiataki's head and long serpentine tail were visible as a dark shape against the fading light. Then they were gone.

"Good work, Wiri," Aihe said and ruffled his hair.

"Think we're in trouble?" he asked, smiling.

"Oh, definitely," she said, looking out over the fiord.

Over the quiet, Rawiri heard someone shouting. He listened carefully, trying to work out what was being said. His eyes followed the sound and found a lone figure stood atop a beached coach.

"Rawiiiiiri! Aiiiiiiihe!" they called faintly.

"Dad! It's dad!" Rawiri said, jumping up.

"Dad!" Aihe called and jumped off the boat.

It took several agonizing minutes to find a path through the remains of town and reach each other, but finally, in what had once been a parking lot, they came together.

Hahona's arms were easily big enough to wrap both up. He pulled them tight and they stood together in the water rocking back and forth. For the first time all day Rawiri felt safe. Ruru and Tipene appeared as well.

"Thank god you're safe," their dad said and squeezed them tighter.

"Where've you been hiding? Been looking for you all night," Ruru said with a smile.

Their dad let them go and looked into their faces, wiping away falling tears.

"My brave kids, my brave, brave kids."

He was crying too.

"Do we have a story to tell you guys!" Rawiri said.

"Hey, is that my truck?" Tipene asked.

They were interrupted by a dark, sleek shape that broke the surface of Milford Sound. It leapt high into the air, letting out a loud whooping call. A long tail whipped into the air, scales rippling with light, and the kiakiataki dropped back into the waters of Piopiotahi.

(IR)RECONCILABLE DIVINITIES
Laura Simons

To be perfectly honest, the lawyer doesn't quite remember how she got here. Well, not *here* – this is her office, she's *supposed* to be here – but here in front of these two people. They certainly didn't make an appointment. She's not even sure if she let them in. They're just sort of here now.

"So," she tries, attempting to claw back some composure through sheer, stubborn professionalism. "What is it I could help you with, Mr and Ms...?" Her voice trails off uselessly when she meets her clients' expectant eyes again.

"Hades," the man says.

"Persephone," the woman smiles.

"Right." The lawyer clears her throat. Something about those names sounds oddly familiar, but she can't quite put her finger on it. "How can I be of service?"

"We need to get out of our prenup."

The lawyer blinks at the woman named Persephone, there is something mesmerizingly intimidating about the green of her eyes. "You need to get *out* of your prenup."

"Yes," she nods.

"And you…both want that?"

"Absolutely!"

Mr Hades' face expresses nothing but agreement and the lawyer is very certain he would be *more* than capable of showing it if it were otherwise. "Well, it's always pleasant to have an amicable split," she says kindly. "And how–"

"We don't want to split up!" Ms Persephone hastily interrupts. "Never!"

"That's exactly why we're here," Mr Hades adds.

"I…" The lawyer looks from the one to the other. "You do realize I am a divorce lawyer, right?"

"Of course," Mr Hades says calmly. "Which is why you should know how to get us out of this." He reaches into his jacket and takes out a document that is nowhere near long enough to be even a standard prenuptial agreement.

The lawyer takes it anyway, glancing at it uncertainly. It doesn't even seem to be real *paper*. Somewhere at the edge of her high school memory the word 'papyrus' dislodges itself in her brain.

"This was drafted by…our families," Persephone supplies helpfully. "We've agreed to the terms for ages, but frankly, we're rather sick of it."

Looking at the document, the lawyer cannot blame her. Not even all her years of studying legal texts have been able to prepare her for this piece of writing. Some of the words seem to flicker before the lawyer's eyes, as if her brain simply refuses to accept them. The names – she knows they are names because they are in places where names *ought* to be – are practically illegible. And the rest of it…the rest of it just makes no sense. Not really. The words are there and they string into sentences, but none of it *fits*.

Time spent in Hades. Time spent on Olympus. Pomegranates… Spring…

With a dull headache beginning just behind her eyes the lawyer looks up again. So she hasn't got a clue what this is about, big deal, half of the law is incomprehensible. You don't need to know all the rules. Not in her line of work. What you need to know is how to find the gaps.

"Let me see if I have understood the situation," she begins, knowing full-well that there was no way she understood it fully. "You wish to circumvent this annual forced separation."

"Yes!" Ms Persephone agrees urgently.

"By any means possible."

"Well, these terms don't actually specify a lack of contact." She pushes the paper back towards Mr Hades, trying not to look at the headache-inducing words again. "It only stipulates the required residence of Ms Persephone." She nods towards his wife. "And it places no restrictions on *your* movement whatsoever."

The couple blinks at her. "What are you suggesting?"

The lawyer smiles. That is more like it. The clients are supposed to be the ones slightly out of their depth.

"I am suggesting," she says pleasantly, "that you arrange a third residence, a holiday home if you will. Somewhere in neutral territory."

"That..." Color is rising into Ms Persephone's cheeks. "...that would be allowed?"

"There's nothing here that forbids it," she replies confidently.

"I do have my business to think of," Mr Hades ponders aloud, but the lawyer can clearly see he's already thinking about how to make it work. If only because his wife seems to be doing as faithful an impression of a blooming rose as a human being should be capable of.

"Of course," the lawyer nods, settling back into her usual confidence. Honestly, most of her days are filled with trying to unravel two people caught up in painful misery. Working with a couple that is fighting to stay *together* is actually a pretty nice change of pace. She smiles.

"In that case, I think there are two matters to sort out. The real estate, and the commute."

SUNG HEROES
Patrick Hurley

The dead boy watched him. His eyes, printed in an old, grainy
newspaper, followed Eduardo throughout his tiny bedroom.
The Chronicle's headline beneath his picture read, *Boy, 14, Takes
Own Life at Golden Gate Bridge.* Miguel Lucio had been his neighbor
Delia's kid. Quiet. Fooled around on computers.

Down in the community kitchen, stale coffee did little to ease
Eduardo's stomach, but it quickened his pulse and washed away
the taste of last night's booze. Accompanying himself with a few
cathartic groans, Eduardo got dressed and grabbed his guitar. He
played an old Gibson acoustic covered in decals from the different
bands he'd been in during his younger days. One long label had
been plastered over all the others:

THIS MACHINE KILLS DEMONS

The sun had begun to creep over the skyline, melting the mist
away, changing the clouds covering the City from gray to golden
purple. Eduardo shivered despite the fact that spring was almost
summer. He'd lived in San Francisco half his life and didn't
understand how a city in California got this cold in the morning.

As his bus approached, Eduardo rubbed his hands to get the
blood flowing. Wouldn't do to start out stiff. Four nights a week, he

played gigs throughout the City. During the day, he bussed tables, worked the kitchen, ran deliveries. Only way he could still afford to live here was by joining a co-op which got him a fold-out bed in a room little bigger than a closet. Weekends were his only free time. For the last ten years, those weekends were taken up by the Bridge.

Longest gig I ever had, Eduardo thought.

He got off the bus and walked to the Welcome Center. Far out over the Bay, the Golden Gate Bridge loomed, its two sets of red towers poking tall and proud through the thick layer of clouds. Suzanne was waiting for him, fiddle in one hand, steaming cup of tea in the other.

"They're loud today," was all she said as she gave Eduardo the carabiner hook with the pass they shared, a pass granted to the select few allowed to busk the Bridge. He nodded, noticing the tired look on Suzanne's face. The music teacher made quite a picture as she trudged toward her bus stop. Like a knight after a long quest.

Of course *los duendes* were loud today. Goblins always were after bad news, and it seemed like every day the news was nothing but bad. He strapped his acoustic over one shoulder, the thick leather band almost as cracked and worn as he was. He tuned the strings (the wet air of the Bay could play hell with them if he wasn't careful). Once ready, Eduardo started walking the Bridge.

Though the walkways had just opened, walkers were already out. Soon as the first got in earshot, Eduardo began to play "Sitting on a Dock by the Bay." Otis Redding blocked *los duendes* pretty well. Evenings before the Bridge closed to pedestrians, Cat Stevens' "Moonshadow" did the job.

As Eduardo played, he checked each walker for that faraway look. After a decade, he'd gotten pretty good at spotting it. Most thought Eduardo and his friends were buskers. They carried donation bowls, but that wasn't why they played the Bridge. They weren't quite like folks in documentaries who stopped people from jumping off bridges. Viewers called those men and women heroes, claimed they'd saved as many lives as EMS workers.

No one knew what Eduardo and his friends did. They didn't know how dangerous the Golden Gate Bridge really was. Probably better that way. Once, while on a ghost-hunter forum, Eduardo read a post that claimed all bridges were haunted. They were in-between places, and as such, open to the supernatural.

Whether *los duendes* were spirits of those who'd jumped or something else, Eduardo didn't know. There were times, as he walked the Bridge at sunset, when the fog was high and the water gold and purple, where it really did feel like the Golden Gate was somewhere different.

Most couldn't see *los duendes*, only hear them on the wind. Their whispers had different effects depending on who heard. Made some so mad so they started swinging fists. Made others tired or sad. Sad enough to walk to the edge of the path and stare at the water far below. If *los duendes* were close, that sadness grew deeper. The face went slack, and they began to climb.

Eduardo strummed and sang, nodding to anyone who dropped spare change, keeping careful watch of the tourists. Not all jumpers were lured by the goblins, of course. Some had their own troubles and didn't need help from the shrouded figures. Ed and the others tried to stop them too, but that was harder, since they often waited until they were alone before making their climb. Sooner the City built that suicide netting, the better.

Now that he was walking, Eduardo felt pretty good. His blood was pumping, the music flowing, and his endorphins began to overcome his lack of sleep. The wind blew pleasantly on his face. The Bay air tasted of salt and the sea. He almost felt like he could relax. Eduardo liked to play classics—Santana, The Doors, Los Lobos—but he wasn't above adding some modern shit like The Civil Wars, or even Taylor Swift if his audience were pre-teens.

Eduardo switched to a favorite, James Taylor, "Fire and Rain." As if on cue, he noticed *los duendes* from the corner of his eye. He sang louder, trying not to let their presence get to him.

Say this for *los duendes*, they were better at waking you up than any coffee.

Ten years ago, Eduardo had been biking the Bridge early afternoon on his way to a gig in Sausalito. He'd noticed Miguel standing there, staring off into the sky, looking a million miles away. Eduardo remembered the boy because his family were friendly faces in the Mission District. He thought about calling out, saying hi or something, but he didn't want to interrupt. The kid looked deep in thought.

Then Miguel reached out to the Bridge's railing and began to climb.

Eduardo fell off his bike, ran toward him shouting, but he was too late to do anything but watch Miguel fall silently over the side. The wind was so loud he didn't even hear the splash as the kid hit the water.

That was the first time he saw *los duendes*, floating just beyond where Miguel had leapt.

They were silhouettes of mist, hooded and stooped, their hands reaching out with long claws. Eduardo opened his mouth to scream, but no sound came out. They whispered to him—fears, doubts, secrets no one knew. Ed felt a command to follow poor Miguel, but then a cool hand touched his arm, and a voice began to sing "Amazing Grace."

That snapped Eduardo out of it. He'd loved that song as a kid in church. To his right stood a nun in her habit. Her voice was deep and strong, and the hooded creatures fled from it.

"What the hell are those things?" Eduardo asked, tears running down his face.

"You can see them?" said the nun, surprised.

Already a crowd had gathered, their murmurs of despair growing louder. Eduardo swayed. "Yeah. They…I think they took my neighbor's son."

His voice choked off in a sob. Far off, sirens began to sound.

"I should have gotten here sooner," the nun said. "Would you come with me?"

Once they were off the Bridge, Sister Esther introduced herself. Long ago, she'd almost been lured off the Bridge by these evil spirits, but was saved by a blues singer, who then asked her to join him and help keep the Golden Gate safe. Sister Esther took to the work. It was she who led them now, all these years later.

"People have enough problems," she'd say, "without these demons."

Since that day, no matter how tired, hungover, or hungry, Eduardo never missed a shift on the Bridge. It was all he could do to make it up to Miguel's family. It would never be enough.

For today at least, Eduardo's music seemed to keep *los duendes* back. Those who walked past him looked untroubled by the floating creatures just a dozen yards beyond the Bridge's fence. With each strum of his guitar, the goblins withdrew, with each verse he sang about fire and rain, they grew dimmer.

After a while, you developed a sense of them. A cold prickle on the back of the forearm or neck. Feeling like you were being watched. *Los duendes* only manifested in one place at a time. When they didn't show, the buskers still played, hoping their music warded the Bridge against the hooded creatures.

Eduardo stopped toward the northern end, set his donation box at his feet, and stayed in one place, determined to keep playing until they left. It usually took a while for *los duendes* to get ahold of someone, so even walking, he could usually get there before anything bad happened.

Not always, though.

Miguel's face stared at him despite Eduardo's best effort not to remember. He almost stopped playing but noticed he'd attracted an audience. A young woman, half his age, the side of her head buzzed and the curly bangs in front dyed green.

"Cool sticker," she said, pointing at the decal.

THIS MACHINE KILLS DEMONS

"Thanks," Eduardo said. He'd seen her on the Bridge a few times over the past couple weeks. Most times busking, people didn't see you. Buskers were background noise, enjoyed or ignored. She saw him. Not just as part of San Francisco's colorful scenery or an old Latino with a gray goatee. Something else.

He switched over to a bluesy "All Along the Watchtower," and began a bit of a shuffle as he sang. She smiled and bobbed her shoulders to the music, but when Eduardo got to the chorus, she looked where *los duendes* had gathered. Their arms were outstretched, their transparent claws shimmered in the sunlight. She shivered, but made no move toward them.

What does she see, I wonder?

Eduardo finished the song, adding a few flourishes until the spirits had almost completely faded. She kept staring out where the remnants lingered.

"Everything all right?" he asked. Sometimes folks would shiver and come out of it, not being able to recall what happened.

"You can see them, can't you?" the girl said. "That's why you all play here."

Ed realized she'd been waiting for a chance to talk to him. A family of four walked by, the dad holding up his phone for a picture. Eduardo pointed at the family and put a finger up to his lips, mouthing the word *wait*.

"Who are you?" he asked as soon as they passed by. He'd recruited for his group a few times, but this wasn't how it usually went.

"My name is Emilia Delgado," she said. "My team was studying places where people are drawn to commit suicide. We were trying to calculate the mathematical influence an act of self-harm has on a specific location."

"What?"

Emilia waved her hand. "Suicide attracts more suicides. Mass shootings inspire mass shooters. People are tribal; we influence each other in ways we're not even aware of. My team was studying that, but then some of us began to notice...them."

"You're studying *los duendes*?" Eduardo asked, feeling a little dazed. Since hardly anyone could see them, he didn't think they could be studied by science.

"What did you call them?" she asked.

The air over the Bay was quiet now; the breeze had died down.

There were still tourists on the Bridge, standing far off, but Eduardo felt no sign of *los duendes*. He led Emilia over to a side alcove so they could sit against the wall.

"*Los duendes.* My name for them. Stories *mi abuela* used to tell. Spanish for spirits or goblins. Sister Esther, our leader, she calls them demons. Thinks they're sent to tempt the unwary." He shook his head. "All we really know is that our music drives them off. It's why the City lets us busk the Bridge."

Emilia looked shocked. "The city of San Francisco knows about this?"

"They only know when we play, less people jump," said Eduardo. "Which is good for business and good for them."

Emilia looked out over the water. "We think they're parasites, some kind of ectoplasmic entity manifesting as a byproduct of psychic misery. Humans do most of the work at first, one act inspiring copycats, providing steady feed. But when the suicides stop, the parasites keep the cycle going themselves."

She stared at Eduardo's guitar and the sticker emblazoned across it. "We never thought to test their reaction to music. I wonder if the mathematical harmonies drive them off somehow."

Eduardo smiled bitterly. "Recorded music won't work. Only live performance."

Emilia looked as though she wanted to ask more questions, but another group of tourists walked by, so they waited, watching the sunlight glisten over the Bay far below.

When the tourists left, the whispering started.

Eduardo...

Los duendes had never called him by name before.

Eduardo...

There. At the point just beyond the high railing where he'd played them off earlier. They'd come back. With reinforcements. Eduardo had never seen so many in one place.

Come join us, Eduardo. We're lonely. Join us with your friend, and we'll no longer be lonely. Come with us, and we'll never trouble this place again. Your friends will be free, the Bridge safe, but only if you come out here and play for us.

"Free?" Emilia asked in a tired voice. He shook his head. *Los duendes* always weighed down the mind, but Eduardo had never felt them so strongly before. He took a step forward and Emilia mirrored him.

Come, Eduardo. Come play for us. Play for us forever.

Another step. To play forever, free of care, leaving the Bridge safe for all. Never wake up poor, hungover, and hungry again…

Sunlight glinted off his guitar, off the sticker across the guitar's body.

THIS MACHINE KILLS DEMONS

His hand felt like it weighed 100 pounds, but he lifted it just enough to strum the strings.

The guitar's note cut through their whispers. It felt like cold water poured over his brain. He looked over at Emilia, who was shaking her head.

Eduardo wished the others were here, but if this showdown had to be a solo act, then so be it. The hooded demons flew at him, clawed hands outstretched, calling even louder. Without thinking, Eduardo's hands began to move across the strings, playing chords of the first song that came to mind. He began to sing, taking his time with the words, words he'd known since he was a child.

Amazing grace! How sweet the sound,
that saved a wretch like me!
I once was lost, but now am found,
was blind, but now I see.

The steady strum pattern and his voice pushed them back, but then *los duendes* began to remove their hoods. Beneath were faces Eduardo recognized. Faces of those who had jumped, who he hadn't been able to save. A young man with a scraggly beard and wide, sad eyes. A middle aged woman who'd leapt without even looking. They stared at him now, eyes beseeching, accusing, and then the last *duende* pulled off its hood of mist and shadow.

"Miguel," Eduardo whispered. His fingers fumbled. The boy looked just as he had on Eduardo's wall. Just as Eduardo was about to give up, another voice began to sing softly.

'Twas grace that taught my heart to fear,
And grace my fears relieved;
How precious did that grace appear
The hour I first believed.

Eduardo stared at Emilia in amazement and began to sing with her. She had a nice voice, a wispy contralto that complimented his own bass. By this point, a crowd had gathered around them. As they sang, the faces beneath the goblin's hoods melted away, revealing nothing but transparent blobs with open suckers for mouths. Though disgusted, Eduardo also felt a strange relief. These weren't spirits; that wasn't Miguel. They were...what had Emilia called them?

Parasites.

With each chord, *los duendes* fell back, fading as Eduardo and Emilia reached a crescendo. As they finished, *los duendes* vanished, and their living audience applauded. Startled, Eduardo and Emilia bowed in thanks.

"Wow," said Emilia, after the tourists left. "Is it like that all the time?"

Eduardo laughed. "Nope. First time they ever took off those creepy hoods. First time they called me by name. Lot of firsts, today."

Los duendes must not have wanted them to meet. From what Eduardo could tell, the creatures were far away. The Bridge had never felt so clean. Maybe this attack had cost them.

"I'm sorry," Emilia said. "I didn't mean to cause trouble."

Eduardo shook his head. "I think you saved us. How'd you know that song?"

"Used to sing it in children's choir," said Emilia, smiling. "First song we learned."

It got Eduardo thinking. Maybe it was time to take Miguel's picture down. Wherever the boy was, it wasn't with *los duendes*.

"It's probably safe to grab a little breakfast," Eduardo said. "After that, I got some friends who'd sure love to meet you."

Emilia smiled at him. "I'd like that."

THE TASTE OF STARS
Carman C Curton

"Listen here, now," Adrian clapped his hands, raising his voice as the primary schoolers poured out of the Baldragon-Dundee Academy van and ebbed back and forth over the rocky beach. "Science and Magic are the same thing, ya know. If you don't understand one, you think it's the other." A boy with wild hair and too many teeth raised his hand, shouting out before Adrian could call on him:

"Where are you from?"

Adrian smiled, "Good on ya, mate. You clocked my accent. I'm an Aussie, I study water and water quality – mostly in Melbourne. Do you know where that is?"

"Yeah," the kids chorused. "It's Down Under."

"Exactly. And just like around here there's a lot of water there... and water–"

"Are you a scientist?" a girl interrupted, her eyes goggled a little too wide and too far apart to ever let her be ordinary. "'Cause you look like a wizard."

Adrian adjusted his glasses, stroked the beard he grew after diving season every year, and went on. "Water is of the stars. It was born at the moment of creation in the center of the universe. And the water right here in front of us has been here since our planet formed." He dipped his hand into the lake, where the rubbish filter had started to hum, and flicked drops onto the kids gathered around him until they screeched.

"But the water, now, it's gone sour. People have dumped shit in it, you know that?" The thunder of kids' laughter roared up at the word. "Shit and plutonium and oil and plastic." His fierce look took in the teachers standing behind the kids. "The worst of everything. But plastic is the worst of all." He stood up and pointed at the nearly silent contraption peeking just above the waves. "Me mates 'n me in Melbourne – we built this to take the plastic out, to restore the water so it can remember what the stars taste like."

Holding up his hands to keep the kids where they were, Adrian stepped backward into the water. Further and further back he went, the water welling up his legs in soft ripples.

"Mister, you still got your shoes on," a blue-eyed boy gasped, pointing at his own enormous, splayed feet.

"Wizards used to ride dragons, ya know," Adrian said. He could feel a shadow just below the surface, rising with building momentum. "But this is the thing, it's not Nessie that's magic, it's the Loch."

He was now a dozen yards from his filter, the tide moving water into its baffles with quiet slaps, the pitch of its revving rising as more and more water poured through the catchments and back out into the deep cold lake behind it.

Kids rushed into the now-churning water, tearing off their anoraks and trainers and wellies as the white wave-caps rose over their squat legs, their joyous screeches and roars echoing off the green hills of the Highlands. Two of the teachers yelled hoarsely at the kids: to get out of the water, to get their kit back on, to leave off. A third plunged into the lake after the transforming children, her dorsal fin uncurling with a *fwump* as she bent to pick up a skinny student whose back curved stiffly.

Adrian was lifted out of the water, firmly astride Nessie,

now, the great beast snorting her joy and confusion at watching the hatchlings return to her Loch. Her wings lifted and her belly expanded as she roared out her greeting and the hatchlings tumbled into the dark water. And tasted the stars.

THE RIPENING
Věra Benedeková

I t was late in the morning when Will walked out of his house.
The weather was balmy, with a many-tiered blanket of clouds
hiding the sun, but the wind that blew and ruffled his hair had an
unpleasant bite to it. Little wonder. October had arrived over a
week ago and brought a definite end to the unusually long summer.
Nevertheless, compared to the reign of heatwaves and droughts
stretching from early June to mid-September, the wistful, misty
October was like a little slice of heaven.

Especially when one could enjoy it with a belly full of grilled
ham and cheese sandwiches and with a large mug of coffee
warming one's hands.

Will sat down on the stairs of his porch for a moment and
quietly savored the autumnal scenery.

The pasture was still green, but showed first traces of the
ochres of winter. Two cows were grazing there, flicking their ears
and glancing at the forest behind the farm every few moments.
All around, mountains were vibrant with blackish-green spruces,
contrasting with amber-colored beeches, patches of gold-leaved
birch and, of course, maples burning vermilion, scarlet and
maroon.

A particularly strong gust of wind suddenly blew from behind the farm and brought a peculiar sound to Will's ears. The snapping of branches and groaning of trees, as if something big was making its way from the depths of the forest. The cows moved to a safer part of the pasture and his trusty cat Violet, who had been weaving her slender body around Will's ankles, growled and ran inside before he could give her some calming scritches.

With a not-unhappy sigh, Will got up and went around the farmhouse and through his orchard, which formed something of a buffer zone between the primordial wilderness of the forest and civilization represented by his small, solitary farm; a buffer zone possessing features of both worlds. On one hand, the trees had been planted by human hands; on the other, though well-maintained, they were very old, with patches of bright yellow lichen on their gnarled branches. The moss-covered, waist-high fieldstone wall, which separated the land of the Maycroft family from the woodland beyond, seemed more like an afterthought.

As Will walked through the orchard, he noticed a huge black shadow looming just beyond the stone wall.

Its shape was hard to describe.

One moment it looked like a spreading oak with a particularly squat trunk, then it seemed to have shifted into an outline of a giant moose standing on its hind legs. Every blink of an eye, every movement of one's head made it change its form, but the closer Will got, the more it shrunk, until it gained the approximate outline of a human, albeit one with about half-a-dozen branch-like limbs and the carmine glitter of distant lights glowing within its torso and head.

Will took another sip of his coffee.

"Good morning, Allauda. You're up early," he greeted the being.

The creature emanated a cavalcade of sounds in lieu of an answer. There was the rustling of dry twigs, the flapping of wings, the cry of a deer, the murmur of a stream. When put together, this amalgam formed words within Will's ears. Or his mind — he was never quite sure.

'*Good day. I was awoken,*' the visitor replied.

"Awoken?" Will repeated with mild confusion. "By what?"

It was still too early for him to have started any machinery. After all, he had just finished his breakfast.

'*They are making sounds.*'

"Who is?"

'*The little ones.*'

"Hm?" Will cocked his head to the side.

When it came to Allauda, the '*little ones*' in question could've been anything from chirping crickets to cows to heavily armed soldiers.

A knotted bough, pitch-black and with a velvety sheen, rose up and gradually assumed the shape of a human arm with fingers pointing somewhere next to the red-headed farmer.

Feeling a sudden bout of unease, Will spun around, nervous about what he might find...—only to come face to face with–

Apples. Hanging from a branch drooping under their weight.

"You mean these?"

'*Yes.*'

"How come you don't know what apples are? You've been here forever."

'*Forever. At the pit of the forest. No apples there. Only here, at the liminal space, where you have drawn me those years ago. Yes. No apples in the pit. No applesss...*' the buzzing of bees explained. The buzzing of bees, the low-pitched sound of ice floes breaking, the pattering of spring rain against freshly sprouted beech leaves.

"So you say they are making sounds?" Will reached for the ripest one and twisted it off.

He put it to his ear and shook it. The seeds inside rattled.

'*Yesss, that sound. It was that sound.*'

"That means the apple is ripe." Will smiled, cleaned it on his shirt and took a large bite.

It was sweet, juicy, and pleasantly cold from the chill of the previous night.

As he swallowed, he felt eyes on his throat. Many eyes.

"Here, have a bite as well," he offered, sensing Allauda's hunger. These honeycrisps were his pride and joy, and he never missed an opportunity to share them.

As he reached out with his hand, the part of Allauda that was his head suddenly spun and shot out, enveloping Will's arm all the way to the elbow. It felt funny, but not unpleasant. Rather like fine silt lifted from the bottom of a pond, thickened and warmed under a summer sun's glare.

Over the years, Will had become quite familiar with that touch. *'Mmmm...tasty. And sweet.'*

"Sweet, huh?" Will chuckled. "I have an idea. How about I grab a basket, and we'll harvest those apples? You'll stretch all the way to the top and pluck them, and I'll wait under the tree with an apron to catch them."

'And then we'll eat them...'

"And then we'll eat them," Will agreed. "Wait here, I'll be right back."

Allauda watched his sun-human rush off.

As he waited for his return, he pulled the seeds of the eaten apple from his stomach. They were already starting to sprout. Pondering his options for a while, he eventually put them back in. He decided to plant them in his pit later on, so there'll be even more apples one day, when his *Willahelm* will visit again.

'...and then we'll eat...' the wind sighed in the branches of the orchard, and Allauda smiled.

THE SCENT OF CHANGE
Laura J Kelly

Some people still call it the Dog Pound though the official name is The Louisiana Rougarou Compound or the LRC for short. It's located just off Highway 10 between Baton Rouge and New Orleans. Sensors, cameras, and God knows what else sits atop the pale blue, 30-foot-high walls. For a quarter mile around, any plant hardy enough to fight back is regularly doused with herbicide to maintain a brown swath that even lizards are afraid to cross. After sundown, the expanse has lighting as bright as any professional football field. All the security is laughable when you consider most rougarous turn themselves in. They still feel safer inside than out.

On the last day I visited my partner Jac, heatwaves rolled up from the concrete adding to the already oppressive atmosphere created by the LRC's looming walls. Friends and family were waiting to enter, clustered together saying little, holding cool bottles of water against the side of their faces, or using hats as makeshift fans. Eventually, a door opened in the wall furthest from the visitors' entrance. Jac strode through, tongue lolling in the heat, his black wavy hair artfully tousled. I smiled at how he always managed to look like he was preparing for a photo shoot. His handsome head swept from side to side, nostrils twitching as he sampled the humid air. When he caught my scent, he stiffened, his eyes found and locked onto mine before he walked into the visitation area.

The security guard behind the check-in counter didn't take his eyes off the Saint's football game on his tablet as he said, "Name."

"Richard Casey."

"Who ya visitin?"

"Jacob Amant."

"ID."

I gave him my driver's license. He looked up long enough to check it against Jac's list of approved visitors.

"This address still current?"

"Yeah."

He checked a box on his list and recited the legal disclaimers in a rapid monotone. "Do you understand that the cause of the change into a rougarou is unknown, and there is no treatment? And do you understand by entering you waive your right to any litigation against the state and federal government, the residents, family of the residents, or employees of the LRC should you experience physical changes?"

"I do."

"Sign here. You have one hour." He turned his attention back to the game.

I handed my laptop and its' thick quilted case to the next guard for her inspection before walking through the scanner. On two previous visits, they hadn't found the knife. I'd tested the hidden pocket using a little serrated plastic picnic knife. This time the test was a full-sized weapon. Still plastic, but so sharp, I was afraid it would shift and cut through the fabric. She held a metal detector over the case, and when it started to beep, she said, "Step to the side, Sir." The guard began running her hands over the surface of the case, inside and out.

Our mamas swore Jac and I bonded while still in the womb, as they sat side-by-side at Sunday Mass. While I doubt the truth of that, there's no denying we spent every waking hour together, often stretching their patience as far as it could go and then some. On summer nights, we'd sneak out at a predetermined time to meet and dart around the neighborhood like bats, dipping in and out of the shadows between houses, down alleys, and climbing fences. When heat stalked the dark streets, we knew which places had fountains in their tiny, manicured courtyards. We held the beast at bay by sticking our heads under the falling water, sputtering and laughing until lights came on, sending us running, leaving wet footprints in our wake.

We were about six years old when some locals discovered a settlement of rougarous southwest of Baton Rouge near the Bayou Sorrel. Until then, the only evidence rougarous existed consisted of a few blurry photographs. The State offered a bounty for bringing them in alive since the Health Department wanted to know if rougarous were responsible for transforming humans and, if so, how they did it. Tranquilizer guns and hunting licenses became hot commodities.

Predictably, the rougarous fought back. When armed strangers close in on you, the options are limited. Survivors were brought in and held in the first LRC, made from a few tents surrounded by barbed wire. I don't remember much about it, though the news coverage was extensive. Old photos and videos show figures using buckets to wash or waiting in line for food with their heads down. A handful stare directly into the camera. One rougarou, in particular, reminds me of Jac. He faces the camera with no hint of shame, no request for pity. Because I never took a picture of Jac after he changed, I printed that photo out and pinned it up where I can see it as I type.

Eventually, the LRC physicians realized most rougarous retained the ability to write and use keyboards unless their hands had undergone more extensive changes. Speech remained impossible because of the differences in head anatomy. When someone leaked their writings to the press, the world began to find out who they were before they turned into a rougarou. One minute someone was a mechanic, a musician, or an office worker, and the next, they were half-dog, half-human. Not one of them could explain why it happened to them.

The residents also described the conditions in the LRC. Beatings were common, as was the indiscriminate use of tasers. The guards placed bets on how many hits it would take for the resident to pass out. Since none of the guards ever changed into a rougarou, even after they had been bitten or scratched, they had proof rougarous were not the means of transfer.

Pressure from international rights organizations and social media became a public relations nightmare for Louisiana. The State had no choice but to build decent housing and ensure residents were well treated. Unfortunately, the evidence rougarous presented no threat to full humans took a long time for folks to accept. People continued to hunt them for sport despite new laws against it. To this day, the occasional rougarou body turns up in a ditch.

Jac and I saw our first rougarou in the flesh when our seventh grade class went on a field trip to the Louisiana Children's Museum. A sheriff's car sped past our bus and then stopped blocking the road. We all rushed to the windows. The rougarou was wearing a disheveled business suit and dusty black dress shoes. He walked along the side of the road, steel gray, dog-head constantly moving, back and forth, up and down. Dressed the way he was, the guy hadn't been one very long. His enhanced sight, hearing, and smell must have made it seem like he'd arrived on a new planet.

The sheriff didn't try to communicate with him, just pulled out a tranq gun and shot him. We watched as he tried to run, fell, and started to crawl. His fur-covered hands grasped at the dirt to pull himself forward when his lower body, the human half, began to fail. Some of the kids started to cry; some started to cheer. Jac joined the cheers until he looked at me, and then he stopped as if his voice had become a stone in his throat. I don't know what he saw on my face. I couldn't have told him if he'd asked.

Later that day, we sat on his front porch steps drinking sweet tea. I said, "Do you believe what Father Michael says about rougarou? That's it's some kinda punishment, and if they repent, they turn back to all human?"

"I heard some do change back. I don't know about the repenting part. Some of the Baptists are saying there's more of them now because it's the end times."

"They say that about everything."

"Yeah, but both churches say there's something wrong with the person if they change. Doctors don't even know what's up."

I put down my glass of tea and asked, "Have you ever thought about if it could happen to you or me?"

"If it were you, nobody'd notice the difference." He grinned and shoved me. I shoved back, and eventually, we succeeded in pushing our fear and questions down to a place where we could tolerate them.

By the time we finished high school, they'd rebuilt the LRC into its present form. The sprawling complex housed medical and research facilities. Despite their efforts, nobody knew what caused adults to change and why about thirty percent changed back in about four months. There were all kinds of theories, genetic predisposition, exposure to toxic chemicals, rare endocrine disorders, viruses. Not even the Catholics believed the old stories that a failure to observe lent or being cursed by someone caused the person to become a rougarou.

The living conditions inside the LRC improved with the rebuild. Barracks became small apartments. Male and female residents were allowed to mingle, though contraception was mandatory. Committees formed and became a type of self-governance, acting as liaisons to the agency that ran the LRC. The improvements made it easy for those of us on the outside to forget about the rougarou. When someone changed, they simply disappeared behind the blue walls.

Scholarships determined where Jac and I ended up for college. So, for the first time in our lives, we went to different schools in different cities. We drifted apart. I can't speak for Jac, but I never felt entirely anchored despite making good friends and having a couple of intense relationships.

When Jac and I reconnected after college, it was like a combination of fireworks and the best home-cooked comfort food you can imagine. We had fights and broke up a couple of times, as most couples do. In the end, neither one of us could see going forward without the other. While our parents weren't thrilled, they'd seen it coming, and if the Pope said we had the right to be happy, then it was okay with them. We moved into a fixer-upper in the Marigny District east of the French Quarter.

Early one night, I heard a thump and a moan coming from the front of the house. My first thought was that Jac fell off the ladder while painting. I hurried into the living room to see him lying on his side, holding his head.

"Oh God, make it stop," he slurred.

"What is it? Did you fall?" I knelt beside him, pulling his hands away, looking for blood. Instead, I saw something out of a painting by Picasso. His jaw looked dislocated, the skin from forehead to chin discolored by purple bruises. His cheekbones and nose shifted as I watched, pushing forward, cracking, elongating.

"Jesus, Jac. I'll call 911." He gave a wailing, unearthly cry when I tried to pull away. He grabbed my arm, his fingers digging in with fierce strength. I put a hand over his, intent on pulling it off so I could get my phone. But instead, I felt the smooth, soft fluff of young canine fur sliding beneath my palm.

I didn't call. Wrapping my arms around him, I struggled to hold on in the face of his greater upper body strength. Muscles spasmed beneath his skin, alternately twitching and turning rock hard as they cramped. Speaking was no longer possible for him or even the ability to cry. He could only whimper and pant. "I'm here. I've gotcha." I kept repeating it until the change was complete, and he lay quiet. After a time, I helped him to the couch, and he fell asleep.

I called his parents and then mine. They both reacted the same way. After some expressions of horror and tears, they said, "It's God's will. We'll light a candle and pray for him to change back."

I was on my own and terrified. You just can't Google how to care for a newborn rougarou. Some of the residents of the LRC posted stories on social media about their experiences with the change. I poured over them, learning what I could. It sounded a lot like some kind of high from drugs or alcohol. They seemed to have difficulty with impulse control, focus, and problem-solving, until they adjusted to all the new information from their enhanced senses. Eating and drinking created new challenges with the changes in anatomy.

I spent some time putting away things that might be dangerous, such as poisons. I needed to do something, and my half-baked logic said to 'baby-proof' the house. With nothing left to do, I sat in a chair, watching him sleep. Jac lay in a fetal position. Black fur, about the length of a Labrador retriever's, covered his upper body and muzzle. The hair on his head echoed his human form, with soft curls from his forehead down his neck. Once well-proportioned, his hands now appeared swollen and chunky with thick finger pads and narrow black curved claws. His legs remained in human form, sticking out from the old shorts he wore for painting. If I hadn't watched the change happen, it might have been easier to believe some mad scientist had contrived to attach his lower body to an animal.

Just after midnight, Jac sat up but didn't respond to anything I said. With unsteady steps, he began to explore our house. For the next few hours, everything seemed to fascinate him. One of the first things he did was sniff and snuffle me from head to toe. I stood stiff, willing myself not to cringe or push him away. I kept repeating to myself, "He can't help it."

I was glad I hid anything toxic as I watched him wander around the house, opening cabinets and closets smelling everything. Paintings and photographs on the walls required minutes of scrutiny as new details caught his attention. Sounds brought him up short, things that I'd never noticed before or couldn't hear, like the faint rustle of my footsteps on the rug or someone walking by on the far side of the street.

When dawn came, I called in sick for me and then for Jac. He watched me make breakfast, pacing around the small kitchen, constantly sampling the air. Eggs, toast, sausage, and grits all started out neatly on plates. The food spread to the table and then to the floor as he pushed it around with his nose, trying to figure out how to use his mouth and tongue. My internal mantra of "He can't help it" wore thin as disgust and annoyance grew. Finally, I left the room to keep from saying something in front of him.

When I came back in, he was on the floor licking up grits. He seemed fine with it until he looked up at me. Then he threw back his head and howled before curling up amid the food scraps, whimpering. His moment of realization at what he was tore me open, and shame for my reactions spilled out. Jac was still there inside, and there was nothing I could do to help him. I sat down on the floor next to him to share his grief as best I could.

By the second day, we worked out how to communicate. We made sure a laptop was always nearby. He pecked away, slowly at first, then with more confidence as he got used to his claws and thick finger pads. Our options were limited. Waiting seemed to be the best choice. If he didn't change back after four months, we'd have to decide if he should go to the LRC. He couldn't stay out of sight forever, and the only other option was finding a place hidden in the swamps. I suggested that as a possibility. Jac snorted and started making huffing sounds. It took me a second to realize he was laughing. I described what he would look like slogging through the water in his best corporate clothes or trying to build a fire on some tiny island. He laughed harder. The more outrageous my description, the harder we both laughed until we were gasping for breath, and just when we got ourselves under control, we looked at each other and started all over again. Gallows humor, they call it.

In the end, the decision to go to the LRC was made for us when a neighbor saw Jac on our little back patio. The guy started shouting, "Call 911!" For a moment, all I could see was that tranquilized rougarou crawling in the dirt.

"We can't wait for them to get here. I don't trust the cops not to hurt you," I said, grabbing his arm and pulling him toward the front door. We ran to our car. Without a computer, we rode in silence. When we arrived at the LRC, I reached over and gripped his shoulder. He turned to me, and I said, "No matter what happens, I'm not giving up on you." He nodded and strode to the entrance with his head up. Guards led him away before I'd even finished giving all the information the intake personnel wanted.

After that, I came home and spent all my spare time researching treatments. I found something among the folk tales no one had tried. Maybe someone had concerns about ethics, or they thought it was too far-fetched. No one believes in curses anymore, so why bother trying crazy remedies? Those things didn't matter to me. If it didn't work, at least I would have tried.

"Sir?"

I turned to face the guard.

"Sir, I'm finished. That zipper on the case set it off again. Enjoy your visit." She leaned a bit closer as she slid the case to me and lowered her voice. "Jac seems a bit down. It happens a lot when someone passes the four-month mark. I hope you can cheer him up; he seems like a nice guy."

"Thanks. I appreciate your concern." I put the laptop into the case and retreated into the visiting area, wiping the sweat from my face.

Jac and I always met in the corner furthest from the entrance. LRC personnel placed a table and chairs under oaks draped with Spanish moss. The shade was only slightly more comfortable, but we take anything we can get during August in Louisiana. When I first started coming, I noticed the outdoor area was much larger than necessary for the number of visitors. People I recognized from my first visits no longer came either because the resident changed back to all human or, more often, because they didn't.

Jac watched me approach with sad eyes. Setting up the laptop between us, I still hoped I wouldn't have to use the knife.

"You're here to check on me again." His fingers clicked across the keys.

"No change then? Not even a small one?" I said.

"You can see for yourself. It's past the time. I've seen it happen to others who came in after I did. I know I won't be leaving. We have to accept it."

"I'm not going to stop coming."

"It's just going to get harder for both of us. I'm taking you off the approved list." He didn't look away from the screen.

"No, Jac. Please just look at me, give it some more time. I need to keep seeing you."

"You know how I feel about you. You're…"

Who would have thought tiny pixels could cause such pain? Processing the words scrolling across the page became too much. I would have to use the knife. Leaving Jac here without the hope of seeing him again would be killing a part of me. Though, if this worked, what I was about to do amounted to the same thing.

As he continued typing, I picked up the laptop case. My hand slick with sweat, I groped inside for the loose thread marking the hidden pocket. A sharp tug would unravel the stitching and open it. I only succeeded in spreading the moisture around. The sweat plastered the damn thing down. There was nothing to grasp to open the pocket. I pulled out my hand, wiping it on the cotton of my pants.

I reached back into the case and tried again. Scraping the surface of the fabric with my nails, I tried to dislodge and lift the thread. There. I pulled. The thread snapped off. I had nothing to grab.

As Jac's typing slowed down, I pushed hard on the lining, forcing it against the knife. The tip sliced through the fabric, barely missing my fingers and giving me enough surface to grab with my thumb and forefinger. I slide it out of the pocket and let the knife rest at the bottom of the case so I could grasp it by the hilt.

Jac was just sitting starring at the screen now. He hit save. As he turned to look at me, I pulled out the knife and sliced it across the back of his arm, cutting through the fur and flesh.

He jerked back and stood, kicking the chair out of the way. His hackles up and teeth bared, towering over me, snarling, every instinct told him to strike. I felt at peace now, watching the blood flow over his glossy coat onto the ground. I spoke my last coherent words. "The old stories say someone can cut a rougarou and remove the curse. The curse transfers to the person with the knife. Sounds crazy, I know. Maybe there's some kind of mutual chemical trigger when you have to hurt someone you care about. If it works, I could change back in a few months. It's worth the chance. I don't think I'm gonna be as handsome as you are, though."

Jac's body seemed to remember his original form and behaved as if it couldn't wait to return to it. Fur fell off in handfuls, his nails retracted. When his jaw cracked, he let out a howl which drew the guard's attention, and an alarm went off. Fortunately, he was almost all human by the time they reached us. Seeing him look so much like the man I remembered made my heart ache. He placed himself between the guards and me to keep them from using their tasers until it was clear neither of us was a threat. Then he knelt beside me, holding me as the bones in my face began to break and reposition.

"I'm here. I've gotcha," he said.

It's been three months. I was right. My head is too big, and despite my best efforts, my fur is a bit scruffy. Jac and I email every day. No matter how often he asks, I haven't let him visit. There's no way I'm going to risk him trying to exchange places with me with what's happening on the outside.

The newsfeeds got ahold of our story, so Jac's using his looks and new celebrity status to full advantage. Yesterday he secured grant funding to start an agency arranging supervised employment for us on the outside. His first contracts will be with federal agencies and law enforcement who want us to detect narcotics. He also made contacts in medical facilities that want to identify scents related to diseases, changes in blood sugar, and low-level infection. Some people are saying it's happening too fast. There are others, just as vocal, who say change can't happen fast enough.

I'm a bit of a celebrity too, which I have to say is a pretty novel experience. There are new lines of research because of what I did. Our chat rooms are in overdrive with discussions about whether someone would choose to change back. Some like their new heightened senses so much they wouldn't dream of it. Others want to return to their old lives. My guess is that most friends and family members wouldn't see them the same way again. I know Jac's parents haven't.

I don't have long to wait before I know if this new me is forever or not. Jac says if I don't change back, he'll get in touch with one of the rougarou he knows and offer to try trading places. We don't know if cutting someone you're not close to will work. Is a desire to change enough without some kind of stronger connection? If it is, Jac could run the business from inside. I guess we'll find out. Wish us luck.

We don't need your prayers.

THE BONE FAIRIES
Mara Lynn Johnstone

"Wait, what are you doing?" Yvette asked. The panic in her voice made Rosalind stop halfway to the cottage door. "Taking the scraps outside?"

"Why?" Yvette hurried over to yank the plate of chicken bones from her guest's unresisting hands.

"For the bone fairies."

"*Why* would you – do you *feed* the bone fairies back home? How are you still alive?"

"What?" Rosalind asked in deepening confusion as Yvette dumped the bones into the fireplace. "If you *don't* feed them, they start nosing around instead of cleaning the woods of carrion."

"What?" The two stared at each other for a moment.

"Do we have different types of bone fairies?" Rosalind asked.

"We must. What does your kind look like?"

"Reddish feathers," Rosalind gestured vaguely. "Like little birds if you don't look too close. They even have beaks, though otherwise they're humanoid with feathers. They crack open the bones of carcasses for the marrow, and they can carry really big ones on account of the magic. They drop them on rocks to split

81

them open. We always leave bone scraps out at the end of the fence."

Yvette was shaking her head, the empty plate forgotten in her hand. "Ours are a terror," she said flatly. "Like huge bugs, with sawtooth arms and mouths to match. Greenish-gray. They'll slice open anything that looks like it has tasty marrow in its bones." She remembered the plate, and moved to place it in the sink. "You do *not* want to invite them closer."

Rosalind's eyes were wide. "I had no idea!"

"I'm glad this came up now," Yvette waved toward the table. "Welcome to my home! Let's go over basic woodland safety so you don't get us killed while you're here."

"Yes, let's!"

Rosalind took the instructions to heart, staying out of dangerous areas and always bringing with her the small pack of essentials, which included a small bottle of bone fairy repellent.

Even so, she somehow didn't expect to ever need it. A lifetime free of such nightmares made her feel on some deep level like this must be an exaggeration. She wouldn't have said so out loud, of course. But she did stay out a little too late into dusk one night, on a search for firewood she didn't have to cut.

Her eyes were on the ground, scanning for fallen branches. She didn't see anything out of the ordinary, and if there was a faint buzzing sound in the air, it didn't bother her survival instincts in the slightest.

Then she passed a dense patch of bushes, and she saw the bear.

The former bear. It was big, it was dead, and there was blood literally everywhere, even splattered on the trees. Its fur moved.

Ohhhh no no no no, Rosalind thought as she scrambled backwards. Hand-sized insectoids were emerging from that dense fur, spotting her and taking to the air. They may have been green-gray once. They were red now.

Rosalind broke and ran with buzzing loud around her. She fumbled with the pack at her hip, dropping things in the search for that tiny bottle. When she found it, she nearly lost it in a fern, but managed to clutch it tight. The cork was slippery under fingers covered in fear-sweat.

Yvette had said that the repellent could be wafted around if the bone fairies were still a ways away, or poured in a circle on the ground if an area needed to be protected. She hadn't said what to do when under *active pursuit*, but Rosalind could figure that out herself.

She wrenched the cork out and dumped it on her head.

Her other hand was already rubbing it into her hair when the smell hit.

Lavender, rosemary, and SKUNK.

Rosalind coughed, her eyes nearly closing as she stumbled forward. She dropped the jar and moved to rub her eyes, but stopped just short. She kept running.

If this is how I die, she thought grimly, *somebody's getting haunted.*

But the buzzing faded slowly, left behind in the deepening shadows of the forest that could keep its darn firewood; they'd burn something else. Maybe Rosalind's clothes.

She finally stumbled up to the cottage in one piece, with no firewood and many regrets. She didn't even have to knock. Yvette smelled her coming.

"Undress over there," she said from the doorway. "I'll get a bucket of water, then grab every tomato in the garden. And a few scrub cloths I don't need back. You don't seem to be missing any bones, so I can only assume it was worth it."

Rosalind coughed and followed Yvette's pointed finger. "Worth it," she agreed. "But barely."

THE OTHER MID-AUTUMN
Jeremy Pak Nelson

The mid-autumn moon hung between the towers of Heyworth Mansions, yolk round and big enough to fill the gap between apartment buildings. Lit living rooms, bedrooms, kitchens, shone starlike on a backdrop of concrete night.

Shingyan never saw the rabbit on the moon. Only a face, looking to the left, mouth open to ask a question. Or maybe exhaling smoke clouds to drift dark on lunar porcelain.

Mid-Autumn Festival brought lights from Hong Kong's apartment buildings into the parks. Children ran with their lanterns, vinyl inflatables vividly illuminated from the inside with LEDs and taking every shape from Ultraman to Pokémon. It's only been a few years since Shingyan had a lantern of his own. He didn't want to admit that a part of him missed it.

A white-haired woman sat on one of the benches. No one in the park paid her any mind, but Shingyan felt a tug at his attention. He couldn't put his finger on why. She rooted around a plastic bag. A squall of children ran past her, little lungs bursting with joyful screams. There was a touch of cold in the air, a hint of winter that reminded Shingyan of dew. Night was his favorite time to be out, especially in the autumn months, not too cold to be uncomfortable, but cool enough not to worry about getting sweaty. He planted himself at one of the park's chess tables and played Crusader Gambol on his phone. For a couple of hours, pixel soldiers and kaiju were all he had to think about. Overhead, the moon traced its arc and appeared to shrink as it rose above the city. With patience and practice one could spot the satellite networks that wreathed the sky.

Shingyan's phone blinked a warning. Running out of power. He had forgotten his battery pack, and – he checked his pockets to make sure – he'd also left the charging cable. He would have to head home earlier, maybe, if he didn't want to be bored all night.

Most of the other kids had gone home, their parents sending insistent texts at them or, for the wealthier ones, being shepherded back by their helpers. If Shingyan left now he might make it back early enough not to be yelled at. Not that Mom needed much of an excuse. Set her off and she'd have at him about being more responsible, about keeping his class rankings up, and their argument dragging everyone out of bed, Dad stepping into the room with face scrunched up from the light, trying to put on his reasonable voice and making things worse. Little Terese by the door, watching. Saying nothing.

Stay out late enough and maybe he can sneak in. Avoid any drama.

The park perched on a foliage-dense hillside of Hong Kong Island. Shingyan traced circles around the climbing gym, peering into the apartments of buildings further down the hill. The ground was steep enough that twentieth-floor apartments were at eye level. The people inside were the size of chibi Gundam figures. Terrace by terrace, apartment buildings colonized the slope.

In a corner of the park a few kids enacted an older tradition. Shingyan remembered – he used to do the same. They congregated around mooncake tins lit from the inside by dozens of red candles. Wax pooled alongside reflected candlelight. 'Cooking wax' was technically illegal, now, but talking a kid out of an excuse to play with fire was not easy.

Shingyan kept his distance. Four children hunched over the fire. They lit one candle with another, tipping them to drip wax footholds to stick the candles down. It wasn't complicated. Simple fun. No school projects to deal with. Maybe too young to worry about secondary school admissions.

Shingyan heard a voice behind him and almost jumped.

"Little kids, always the same." It was the woman from the bench. She stood a step or two behind him, but her eyes were on the fire. "Tell them all you want, but some won't listen." She looked at Shingyan. "Are you one of those kids?"

Well, he thought, screw her and her attitude. He walked away. Who had time to deal with strangers telling you off? Had plenty enough at home. But what Shingyan didn't have at home was junk food, so he left thinking of McDonald's. Behind him he heard the woman heave a hacking cough. He didn't look back. If she was a spitter he didn't want to see it.

Shingyan finished the last handful of fries when he wandered back to the park. Past midnight, only a few determined stragglers remained. Some, like him, no doubt valued time outside their cramped apartments. Others, maybe, with families too lenient or neglectful to make sure the children made it home. But most of those kids didn't stay in the parks, much, there was too much else to do. Shingyan loved that about the city. Walk around at almost any hour and you wouldn't be bored. Not unless you're out in the bloodshot predawn hours when fresh newspapers were stacked on sidewalks, when restaurants prepared service for the earliest shift. Even then, there were the gaming cafes that never closed, fast food restaurants that doubled as extended dining rooms for the crowds. But all that needed money, and Shingyan hadn't gotten his allowance in weeks. Hadn't earned it, his parents said.

The older lady was still there, standing in a planter ankle-deep in shrubbery. She was bent over, messing with something on the ground. Shingyan heard a cat's meow, almost a phone notification's chirp, and only then did he notice the cats. Tabby, calico, ginger and black, at least a dozen wound their way through trees and fences to approach the old woman in the planter. She held cans of food. She opened one, upended its contents into a small dish, and placed it beside her. A bag at her feet bulged full with more cans of cat food.

"There are some kids," she said, as if they'd been talking all along, "there are some kids that are particularly naughty, stubborn. Doesn't mean they're bad kids. You have to find a way to let them mature." She bent down for another can, and he wondered if it hurt her back at all. Not that he cared, or even had any idea of what the woman expected of him. How were you supposed to respond to unprompted lectures? So he said nothing. Maybe it was the price to pay for watching the cats. There were maybe fifteen that Shingyan could see, though he caught glimpses of more in the trees, waiting.

"What about you?" she asked. "Are you too old to be setting things on fire? Are you rebelling? Do you do your homework?"

Silence wasn't always the right answer, but at least it wasn't usually wrong. To appreciate the cats in peace was too much to hope for. Shingyan's family absolutely did not have room for pets at home; three hundred and fifty square feet didn't leave room for much of anything. Not enough for arguments, certainly.

The woman dropped one of the cans. It hit the ground and rolled. Without thinking, Shingyan reached out with a foot and stopped it.

"Not bad," she said. "You play on a team?" As if she hadn't been hectoring him a second ago.

"Tryouts are next week," he said.

"Work hard, that's what coaches like to see. Work hard and you'll make it in."

He nodded.

The park still had the old yellow streetlights. Didn't feel as clean as the new LED ones. But not as much eyestrain, he thought.

Terese would always complain about the extra shadows the new multi-bulb lights cast.

Shingyan stepped closer to have a better look at the cats. They paid him only as much attention as they needed to determine he had no food to offer, and then they were all eyes on the old woman. When she finished with the last can, she tied the plastic bag up with a tight knot. "For the smell," she said, and rolled one shoulder, then the other.

"Maybe you're a good kid. I can tell that there's some rascal in you, or else you wouldn't be up so late, there's school in the morning! But a good kid. Let me show you something."

She fished under her jacket, which was a thickly-padded puffer jacket far too warm for the weather. Mom would have approved. She was always telling Shingyan to put something on when he headed out. The woman pulled out a pair of spectacles. They looked ancient. He might have seen the exact same pair in sepia-toned photographs from a century ago. Round black frames. She held them out.

"What are you standing there for? Put them on," she said. And she was right back at nagging him.

"I've got glasses," Shingyan said.

"Wear them in front, your nose is definitely big enough to do the job."

If curiosity hadn't gotten the better of him Shingyan would have left. Not that he had anywhere to go. So he put them on, fully conscious of how ridiculous he looked. Sure, Shingyan had plenty of friends in school, but he knew he wasn't enough of a trend-setter to get away with what was happening on his face.

The lenses were smudged. He wiped them on his shirt, and looked again. No help. Through the two circular lenses was a world full of mist. And he realized that's exactly what he saw. Through the old woman's glasses, mist drifted through the park like a winter dawn at the top of the Peak.

"The full moon lights everything up real well," she said. He turned to follow her voice, and through the glasses *she* was different, her eyes as bright and as lively as his little sister Terese's, but apart from the eyes she was still very much the same woman who fed cats – and probably did so every night.

"There are more interesting things to look at, knucklehead." She grabbed his arm and turned him around to face the apartment buildings closest to them. He would have to lean back to see to the top, but he didn't need to look that far.

From the tiled facade of the building came a stream of fog, like breath in cold air. An open window let out the unmistakable clatter of mahjong tiles being shuffled on a table. He could almost hear the voices of people speaking over the noise. As the clatter died down, and the game began, the mists that streamed from the building changed. They took on shape. They looked...almost like puppets, like tiny cloud people pulling themselves from the stream. A few faded away, broke apart as if dispersed by a breeze. Others ran through the air, disappearing into another apartment or up the hill into the mountain.

There was more. Something inside the little cloud people, odd regular shapes. Symbols. Bewildering until Shingyan recognized them from the mahjong tiles. Round circles of the coin suite tumbled in the stomach of one of the puppets. A peacock in another. Four humanoid figures with arms linked drifted overhead, each of them carrying within one of the cardinal directions, 東, 南, 西, 北.

"I would have picked better company if I knew you were the quiet type. Quit gawking, we have work to do." She waved with her hand as you would at a dog. Shingyan felt like he had to tear his eyes away. Over and over, the words *it seems so real* repeated in his mind. But that seemed such an inadequate thing to say. He followed.

They left the park and walked along the sidewalk to the busier part of the neighborhood. Shingyan thought to take a picture through the lenses with his phone, but the battery had already given out. *Typical*, he thought. But a small part of him also couldn't help but wonder if the evening would have been possible otherwise.

Most of the stores were closed, now, and even through the glasses there didn't seem anything special about most of the street. Except, he noticed, for the staircase that led down to the basement cybercafe. The place was full of the opaque mist. It pooled in the stairs. Every now and then a tendril reached out, as if part of something alive, to test the air.

"What is all this? What are we doing?"

"Looking for something. What's the point of a Mid-Autumn Festival if you don't go out and look for spirits? Make some friends?"

He pointed at the mist. A mist-figure, about the size of a toddler, crawled up the stairs. At its heart a gemstone sparked. "Are those spirits?"

She made an exasperated grunt. "Don't be absurd. Does that look like a spirit to you? It's barely a thought. It'll be gone by sunrise, and it'll only last that long because of the season." She pointed one hand at the alleyway behind the supermarket. In the light her liver spots stood out. He thought of animal print.

"That," she said, "is promising."

It took Shingyan a moment, then he realized she pointed at a cat. A white-and-ginger that reminded him of a Fanta ice cream float. Terese's favorite.

"The cat?" he asked. Despite all the strangeness that had already happened, the strangeness that drifted in eddying mists around them, to imply the cat was a spirit seemed beyond ridiculous.

"Of course not. But if we follow, give it a nudge…"

They trailed after the animal. The cat's tail crooked in the air, almost like a taunt. When the creature noticed them following, they slipped into the alley between the supermarket and a cha chaan teng. The restaurant was only now closing up for the night, the last customers at their tables washing down fried noodles and pork curry with Tsingtao. Phantom beer bottles rolled through the windows to vanish in the street.

Water stains streaked black where the walls of the alley were scarred by years of air conditioner drip. It smelled of stagnant water. Like a pond left too long to gather algae.

A surprisingly strong hand grabbed Shingyan's elbow. "We wait here," she said, "and watch."

The alley walls were marked by more than stains. At irregular intervals, scattered on the walls, were small white lights. Like upturned bowls. They blinked on and off, but gave little light.

Under one of the lights, the cat paced, nosing the ground. They rubbed a cheek against the wall. And above the creature, the light grew.

It didn't become brighter. No, it grew how a plant grew, extending from the wall, a pale ghostly stalk. It had, Shingyan realized, a face. Every one of the lights wore a face. A wall of hanging masks, Shingyan thought.

He saw what happened next, but didn't understand it. The stalk turned down and wrapped itself around the cat, who seemed not to mind, nuzzling against the ghostly appendage. Shingyan peeked over the glasses the old lady had given him, and without the help of the lenses there was only a white-and-ginger cat turning in on themself in the alleyway.

The other faces watched. They might have watched the two people standing at the mouth of the alley, but to Shingyan their small eyes seemed directionless, almost dead. But he thought there was nothing to fear from them, sensed no animosity from the many painted masks. Or maybe he just wanted to pretend not to be afraid.

The light stretched from the wall, thinning like chewing gum until it snapped away from the concrete and wound around the animal. The two convolved, spun like the patterns of a gymnast's ribbon.

Then the light was gone, leaving only a cat. Who seemed normal. Maybe a bit bigger than before. The faces on the walls receded into concrete. Shingyan thought of a snail's eyes, how their stalks shrunk away into themselves.

"You're lucky, son, that's not something you see often, even on nights like these. Give it a few decades and the little nubbin might transform completely."

Shingyan didn't understand what she meant. The strange ghostly display? Then the cat turned around, as if they'd heard. Shingyan met their eyes and couldn't move. It was like he became one of the faces in the wall, rooted in place, no limbs, no body, only his eyes meeting the all-too-human eyes the cat now wore. The eyes that came with a human's nose and small, smiling, human lips.

A hand swiped the glasses from his face. "It's not polite to stare, kid, didn't your parents teach you?"

With only prescription lenses, the cat looked like any other cat. Except, maybe, with a knowing look. In the dim alleyway they shone. The cat turned and left, as though there was all the time in the world.

"Was that – what was that?"

"Don't be daft, you know what you saw. Must have been an old cat to become a 猫精 so easily." She gave one of her hacking coughs, and that shook Shingyan out of his trance. For all her lecturing she could do with some manners. Maybe she was too old to care.

"That can't be right," he said. Without the antique glasses the alleyway looked like any other urban crevasse, moldering from too little sun. But he couldn't dismiss what he'd seen.

Shingyan's guide waved a hand at him, as if he'd been bothering her instead of the other way around. "It's far too late for kids to be wandering about. You better head on home or your parents will worry."

They wouldn't, he was about to say, but she gave a look and Shingyan couldn't get a single word out. She tucked the glasses back inside her jacket and left him there, stuck fast at the mouth of the alleyway. Her shuffling steps carried her faster than he would have thought possible, and in moments he stood alone. The last of the diners made their way out of the restaurant, singing football songs with breath stinking of stale beer. For a moment, the old woman's eyes had caught the streetlights, and her pupils shone gold.

Shingyan turned the lock as quietly as he could, but in the narrow hallway outside his family's apartment every sound magnified off tiled walls in endless echoes. He pulled the metal gate to the side, and thought for the hundredth time that he needed to write a note to remind himself to oil the hinges. Despite the noise, when he opened the door the living room waited empty, dark but for the city's evening light cast in windowed shapes on the floors, on the bookshelves, the television. Passing cars ten floors down swept their headlights across the room as if a lighthouse in the distance revolved its guiding lamp over the city.

A door opened, and his insides tightened up, ready for an argument. But it was the other bedroom door. Terese stood there, still small enough she had to reach up for the doorknob.

"Sorry I woke you," Shingyan said.

"It's really late," she said, still half-asleep. "Or really early."

"Come on," he said, and nudged her back inside. She fell back into her blankets and wrapped them around herself. He could almost hear her words, even if she didn't say them out loud: *Like a cocoon.* Shingyan went up to the top bunk, trying his best to be quiet. The bed creaked with every step.

"I can't sleep," Terese said.

"I can't either."

A car drove past, and lines of light crept through the blinds to sweep the ceiling.

"Can you tell a story?"

"Shh, don't wake Mom."

A breeze came in through the open window, and the blinds chattered to themselves. If he waited, she might fall asleep on her own.

"Please?"

What would he see, if he wore those glasses now? What would the apartment look like from the outside?

"Okay, but you'll have to sleep after," he said. "And you'll have to keep it secret."

"I promise," Terese said.

He'd never forget tonight, he thought, but what was there to show for it? Memories, ones he didn't know if he could even trust. How long since he properly slept?

"I promise," Terese said again, and Shingyan gave in.

"Do you," he asked his sister, "believe in spirits?"

THE CREEPING HORROR
Stacy Noe

Some say Eldritch beings are ancient, unknowable, all-powerful. They exist in liminal places and come and go at will. They wait, breathing the same air, seeing the same things, hearing your words, all without your knowledge; until they wish you to know they're there.

The Being did not consider themselves any of those things. They were simply power. Energy. A force of nature, an entire universe. They existed outside of time and place, their thoughts, and their motives their own. Too vast, too beyond the comprehension of mere mortals.

Choosing to leave their precious blackness, their eternal nest of stardust and black holes, had taken only one thing: the call of a single soul, one they would give up almost anything to possess. One that, when they completed their hunt, would be only theirs.

One perfect soul, the only of its type. Black, nearly as black as the Being's. Stained such a dark red with so much blood, they begged to be taken, captured, and dragged back to the Being's inky lair.

They waited with the patience of one eternal. Even out of their element, the Being moved silently, undetected by mortal instruments, beyond mortal perceptions. Gliding from shadow to shadow they stalked their prey, prepared to consume it whole.

Their prey was close, so close they could smell the blood on them. It was the only soul so stained that it called out to them. Begged to join them. The Being, for the first time in its eternal existence, was tempted.

Soon, they entered their prey's vicinity. Closer. Closer they crept, still clinging to the shadows. The temptation was too strong, the call too loud. For the first time in eons, they felt impatience tugging at them, pulling them closer, drawing them from the shadows. They reached out physically, for the first time in so, so long. Their want enveloped them, seized them, creating a longing they had only felt once before. They closed in on their prey, still unaware of the precarious predicament they were in.

So close, so close, so close. Closer. They were finally within reach of their greatest desire. They closed their fingers...

"Jenny," her brother said, not looking up from his book, but placing a protective hand over his bag of jerky. "Knock it off."

"Dang it," Jenny grumbled, then slunk back into the house to find something else to eat.

CHANGELING
E M Lamdan

Charlotte was a savvy parent – all of her friends agreed. She had fussed over Willow's development since the moment the child had been born, charting milestones and reveling in the ones her daughter hit early. Willow spoke her first word at eight months – a loquacious infant, an intellectual, a gossip! She pushed herself up on wobbly, doughy legs at ten months – an athlete, Colin said when he heard about it later. A dancer, Charlotte corrected, and he agreed, yes, a dancer.

Parenting was exhausting, but the big house and the manicured lawn and the careful maid helped Charlotte relax, from time to time. If she set her daughter down in the soft grass of the backyard, the child would waddle halfway up the hillside away from the house, then lose her footing and roll back down, laughing. As she grew into a toddler, she would get farther up the slope, closer to the tree line at the top. Charlotte would sit on the back porch of the house, one eye on Willow and another on a magazine. She knew there were extra eyes, too; the housekeeper's careful vigil from the kitchen window, or her mother-in-law, wary like an elderly warden surveying a prison yard.

One afternoon, Willow made it halfway up the hill without losing her balance. She continued up the rise with a resolute focus, tiny arms swinging to keep herself upright. Charlotte smiled lightly, and turned the page of her magazine. Lace was out this summer. She made a mental note to take down the curtains that framed the front windows.

"That child is going to the trees," Colin's mother said in her round accent. "Are you going to stop her?"

"Why should I?" Charlotte hooked a sharp nail behind the corner of the next page. "She's only playing, Siobhan. It's normal for a child this age to run around like that. She'll come back down eventually."

"She's almost to the top."

"Willow," Charlotte called absent-mindedly, "don't go too far from the house, sweetie."

Siobhan didn't seem content with the warning. She let out a sharp breath and shuffled after Willow, a fierceness in her gaze. Her knobbly joints gave her gait a different awkwardness, and Charlotte closed her magazine with a frown. The old woman tottered after the toddler, a race between cumbersome age and unwieldy youth, until Siobhan was able to snake her bony arms around the giggling baby and scold her, "Stay away from the woods, child! Don't you see the mushrooms? There are faeries in the trees."

Willow laughed, and Charlotte scowled, her gaze darting to the neighbors' backyards to assess their reactions. Their porches were empty. Relieved, she sighed and returned her attention to the magazine.

Stained wood was out this year. She would have to get the kitchen remodeled.

When Willow was around three years old, her constant bubbly laughter died down, to be replaced with an owlish seriousness. Of course, Charlotte was instantly concerned, and of course, she brought her daughter to various specialists. The doctors proclaimed her healthy as could be, and referred the family to a psychiatrist, who proclaimed her autistic.

It all made sense – the way this toddler never cried, until she screamed. The way her babbling words had been replaced by eerie silence. The way she lined up her toys, and when she ran out of toys, began to make rows of everything: shoes, stones, and once she was old enough, words, cultivated into scrawled lists. Charlotte grieved the loss of her precocious child, and thought about what Siobhan had said so long ago, her warnings of the fair folk coming in the night to replace children with something alien. Charlotte didn't believe Colin's late mother, but she could see where the superstition came from.

She took her daughter to ballet lessons at Colin's suggestion, but Willow wailed and flung taut fists against the floor, writhing as though there was physical pain in having her posture corrected, in moving with grace. Where was the little dancer her baby had been? This child was flat-footed and inelegant. When she was reprimanded, when her form was corrected, she collapsed to the ground with her hands flapping before her face, eyes screwed shut and teeth pressed over her bottom lip. The rest of the mothers whispered amongst themselves and shot Charlotte pitying glances. She stopped taking Willow to ballet.

These days, Willow spent her time in the garden. She ran her hands over the stems and drew pictures of the leaves. When she wasn't outside, she was cross-legged on the floor, making her lists. She would sit with her flaxen hair falling in a sheet around her shoulders, soft silken ripples down almost to her waist, focused with surgical intensity on towers of words arranged into precise columns. Charlotte often had to tie Willow's hair back in a thick braid to keep it neat. Whenever she did, she let the fine strands run through her hands like water and silently cursed the child. At ten years old, Willow should be old enough to delight in her perfect hair and doe eyes. Old enough to comb it with the same diligence as her classmates. Old enough to do more than gather it into a sloppy ponytail and ask if she could cut it all off.

Charlotte leafed through Willow's lists sometimes while she was at school. It was her duty as a mother; every blog she had read told her to keep tabs on these sorts of things.

On wide-ruled notebook paper, a list of the types of flowers in the garden out front:

blue jacket hyacinth
reine hortense peony
daffodil
coneflower
marigold

And a list labeled *"friends"* – twenty-seven names long, names that Charlotte had never heard:

Julia
Charlie
Rachel
Daniel

It was impossible for Willow to have twenty-seven friends. When she spoke to people, her voice was too loud and too quiet, and she changed the subject with the subtlety of a cudgel. She came home from school every day with her careful braid loose, her shirt rumpled, her posture hunched.

Whenever Willow was at school, Charlotte tried to focus on her landscaping. Peonies were out this year. She had to dig up the flowerbeds and plant geraniums. More importantly, she had to do something about the flat-capped mushrooms that had spread in arcs across her lawn, encroaching on the garden.

The switch occurred on a Tuesday. It must have happened while she was at school, because she walked to the bus with her gaze fixed on the concrete, her arms stiff at her sides. But when the bus pulled up at the end of the driveway, Charlotte watched through the windows as her daughter flounced down the steps.

She opened the front door and leaned over the threshold. "Willow, sweetie–"

Willow ran across the front lawn. She looked up at the door, and her face brightened into a dazzling smile. "Hi, Mommy!"

Mommy?

"Did you have a good day at school?"

"Of course!" Willow bounced up the steps, and Charlotte stepped back to let her inside. "Julia invited me over after school tomorrow. Is it okay if I ride the bus with her?"

Charlotte returned her daughter's smile, a rigid expression. "Ride the bus with her?"

"I promise I'll do all my homework."

"Of – of course, sweetie. Does Julia's mom know you're coming over?"

"Yeah, Julia said she would ask tonight." Willow shrugged off her backpack and stood on tiptoes to hang it off a hook near the door. She didn't wobble in the slightest, and when she turned back to Charlotte, she looked up and met her mother's gaze directly. "Also, some of my friends were talking about doing gymnastics. Can I try a gymnastics lesson?"

Charlotte opened her mouth to respond, but found herself speechless.

"Mom?"

"Um – yes, of course. Gymnastics lessons." Charlotte shook herself. "Willow, I took you to ballet when you were five, and you hated it. I had to drag you out of this house kicking and screaming."

"Ballet was boring," Willow said. "My *friends* do gymnastics. It'll be fun!"

Charlotte thought back to the list. *Julia Charlie Rachel Daniel....* "Does Rachel do gymnastics?"

Willow nodded. "Her and Julia go after school, three days a week. Rachel says she's gonna go to the Olympics one day."

"That's nice." Charlotte forced another smile.

Willow ran past her into the kitchen, and Charlotte took the moment to steady herself against the banister. It had taken all of a minute, but it was the longest conversation she'd ever had with her daughter.

Charlotte thought of this Willow as New Willow. New Willow met her gaze and smiled and laughed and sat quietly and finished her homework. She asked for help with a few tricky math problems, her brow furrowed in frustration but her hands still upon her lap. Her hands had been motionless since she'd gotten home from school, folded politely as she listened to Charlotte butcher an explanation of fractions. She didn't scream, or cry, or rock, or flap. She didn't draw flowers in the margins of the notes.

After an hour of painless math, Charlotte sat back in her chair. "Do you want to come with me to the garden and plant the new geraniums?"

Gardening was one of the only things that piqued Willow's interest. She had a fixation with the flowers. She was quiet in the garden, as she turned soil to make room for new growth and ran her fingers over the silky petals of the tulips with eyes closed. Daily, Willow would talk about the flowers, but not about their beauty or the pop of color they could bring to the front of the house. It was always some ramble about angiosperms, vascular development, plant reproductive morphology—

"No, thanks," New Willow muttered. She leaned over the table, scribbling an answer to one of her math problems. "I have to finish these so I can go over to Julia's tomorrow."

"Are you sure? I just ordered them from the flower shop. They've been sitting on the back porch—"

"I'm too busy. Besides, I don't wanna get my hands dirty. Rachel did my nails during lunch."

Charlotte squinted at her daughter's hands, and sure enough, there was a thin veneer of glittering polish on each fingernail.

Unsettled, Charlotte got to her feet and went back to the foyer. She dug through the closet for her gardening gloves, and her chest tightened – wasn't this what she wanted from Willow? The focus, the friends, the colorful nails?

When she stepped outside, a wide-brimmed hat pulled low over her face, she noticed that the mushrooms had reached the edge of her flowerbeds.

Charlotte was in bed, but she'd been unable to sleep. She knew that Colin wasn't asleep, either, because he wasn't snoring as he usually did.

Eventually, he pushed himself upright. She couldn't see him in the dark, but she could hear the squeak of the bedsprings beneath his hands. She closed her eyes, feigning unconsciousness.

"Charlotte."

She sighed through her nose. "Yes, dear?"

"Have you noticed—"

"Noticed what?"

"Willow," Colin said. "She's acting different."

Charlotte rolled to face him, her hands still cupped beside her face. "Different how?"

"I can't explain it," Colin said, though Charlotte could've, easily. "There's just something *off.*"

"Off? She seemed fine when she got home from school yesterday."

"Yes, but—"

"Better than fine. She was smiling. She didn't have her nose in that notebook."

"But she always has the notebook, and she's never smiling."

"Smiling is good, Colin," Charlotte said wryly.

"It's unusual, that's all." Colin shrugged. "She wasn't out in the garden, either. When I come home from work, she's usually out there, looking at the plants. And when I came in—"

"Yes?"

"She said she had to finish her homework, so that she could go over to a friend's house tomorrow—"

Charlotte interrupted him with a soft laugh. "Honey. Do you hear yourself?"

"I'm telling you," Colin insisted, "there's something strange going on."

"Colin, maybe she's just getting older. Maybe she's just growing out of her awkward phase." Charlotte loved that explanation. She'd been told that it was often the case for girls, that they worked their way through autism and were molded and shaped by their peers into passable facsimiles of normal teenagers and normal adults.

Colin still seemed unconvinced.

"This is a good thing," Charlotte reassured him. "Doing her homework? Making friends? It's a lot better than spending all day staring at plants, isn't it?"

Wasn't it? Her perfect daughter with her perfect friends. A good student. A gymnast, maybe. Charlotte pictured gymnastics meets; gossiping with the other mothers, watching her child traverse a balance beam with a dancer's elegance. She turned away from Colin, and after a few minutes of silence, he settled back onto the pillows.

She would have to convince him to have a shelf put up, for the trophies. Something simple, minimalist. Bookcases were out this year.

Charlotte woke up at seven, as always, to style her hair and apply mascara. Colin rose at eight to prepare for his workday, which meant that the quiet of the morning was disturbed. Most mornings, Charlotte managed to put together her face and smooth her hair within the hour, before Colin's weary stumbling became too much of a distraction.

Once she was satisfied with her reflection, she shuffled to the kitchen to brew coffee for herself and her husband. As she meandered down the hall, she paused outside of the door to Willow's bedroom. Her daughter had always been difficult to wake in the morning.

"Willow, sweetie–"

The sheets were pulled back and rumpled; she was already awake. Charlotte craned her neck, peering through the open door. There was a light on in the bathroom. Charlotte tiptoed through the room to stand outside the threshold.

Inside, New Willow leaned toward the mirror. She ran a flat brush over her platinum hair, detangled it over her palm, and let it fall in a curtain around her shoulders. There was a focused intensity in her eyes as she drew the brush through the soft strands, then gathered up her hair and began to twine it into a thick French braid.

"Willow, sweetie," Charlotte said.

She jumped, letting the hair spill from her hand. "Mom?"

Charlotte was silent for a moment. She walked over to the mirror and stood behind her daughter, staring at both of their reflections.

"You should wear it down," she said finally. "Braids are out this year."

A month later, at her first gymnastics meet, New Willow walked the balance beam with light-footed grace. When she posed and smiled at one end of the beam, it wasn't the approximation of a smile that Charlotte had become accustomed to. One of the coaches draped a cheap medallion around New Willow's neck, but Charlotte was more proud of the way the other girls gathered around her and laughed and chatted excitedly.

New Willow talked non-stop on the ride home – something about an out-of-state competition, and how the whole team was going to stay in a hotel. How she'd never had a sleepover before, and wanted to invite Julia and Rachel and Kathleen, a new girl, to come over and spend the night. Charlotte listened quietly, basking in the glow of her daughter's excitement, but also nervous about the prospect of the other girls coming into her house. Their mothers would drop them off; they would come inside to inspect the home, and that meant everything had to be immaculate.

When they arrived at the house, Charlotte found Colin in the living room, crouched beside the mantel. He frowned at the seams of the wood, then glanced up as Charlotte approached.

"You see that?" He gestured to the edge of the fireplace.

Charlotte looked. Flat discs of bracket fungi had formed throughout the corner of the mantel and the wall. They were ringed with rippling bands of brown and white and orange, and they triggered an instinctive disgust within her. She wrinkled her nose.

"What is that? That's absolutely *nauseating–*"

"Mushrooms, Charlotte."

"Eugh – how did they get in here?"

Colin scowled at the fungi. "Beats me. But there are more of them in a few places upstairs. I think we probably have to call someone about this."

Julia and Rachel and Kathleen ran through the house with New Willow, laughing as they bustled through the living room and thundered down into the basement. They carried pillows and a box of cookies and scrapbook materials. Charlotte had expertly kept their mothers in the foyer for a light chat before sending them on their way, but she knew they'd scanned every inch of the house within eyesight.

She watched the girls from the couch, curled up with a glass of chilled white wine. Opposite her, Colin leaned back in his armchair. Neither of them looked at each other, nor towards the kitchen, where a tangle of vines creeped through the open throat of the sink faucet.

"Mom! Mom!"

Charlotte didn't look up from the sink. She positioned the hedge trimmers around the thickest rope of vine and squeezed the handles. The effort made her wrists ache; these tendrils were stubborn, like fiber-optic cables that grew at least a foot a day. Sometimes, Charlotte thought she could hear them spreading through the pipes, leaves whispering against the metal.

"Mom!"

New Willow rushed into the kitchen, and Charlotte finally dropped the shears and turned. The child's cheeks were flushed, her eyes shining as she held up a folded piece of paper.

"What's this?" Charlotte crossed the room, trying to ignore the way the hardwood floors sagged beneath her feet, and took the paper.

"My report card," New Willow said breathlessly.

Report cards were always a trial. They spanned the full range of the alphabet, and came loaded with teachers' disappointments and mumbled excuses. Normally, Charlotte would have been dreading report card day, but last night, large fungal trellises had appeared along the doorframes in the master bedroom. All she could think about was the decay that had begun to take root in the drywall. The whole house smelled like mildew.

Charlotte gave New Willow a purse-lipped smile and unfolded the paper. Her eyes scanned the row of letters in the right column: straight As. When she lowered the report card, New Willow beamed at her.

"I got straight As!"

"That's great, sweetie." Charlotte tried to sound genuine. Any other day, she would have been thrilled. But today, she could see the vines crawling back over the lip of the drain. Her gaze darted to the corner of the kitchen, where a cluster of red-capped toadstools had blossomed behind the toaster, and a shudder ran down her spine.

"Charlotte." Colin's voice drifted in from the foyer.

She folded the report card back up. "We're in the kitchen, dear."

Colin's face was severe as he marched in. He dropped his briefcase by the entrance, went straight for the liquor cabinet, and poured himself a short glass of whiskey.

"Don't you think it's a little early for—"

"Charlotte, there are *mushrooms* growing in our kitchen." The ice clinked in his glass as he picked it up. A nerve twitched in his neck.

"Yes, I noticed that."

"Why are there *mushrooms* in the kitchen?"

"We must have a mold problem," she said, as though this was common, as though she'd seen it countless times in other homes.

Colin leaned towards the sink. "Why are there vines growing out of the drain?"

"I managed to trim the ones that were in the faucet."

"That doesn't answer my question, Charlotte." Colin's voice was sharp enough to slice the trailing plants. He took a sip of the whiskey.

"Dad," New Willow chirped, "I got my report card today."

"She got straight As this quarter," Charlotte added.

Colin took a longer drink from his glass. He didn't respond.

"Aren't you *proud?*" Charlotte pressed.

He stared into the whiskey and gave a noncommittal grunt.

Charlotte scowled at him, then marshaled her face back into a smile as she turned to New Willow. "Sweetie, why don't you go upstairs? I'll take you shopping in an hour – just a little reward for doing so well in school."

As New Willow rushed off to her room, Charlotte rounded on her husband. "What's wrong with you?"

"What's wrong with *you?*"

"Our daughter just brought home a straight-A report card," she snapped. "Can't you find the wherewithal to congratulate–"

"Charlotte, our fucking house is rotting!"

Charlotte blinked, taken aback.

"There are plants growing in the pipes! I tried to take a shower this morning and the water was full of mud and leaves–"

"We can hire a specialist to inspect it. I'm sure it's a–"

"Bull*shit*. This isn't just a normal problem."

"What are you saying?"

Colin's scowl deepened, and he set the tumbler down on the granite island. "I don't know. This is freaking me the hell out."

"You sound like your mother," Charlotte said archly, raising an eyebrow. "You really shouldn't be drinking this early in the afternoon."

Colin glared at her. "Well, I would try to grab something to eat, or get some water from the filter. But all our water is filthy, and there's mold in the cabinets, so I can't, can I?"

"Colin, this isn't my fault."

"Are you sure?"

"Is that supposed to be a joke?"

"No."

She drew herself taller. "What are you trying to say?"

"I don't fucking know."

"Stop swearing," she said. "Willow will hear you."

He laughed, a harsh sound, and shook his head. "Charlotte, you and I both know that's *not* Willow."

"How dare you," she hissed.

"That's not Willow. That could never be Willow. But I guess it's fine, now that this *creature* is getting good grades—"

"Shut up, Colin!"

Colin reached for the glass. "I can't live like this, and neither can you, but you're always gonna be too stubborn to admit it."

"It's not that bad," Charlotte said. A pang of desperation sank into her chest like the colorful circles of rot spreading through the walls.

"This place is a hazard." Colin took another drink, then tipped his head back and breathed through his nose. "There's mold in the air."

"You can't even see it from outside the house. It's probably an easy fix."

"Charlotte, just go," Colin sighed. He suddenly looked weary, as though this conversation had drained all of his energy.

Tears stung at Charlotte's eyes, and she stomped out into the foyer. "Willow," she called, "come on, we're heading out."

Charlotte returned with an armful of shopping bags – new clothes that New Willow had chosen herself. Shopping with her daughter was as fun as Charlotte had always dreamed; it allowed her to take her mind off the fight with Colin. But as soon as New Willow skipped up the front steps, everything came rushing back.

She would have to apologize to him. He'd been rude and surly and unpleasant, certainly, but she didn't want the bad blood to fester. Sometimes it was better to lie, if only to appease him—

New Willow flung the door open and skipped inside. Charlotte followed, and as soon as she stepped over the threshold, the bags dropped from her arm like a line of dominoes falling.

The vines had left the sink and spread across the floor. They were wrapped around the banisters on the stairs; a spiderweb of tendrils covered the stained wood, working its way into the seams between the boards. Polypores dotted the walls, and ferns had sprouted in the corners. The place smelled like wet soil and fungus, and there was a thin sheen of moisture running over every surface, as though it had recently rained indoors.

Charlotte gagged at the sight of it. Her hand flew to her mouth, but she was unable to stop the horrified squeak.

New Willow leaned around the wall at the entrance to the kitchen. Where her fingers gripped the exposed wooden skeleton of the doorframe, the wood crumbled. "Mom," she said, her voice calm as though nothing was out of place, "Dad left a note for you on the counter. Is it okay if I invite Julia over later tonight? We're supposed to study algebra together."

Charlotte walked towards the kitchen in a trance. It was difficult to avoid stepping on the mushrooms, or tripping on any of the vines. She ignored New Willow, brushing past her to reach for the sheet of stationary on the center island.

"Mom?"

I'm staying at the Hampton. Already cleared out the closet. If you have the good sense to move out, go to a different hotel.

Charlotte crushed the paper in a shaking fist.

"Mom?"

"Go to your room, Willow," she snapped. She couldn't let anyone see the house in this state. As New Willow left the room, showing no signs of disappointment beyond a sigh, Charlotte yanked the drapes closed over the kitchen windows.

The trees behind the house. Yes, that was it – this blight was coming from the sparse woods at the edge of her backyard. She didn't know how it spread, or why, or what she could possibly do about it, but she felt that it was the source of the problem, and that there were few problems that couldn't be solved with a determined confrontation. She wasn't yet willing to agree with everything Colin had said, but there was definitely something unnatural about what was happening inside the house. If she could banish the vines and the fungi and the bracken from her home, perhaps she could call him and let him know that everything was back to normal, that it was all okay again.

When she reached the tree line, the temperature seemed to drop – from the shadows, she told herself. Here, the mushrooms weren't as numerous as they were inside the house. They were the same as they had ever been, clutches of peaceful spores gathered together away from the edge of the uniform grass.

Had the foliage always been this thick? Had the forest behind her house always been deep enough to grow dark, the trees tall enough to make her sway on her feet as she craned her neck upwards?

When she looked back down, a chill flashed through her. Within the trees, her gaze fixed upon the ground, was Willow.

Old Willow.

There was a viridescent cloak draped around her shoulders, a robe of moss that sprouted crocuses from the lining. Her hair was cut short, little more than a jagged tuft of platinum blonde. She wore a crown of tendrils, woven with hyacinths and lilies-of-the-valley, and her wrists were wreathed with vines. Willow smiled at the ground, a shy, secretive smile, like she was enjoying a private joke that Charlotte couldn't begin to understand.

"Willow, sweetie?" Charlotte breathed.

The child didn't look up. She watched the ground, and Charlotte followed her gaze. A dozen tiny sprouts bloomed out of the earth at Willow's feet. They curled around themselves as she rocked back and forth, shifting her weight.

"They're fragile," Willow said. Her voice was too quiet, but it carried as though the trees were passing her words along. "When they're growing, they're very fragile."

"Willow." Charlotte's eyes stung as she stared at the plants. "Did you do this to the house?"

Willow ignored her. "It's hard to tell what something is going to grow into, when it's still small. But look at the leaves."

The leaves unfurled from the quivering stems and spread into wide, flat blades. Charlotte sniffed. She recognized these weeds; she'd spent long enough pulling them from her garden.

"This is crabgrass," Willow said.

"Willow, please. Please – don't do this to my house."

"Crabgrass belongs here," she continued. "It's supposed to look like this. The grass should never all be the same."

Charlotte tried for a watery smile. "Willow, sweetie, please. Why are you doing this?"

Willow flapped her hands – self-stimulatory behavior, the psychologist had called it – and more shoots sprouted from the dirt; a patch of clover began to blossom, white flowers materializing through the blanket of green. The clover began to creep towards the edge of the forest, towards where Charlotte stood on the verge of her once-pristine lawn.

"My house is rotting," Charlotte whimpered. "It's all falling apart"

Willow looked up, and the smile returned to her face. It was sharp now, vindictive, as though she'd been taught the expression by foxes. She flapped her hands again, her palms falling inwards from limp wrists, and the clover and crabgrass and crocuses went wild. A verdant river coursed through the trees and lapped at the trunks. The leaves sighed as they flared outwards, rippling into the cropped fescue turf of Charlotte's perfect lawn.

Charlotte turned to stare as the wave tore up the grass. Flowers bloomed at random, different colors in uneven patches. Bushes exploded from the topsoil and shredded the ornamental monoculture. In Charlotte's careful flowerbeds, mushrooms ate through the mulch and climbed the sides of the house. Fungus and vines snaked their way into the wooden siding, and to Charlotte's horror, it began to split.

The walls splintered. The wood cracked. And the side of her house began to disintegrate, revealing the rotting interior.

Charlotte screamed.

The neighbors filtered onto their porches. Even from hundreds of yards away, Charlotte could hear their gasps, see their shaking heads.

New Willow, up in her bedroom, sat cross-legged in front of the mirror and brushed her hair. She seemed oblivious as the last of the outer wall crumbled away and vines snaked around the glass, as toadstools the size of car tires bloomed across the floor. Charlotte fell to her knees in the jumble of plants.

"Don't worry, Charlotte," Willow said behind her. "Mushrooms are in this year."

ADONIS IN FURS
Dan Micklethwaite

His mighty heart speeds in his supersized chest and his giant feet scatter the dirt as he runs. And though his massive hands rattle this little black box, he takes care not to catch it on boulders or boughs.

He can't quite believe that he's actually found one, all of these years since he'd learned what they were; all of these years since he'd learned about humans, from the racket they made and the rubbish they left.

Most of their cast-offs he had also rejected, but there were some things his pride simply couldn't ignore – those scraps and thin-cut skins of trees, with the markings across them like smoke-sickened grain, beside which were placed even grainier pictures; most of them faces, some of them his.

His intensity ebbs, as he recalls them in turn, as if sparked by the sunbeams that spear through the canopy. A ragged array of his hideous features, hazy and flat like some roadkill he'd seen.

He had crumpled the first in a ginormous palm, and hurled it as far through the trees as he could. But it nagged him for days, and he had to retrieve it, to study it closer, as though it revealed the full truth of his being; as if it counted for more than a common reflection, the good-looking glimpses he'd caught in the stream.

His heart is still racing, but aching as well.

He'd found other such images in the following months, and taken them back to his best-hidden den, partly to stop other animals seeing, and partly to nurse his scarred ego in peace. He had pinned them to wall moss with briar-thorns and pine needles, and stared at them daily for hours on end. He had brooded for years in the forest's dark reaches; despaired at his chances of finding a mate.

He hits out in anger at bushes and branches, and a bellow bursts forth from his humongous lungs. His gargantuan feet are beginning to falter. Doubt like a beaver gnaws at his plan.

Except now he remembers how everything changed. How he finally came to perceive his misjudgment: that his vicious self-loathing had been undeserved. The fault was not with how he looked, but instead with the way humankind looked at him. And the way that they handled those little black boxes, like the one that he bears up this mountainside path.

The first time he had properly seen one in action, he had believed it was a gun, and darted for cover. It was only weeks later, when he noticed the moment in stark black and white, that he realized his features weren't actually ugly, it was just that the image was so badly blurred.

He soon reconsidered the rest of his gallery, and compared to the portraits of Hollywood hunks – salvaged from newspapers strewn through the forest – the pictures of him were distorted and crude. They were frequently plagued by inadequate lighting, and most had been lacking in focus and zoom. People, it seemed, were afraid to come closer, to request his permission before taking a shot.

But he can't let their fearfulness shape how he lives.

Not any longer.

He has come to the end of his frantic ascent, to this one remote spot where the blue sky shines clearly. It is the middle of the day, and no shadows will bother him, and the backdrop is stunning in every direction. He couldn't have picked a more suitable scene.

He waits for his pulse and his breathing to settle, before making his way to the heart of the glade. He tries to prevent his titanic toes twitching, and his huge, hairy fingers from smudging the lens. He smooths down the fur on his head and his chest, and rehearses his suavest, most elegant poses. Then he raises the box at arm's length, angled downwards, and flashes his biggest, most brilliant grin.

COILED IN SHELLS OF LONELINESS
J Moffatt

Riher is a bilious cunt.

King of the Gods, they call him. Master of the Skies.

He is master of nothing but his own asshole.

When his precious ego couldn't take it anymore, when he got too puffed up to see the truth before his very eyes – that he was ineffective and useless, king only of the pathetic, groveling sycophants surrounding him – he cast us out.

The Fallen is what they call us. I am Azriel, the Fallen.

Banished to Earth, home of the wretched, the mortal. Humans. They are truly hopeless and weak, here for the blink of an eye, and for what?

They are staring at me now. Yes, I must look fearsome to them. The beauty of an angel is dependent upon who regards them. A pure soul will see me as I am, radiant and powerful, glowing skin over sinewy muscle. But one with a dark soul will see me as a monster, shriveled, with yellowed fangs and claws. I stare back. I can tell who in the crowd is a monster themselves.

When I bore of dramatics, I jump down from my perch and begin to stalk towards them. The crowd scatters, except for one man who remains rooted to the spot. He is large, for a human, nearly as large as me. His skin is ochre, not as dark as mine, and, of course, rougher, marked by age and accident. His eyes are scanning me up and down. I stop in front of him and he does not flinch. He is upset.

"What the fuck?" he growls.

I frown. I am not sure what he is asking. So I wait.

"You broke my framing," he adds, pointing back to where I landed.

I look. Yes, some of the wooden beams do seem to have splintered. I turn to face him again. His clothing is coarse and dirty, a menial laborer of some sort.

His eyes are searching my face. He looks less angry now. "Are you okay, buddy?" he asks after a pause.

"Of course," I sniff. Ridiculous question.

"Well, fuck, mate." He takes off his yellow helmet and rubs at his bald head. "You're naked in the middle of a construction site."

Oh, yes, clothing. Humans insist on it. So tedious. "Do you have anything I could wear?" I sigh.

He looks confused, but then he shrugs. "Yeah, in the office, I think."

He turns and walks across the dusty lot into a battered white and blue trailer sitting at one end. I follow him, ignoring the other humans as they chatter and whisper about me.

The inside of the trailer is as filthy as the outside, except it is darker and smells worse. Gods, what *is* that stench?

The man is rooting through a locker and pulls out a pair of rough coveralls. He hands them to me. "Here, these should fit."

I raise an eyebrow. Vile. "Is this all you have?"

He looks amused. "You're even bigger than me. You're lucky I have this."

I suppose he is right. I will need something. Reluctantly I step into the legs and pull it up over me. It feels wretched and smells like the trailer.

He finds me some boots, too. "So…" His face grows serious again. "You broke my framing."

"What do you want me to do about it?" The boots pinch my toes a little.

"I'm behind now. Could use your help fixing it."

This is fair, and I am strong and do not tire easily. I nod.

He looks relieved, but before he turns to go he holds out his hand. "Name's Oman."

"I am Azriel." We shake. As expected, his hands are rough.

"Nice to meet you, Azriel." His voice is gentle though.

The work is easy. I hoist the beams high and hold them steady as they are secured. Oman looks pleased and we work until the sun begins to dip below the horizon.

The other humans say goodbye to him warmly, but cast wary glances at me, skirting wide as they leave. The site is quiet as I watch Oman lock the office door.

"Would you like your clothing back?" I ask. It is warm against my skin now and I would prefer to leave it on, but he may need it returned.

He looks amused again. I am not sure why he finds me so funny. "I guess you'll need to keep it for now. Maybe you can bring it back tomorrow?"

"All right."

We walk to the gate and he locks it behind us, nodding to the arriving security guard. I follow Oman to his car, because it is as good a direction as any.

"Where did you come from?" he asks suddenly, pulling his keys out of his pocket. The question is blunt.

And Riher may be a cunt, but I am proud. "I was… sent away," I say, hoping he leaves it at that. He does.

"And do you have a place to stay?"

"No," I say simply.

He shifts his feet, looks at his keys, deciding. "Look…do you want to work for me again tomorrow? You can stay at my place tonight. It's not much, but…"

Well, as I said, I have nowhere to be.

We listen to music in the car, tinny, frantic songs that beat twice as fast as my heart. Oman seems to enjoy it, his head bobbing along. I see him glancing at me while the breeze from the window blows my hair back.

And indeed, he is correct, his place is not much. I look around at the drab, well-worn furnishings in the cramped apartment. Everything is impeccably clean.

"Beer?" Oman asks, dropping his keys on the counter and opening his fridge.

"Yes," I say, suddenly aware that my hands and face and coveralls are covered in grime. "But," I gesture at myself, "I am very dirty."

"Oh, that's okay, don't worry." But he sees the expression on my face. "Would you like to shower? I can find you some clothes that should fit."

"Thank you," I say gratefully. In the warmth of his apartment, I am desperate to get out of these rags. I can feel the dirt boring into my pores. I pull the zipper down and peel the scratchy fabric off my skin.

Oman opens his bottle and his eyes widen when he sees me naked again.

Oh, right. Modesty.

"Uh..." His eyes start to slide down my body, but then wrench back to my face. "Bathroom is down the hall, fresh towels in the cupboard. Help yourself to the shampoo, and…whatever else you need."

The shower feels heavenly. I sniff all the bottles and use the one I like best all over my skin and hair. I scrub away the grit of the day, watching it swirl down the drain.

When I get out, dripping onto the floor, I see clean, folded clothes waiting for me on the counter. I like what he has chosen for me. A white t-shirt, a loose, faded blue sweater, and gray sweatpants. They are soft and well-worn, and smell like him.

"Thank you for the shower and the clothes," I say, once I have shuffled back to the kitchen.

Oman turns and smiles when he sees me. "Do they fit okay?" He hands me a beer.

"Yes, thank you." I twist the cap off and take a long pull. It is quite good, rich and earthy.

Oman turns back to the stove where he is stirring something. Then the smell hits me and my mouth waters.

"What are you making?" I ask, going to stand next to him.

"Red curry." He lifts a spoon to my mouth. "How does it taste?"

I close my eyes as the sauce washes over my tongue. Incredible. "It is delicious," I tell him, licking my lips. "You are quite talented."

He chuckles and looks pleased again. "My mom taught me."

"May I help?"

"It's just about done. Could you serve us some rice?" He nods at the pot on the stove and the bowls sitting out.

When we are settled at the table a silence falls as we eat. I will give humans this: they make wonderful food. I do not actually *need* to eat, but I enjoy it, and it does keep me stronger. Plus even I can admit that I am more amiable with a full stomach.

Oman must have questions, but he does not ask them. Instead, he describes the tower we are building, and tells an amusing anecdote about his cement truck driver. I go back for a second helping.

Oman's voice is soothing. I am starting to feel the effects of what has been quite a long day. The Earth's gravity weighs down on me much more strongly when I am on it.

Oman sees me drooping. "I'm sorry, it's late. You must be tired."

"Yes, I would like to sleep," I admit.

He collects my empty bowl. "I'm sorry, I only have one bed..." He trails off, looking sheepish. "Is the couch okay? I'm not sure you can even fit."

"The couch will be fine, thank you." Truthfully, I can sleep anywhere.

Oman hands me several blankets and says goodnight, disappearing into his bedroom. I curl up on the threadbare cushions, running my hands over the soft fabric of his sweater. I wonder where I would be right now if I had not met him.

He wakes me in the morning with a gentle hand on my shoulder.

I have never slept so soundly. The clothing he lends me for work is comfortable, no more scratchy coveralls.

The job is easy, and pleasant. I can exert my body while my mind wanders. I heft bags of cement mix, load pallets, lift beams. I do whatever Oman needs me to do. He gives me a sandwich and an apple to eat at midday. Then, at the end of the day, an envelope.

"What is this?" I ask.

"For today. You did good work. You're worth at least two others."

I open it and see it contains money. I hand it back to him. "I have no need."

"But you– "

"You have fed me and clothed me and housed me. You keep it."

He looks at me a moment, then nods, and tucks the envelope back into his clipboard. "Can you stay? Working here, I mean?"

I hesitate. I had not planned to linger.

But he sees my pause. "You can stay with me," he offers. There is a hint of something in his voice. I wonder if it is hope.

"Yes, I will stay."

We fall into a routine. Oman makes dinner each night – rich soups, thick stews, spicy stir-fries. We talk at the cozy table, our legs slotting neatly together underneath, until it is late and we are both ready to let sleep take us.

After a week he invites me to share his bed. It is easily large enough for both of us, he tells me. The couch is rather cramped and it would feel good to stretch out, so I accept his offer. I am careful not to encroach on his half of the mattress, but I am comforted by his warm weight next to me as I drift to sleep.

He tells me all about his life. The small town he grew up in, and how he came to be here. The way he broke his arm falling out of a tree when he was six and how he had to conquer a fear of heights for his job. The way his three older sisters would nag him like he had three extra mothers, but love him like he had thirty.

I do not talk about myself. I am already breaking almost all of the rules. I am meant to wander the earth alone, you see. Miserable, a creature to be feared, driven away from any refuge I might find by small, fearful human minds.

But I am not alone, am I? Our lives weave together in a thousand small ways. I learn to use the toaster to make us breakfast. I like the feel of his hip brushing against mine while he cooks and I set the table. The smell of his laundry detergent comforts me when I put on fresh clothing. I discover I like making him smile.

At the construction site, I work harder than ever, lifting and hauling and building, wanting to prove I am worth *ten* others. And then one day... It is awful. One of the new workers is not watching where he is going, and he has not loaded his wheelbarrow properly. Careless fool. He loses control and it tips over, sending a shower of broken concrete chunks down to the level below, where Oman is standing. I do my best to divert the cascade from landing directly on him, with a subtle flick of my fingers, but one stray piece bounces off his hardhat, then leaves a gash on his forearm.

I am furious.

There are protocols in place, first aid attendants who flit around Oman and tend to his wound. I glare at the man responsible and he flinches away from me. He will not dare to meet my eyes again.

Oman insists he is fine, but he is sent home early after the attendants have determined there are no broken bones. He sinks onto his couch with a sigh as I hover anxiously.

"What can I do for you?" I ask.

"I'm okay, Azriel."

I fold my arms, giving him my firmest look.

He relents. "An ice pack and some painkillers, then." He directs me where to find them.

"I can make dinner," I offer, once he is settled comfortably.

"Nah, we can just order pizza..."

He has cooked for me seventeen nights in a row. "I would like to cook for you."

"Okay." He smiles softly. "I was going to make sweet potato soup."

"Excellent."

It is not excellent. It is lumpy, and the ginger is overpowering, but Oman insists it is delicious.

After I have tidied up from dinner – cleaning, I can do – I kneel in front of Oman to change his bandage. I carefully peel back the gauze and appraise his wound. It looks angry and inflamed. Well, why stop breaking rules now? I place my hands on either side of the gash and close my eyes. My light flows into him, by the grace of the gods.

I feel the infection ebbing, dissolving, drifting away into the ether. I exhale deeply and open my eyes. The redness of the wound is fading. Then I feel a tingle from touching him which has nothing to do with healing.

Oman is watching me. His eyes feel hot on my skin. "Thank you," he says simply.

Then he laces our fingers together and pulls me towards him. I rise up onto my knees and rest my other hand on his chest. I can feel his heart beating in time with my own.

"Azriel," he says.

I close the small distance between us. Our lips meet.

We kiss slowly at first, as we explore this new world. I can taste the beauty of his soul. Feel its goodness deep within me. It is sweet and warm, a tender thing waiting to be seen.

Then our kiss changes. It is more urgent. Needy. I realize I am gasping, groaning, into his mouth and I need more, so much more. His arms are tight around me, and I hope he will never let go. I want all of him.

We make love on his dingy couch, but together we are transported to another plane. Not the one that belongs to the gods, cold and calculating, but one where nothing exists but the two of us, and the way our bodies move together as if they were always meant to.

I think to myself, as we are wrapped in one another's arms, it is funny how I thought his skin was rough the first time I saw him. Now, under my lips and tongue, it is as smooth as any god's.

Much later, when we are tangled up in our bed and the sun is almost ready to reappear, Oman whispers to me, "How long will you stay?"

"As long as you want me," I tell him.

There is nowhere else.

WHAT'S GROWING IN FORT CUNNINGHAM

Calen MacDonald

On an otherwise placid April afternoon, Mable Paige discovered a disembodied limb on her walk home from school.

Mable had a habit of slipping out of Fair County Middle just before the last bell. The problem was, at the 3:15 pm dismissal, all the other Fort Cunningham kids would gather to walk home. They congealed in little fission-fusion groups, chatting about boys or girls or the internet. Mabel always left promptly at 3:10 pm so as to avoid this crowd. It wasn't that she didn't want to talk about boys or girls or the internet, just that she didn't have anyone who wanted to talk to her about them.

So Mable Paige walked alone on that April day. And there the limb suddenly was, at the intersection of Carmichael Street and Jameson Avenue. It sprouted from the ground like a surrealist lamppost, standing easily eight feet tall. The wrist was bent just so as to hang lackadaisical. Its flesh was a sickly gray that only added to the alarm of the whole situation.

Mable Paige didn't scream when she saw it, but that didn't mean she wasn't scared. Her first instinct was to look around in case the owner of the gargantuan arm was still around, but the street was empty. Just hours ago Mable had walked the same route on the way to school, unimpeded by giant arms. Now, she stood transfixed. Almost reflexively, her own arm slowly rose up, and Mable found herself softly waving at the gray limb. Its elongated fingers flexed dully, but not in a way that made Mable feel acknowledged.

Mable Paige took off running and she didn't stop until she made it home. Hours later, the Fort Cunningham Daily Shouter would track her down for an interview. The only quote they could entice from the morose child read, "I don't think it would've been as scary if it had waved back."

Fire Chief Georgio Clements was deployed to the scene in response to a frantic 911 call placed by Mable Paige's mother. Georgio didn't take the call too seriously. However, the last fire in Fort Cunningham was half a decade ago and Georgio loved to drive the fire truck. Sirens blaring, Georgio rolled up to a growing crowd gathered around the arm, the hand looming above their heads. Ignoring the onlookers, Georgio began his work with aplomb. In no time at all, he had established a perimeter cordoning off the limb. Georgio loved to establish a perimeter.

With a perfect square of caution tape in place, Fire Chief Georgio Clements set himself to the delicate task of examining the arm. Poking and prodding strange limbs barely fell under his purview, but there was no one else up to the task. The arm was surprisingly docile. It didn't seem to notice his investigation at all. Even when he got in there really deep with his Fort Cunningham Fire Department pen, it remained passive. Georgio worked his way up from the base of the arm to as high as he could reach. As his observations revealed little, Georgio decided he would have to delve deeper. And so, Fire Chief Georgio Clements went to retrieve a jackhammer from his fire truck.

Throughout the investigation, the crowd of onlookers had continued to grow. Amongst the concerned, the curious, and the panicked was the 3:15 pm crowd from Fair County Middle. Talking about boys and girls and the internet paled in comparison to the allure of a disembodied limb. The few kids who were lucky enough to have smartphones were already flooding social media with news of the mysterious appendage. Those who couldn't immortalize the moment in pixels did so in memory, sneaking up to get a closer view whenever Fire Chief Georgio Clements turned his back. The boldest of these thrill seekers was Jeremiah Brown. Jeremiah had entered Fair County Middle School on that April day with not only a brand new pair of shoes, but a fresh haircut to match. Both of these attributes went unnoticed by his classmates. Jeremiah had chafed under this slight all day, but the arm's sudden appearance offered a chance at redemption.

Jeremiah kept his eyes trained on the Fire Chief. As Georgio disappeared to locate his jackhammer, Jeremiah found exactly the window he was waiting for. He moved quickly, but with great care, slinking beneath the caution tape perimeter. Just before doing the deed, he turned back to find his crowd of friends looking on with bated breath – his moment had finally arrived. Emboldened by their attention, Jeremiah dug the soles of his new shoes into the ground. With all the force he could muster, he jumped upward, stretching his arm as far as it would go, and gave the gray hand a hardy high-five. The resounding slap drew the attention of everyone in the nearby vicinity and the ire of Fire Chief Clements. Jeremiah was promptly removed from the caution tape perimeter by the scruff of his shirt. Jeremiah didn't mind the extraction or the scolding; he had won his moment in the spotlight.

As the afternoon progressed and the middle schoolers were summoned home by concerned parents, Georgio got to work with his jackhammer. Rerouting power from the Ragtime Cinema on Carmichael Street, Georgio got to work tearing up the road. He took great care not to nick the arm itself; Georgio had no desire to inflict pain on any other creature. What soon became apparent was that the arm extended much farther beneath the ground than Georgio had anticipated. As the sun slunk below the horizon, the moon rose to find Georgio waist-deep in a hole of his own making. The fire chief was beginning to get disheartened. His hours of work had uncovered nothing more than a continuation of the impossibly long arm. He hadn't even reached the elbow.

Fire Chief Georgio Clements hoisted himself out of the hole, coated head-to-toe in dirt, to find himself face-to-face with Mayor Valexia Doubleday. The Mayor had chosen blue as her primary color for the day. Her tailored blazer was a deep azure that was echoed in her lipstick, her nail polish, her shoes, and the tips of her braids, piled on top of her head like an impossible hat. Always clutched in her hands was a clipboard, a new color each day to suit her outfit. There was an air of impeccability to the Mayor that had always in equal parts intimidated and impressed Georgio. In her presence, the crowd seemed immediately more at ease. Even the arm seemed to loll less menacingly.

"Chief Clements, I have been informed of the situation. How goes the excavation?"

"I've been digging for hours ma'am. There's no end in sight."

The Mayor pursed her lips and made a swift note on her clipboard.

"Then we shall have to dig deeper."

And dig deeper they did.

Georgio spent the next two days grinding apart the pavement, cleaving out a 10 foot radius around the arm. When this revealed nothing more than a now-eighteen foot tall arm, Mayor Valexia Doubleday called in a full construction crew. The intersection of Carmichael Street and Jameson Avenue became a dig site. Days turned to weeks with no revelations aside from an increasingly longer arm. Still no elbow.

A few days into the excavation, Mable Paige paid the dig site a visit. Since giving the local newspapers her quote, Mable had spoken a scant few words. At her mother's insistence, she began to see a child psychologist. This psychologist convinced Mable she was suffering from a litany of traumas brought on from the harrowing event. Exposure therapy was prescribed.

And so Mable Paige visited the dig site. Worming through the crowd of fifteen or so onlookers, she reached the caution tape perimeter. She couldn't decide if the arm was more or less frightening now. It seemed much bigger than when she had first seen it, but she wasn't sure it was the bigness that had frightened her in the first place. One thing was for sure, it was nice to not be alone in seeing it.

Mable was always alone in her nightmares. Even when the arm appeared, it was far off in the distance and it never acknowledged her. The child psychologist had told Mable that experiencing nightmares was an important part of processing her traumas, but she had stopped sleeping most nights.

"It's pretty cool, isn't it?"

Mable was stirred from her thoughts by a voice to her right. She recognized the boy from school, although he had never spoken to her before.

"You know, I high-fived it. I'm the only person in town who's touched it. Even Chief Clements has only poked it with a pen." The boy smiled at her, his face flush with the expectation of praise. "Hey, I know you, right? You're Mable? We go to school together. I'm Jeremiah."

The boy, Jeremiah, extended a hand, which Mable tentatively took. Jeremiah had an emphatic handshake.

"You're really quiet Mable."

"I'm processing my traumas."

"Cool."

The two chatted until Jeremiah was called home for dinner. Actually, Jeremiah did most of the talking, but Mable found she didn't mind being talked at, in fact, she sort of liked it. As she turned to head home herself, she gave the hand a tentative wave. It remained apathetic. Mable would later tell her mother that she no longer wanted to see the psychologist, although she would continue to visit the hand.

Mayor Valexia Doubleday shut down the dig site after three weeks of uninspiring progress. The arm had proven immeasurably long, and, with a quarry-sized hole dug in the center of town, the Mayor could no longer justify the excavation.

Throughout the lengthy process, Fire Chief Georgio Clements developed a budding respect for the arm. He liked seeing it every day. It was harmless and it gave him the opportunity to do his job. And Georgio loved to do his job.

On the whole, Fort Cunningham had come to agree with Georgio. Fewer and fewer onlookers had returned to gape at the strange sight. Instead, passersby took to offering friendly waves. The arm was the topic of much pleasant conversation. The students of Fair County Middle School practiced their persuasive writing by crafting essays arguing to give the arm an official name. Popular choices included "Army McArm," "Mr. Hand," and "Susan."

The Fort Cunningham Historical Society had also cottoned to the arm quickly. Within the week of its discovery, there was a petition to designate it a historical landmark. Chairman of the Fort Cunningham Historical Society Oxton Taller set himself to constructing an intricate record of the arm's short history. He even conducted a full historical interview with Mable Paige. In his forty years as Chairman, Oxton had never got to conduct a historical interview. Mable found the mustachioed enthusiast comforting and she was happy to speak to him regularly. In no time, Oxton had a densely compiled report advocating for the arm's landmark status. It clocked in just shy of five hundred pages, stuffed with photographs and artistic depictions of the arm as well as hundreds of personal accounts from the day of the arm's discovery.

When the Chairman's appeal made its way across Mayor Valexia Doubleday's desk, she crumpled her face into a sour expression that smeared her cherry lipstick. The Mayor had poured her heart into Fort Cunningham. She wouldn't allow the town's legacy to be hijacked by an errant limb. She alone had put the town on the map. She had overseen the construction of the Fort Cunningham bike path. She had saved the Ragtime Cinema through clever use of zoning laws. She had personally restored the Fair County Memorial

Garden to health. No. Mayor Valexia Doubleday wasn't one to be outdone by a simple limb. The arm would have to go.

The next morning, an early print edition of the Fort Cunningham Shouter made the announcement public: the arm was to be cut down. The news spread across Fort Cunningham like a great conflagration. It made Jeremiah Brown feel hollow in a way that he couldn't quite explain. A compulsion that was altogether foreign to the preteen compelled him to run as quickly as he could to the intersection of Carmichael Street and Jameson Avenue.

Upon opening the paper, Chairman of the Fort Cunningham Historical Society Oxton Taller turned sheet white and passed out into his bowl of breakfast porridge. He would continually discover bits of crusted oats hidden in his mustache throughout the coming days.

Mabel Paige's mother threw the newspaper away so that her daughter might never see its contents, but Mable, tantalized by the promise of forbidden knowledge, fished it out of the recycling bin.

Fire Chief Georgio Clements never had the opportunity to learn the news from the paper. At 7:00 am he was awakened by the rapping of a deliberate hand on his front door. Mayor Valexia Doubleday stepped into his foyer without invitation and produced the hatchet that she had already retrieved from the fire station. She explained her intent from outside Georgio's bedroom door as he dressed. The idea of cutting down the arm as if it were an overgrown tree sickened him. And yet, he could see that the Mayor was right. A town like Fort Cunningham couldn't have an arm growing at its heart, it was simply too strange.

All this Georgio rationalized to himself as the Mayor started up her car. When she turned the corner to Jameson avenue, his heart sunk to the tip of his rubber boots. Amassed there was a crowd of citizens, many of them treading on the newly replaced asphalt and breaching the perimeter he had so carefully laid. And, as always, the arm remained.

Mayor Valexia Doubleday parked as close as she could to the gray limb. She intended to remain in the safety of her car, but she unlocked the passenger side door to allow Georgio to get on with the deed. Georgio steeled himself by clenching and unclenching his jaw six times and running his fingers along the length of the axe handle. A medley of faces watched him exit the car. Concern, glee, confusion, and the occasional glint of despair played across the crowd. A lump formed in Georgio's throat. All of a sudden he very much did not love his job.

Like a school of fearful fish, the crowd parted to allow Georgio access to the arm. But, as his path slowly formed, one figure stood obstructing it. Jeremiah Brown was again made all too aware of the difference in stature between him and the Fire Chief.

"Step aside kid." Georgio was similarly cognizant of the optics of the situation. A big lumbering man. Equipped with an axe. Facing down a child who was just cultivating his first chin hairs.

Jeremiah stood in a fashion that he hoped looked indignant. He dug his heels into the ground to prevent his legs from shaking. They trembled nonetheless.

Fire Chief Georgio Clements took a step forward. Jeremiah remained rooted.

Georgio approached in a methodical fashion, planning to simply sidestep the child. But, just as Georgio prepared to lunge, Jeremiah scampered backward and latched onto the arm. He scurried upward with a newfound desperation. Finding purchase on the smooth skin was difficult, but Jeremiah managed to muscle his way to the top. The oversized hand was just large enough to cup Jeremiah's undergrown torso. The arm remained as passive as ever. Perched atop it, Jeremiah felt it was no more aware of him than an oak tree would be a squirrel. With the crowd below looking to him expectantly, Jeremiah confronted the reality that he had acted with very little intention and even less of a plan.

Below, Georgio felt a wave of relief. With the kid absconded atop the arm, he surely couldn't chop the thing down.

"Well?" Mayor Valexia Doubleday had rolled down the car window. "Get on with it."

"I can't ma'am. The kid's up there."

"It's a short fall. He'll be fine."

Jeremiah Brown's eyes widened as hesitation mingled with duty in Georgio's mind. He took a meager step toward the arm and raised the axe, but his shoulders slumped mid-swing and he dropped the axe half-heartedly.

"I'm not gonna hurt the kid ma'am. Surely we can wait 'til tomorrow to chop it down. It's not causing anybody any trouble."

Only now did Mayor Valexia Doubleday emerge from her car, gingerly placing her red clipboard atop it. She slammed the door shut with purpose, sending a shiver down Georgio's spine.

"Chief Clements, I'm disappointed."

The Mayor picked up the axe. Its red head complemented her rosy beret and slick-cut pantsuit. One look sent Georgio stepping out of her way. With an unpracticed hand, the Mayor lugged the axe up over her shoulder, garnering all her strength for a hefty swing. The crowd drew a breath in unison. With a wobbly motion that threw her off balance, the Mayor struck into the arm.

For the first time, the dull gray of the arm's flesh was interrupted by a growing patch of crimson. The deep red slit looked like the first cut into a summer watermelon.

One swing alone hadn't sufficed to fell the minatory limb. Although the exertion of the first strike left the Mayor panting, she reeled the axe back with gumption for the denouement. She shifted all of her weight backward as she lifted the axe head high, mustering the strike that would finally cleave the dreaded limb. Suddenly, the axe became much heavier in her hands, too heavy, and she was flung backwards head-over-heels.

Seized by an unfamiliar confidence, Mable Paige had emerged from the crowd and sprung herself upon the axe in the Mayor's hands. The weight of her tiny form was just enough to offset the Mayor and land the two in a sprawling heap. Mable found herself still clutching the axe, its blade making the tiniest of cuts into her forearm. As red blossomed from the cut she scampered to her feet and did her best to drag the axe alongside her. The Mayor righted herself as well, still developing her understanding of the situation.

Mable placed herself before the arm, Georgio, and Valexia, menacing them with the axe as best she could. Above, Jeremiah still clung to the hand. The crowd had yet to release its held breath.

Taking stock of the situation, Mable could see Jeremiah was struggling to remain in his lofty perch.

"Would you like to come down Jeremiah?" Mable said in a tinny voice like an antique bell.

"Yes, very much," responded the boy. Initially delicate, the climb ended with a drop that would certainly leave a bruise. The Mayor watched Jeremiah's descent wordlessly. As the boy scampered to his feet and stood alongside Mable, the Mayor's entire demeanor changed, her posture shifting to appear genteel as she stepped forward.

"Put down the axe little girl." The honey of her tone failed to mask the malice of her intent. "You might hurt yourself."

"Stay back!" Mable had never shouted at an adult in any fashion and here she was threatening one with an axe. In the crowd, she spied her mother, paralyzed by shock. She must have followed Mable after she slipped out of the house.

"The arm, it's…" Mable trailed off as she briefly failed to force words past the lump in her throat. "It's not hurting anybody."

A murmur passed through the crowd. People seemed to agree that the arm was, in fact, not hurting anybody.

"It's a guest in our town and it's…it's not fair to treat it like this." Mable paused and collected her thoughts. "I used to be scared of it too, but it's not actually bad. It's just a little weird."

Mable's mind raced, trying to find some way to make salient the thoughts jumbled in her head. In a moment of inspiration, she thrust her arm up into the air, parallel with the limb looming behind her. Her skin was stained from her axe wound.

"Look! It bleeds just the same as any of us."

This small gesture of sameness seemed to turn the crowd. Mable looked toward her mother once again and was surprised to find a hint of pride. Mayor Valexia Doubleday however, was not so easily convinced. As Mable raised her arm, the Mayor lunged toward the axe, but found her path interrupted by Georgio. He placed an arm on her shoulder with a gentle, yet firm grip.

"Ma'am, we're not hurting that thing."

Georgio extended a hand to Mable, gesturing for the axe. Tentatively, Mable released it. Relief washed over her the moment it left her hands.

The next few days were a blur for Mable Paige. The Fort Cunningham Shouter took to her with a renewed interest, plastering her across the front page of the special Sunday edition. Mable's mother grounded her for the remainder of her life, a sentence which struck Mable as surprisingly lenient. The whole incident didn't change Mable's situation at Fair County Middle School as profoundly as she had expected. Other kids started to take notice of her, but in a way that seemed sheepish. They would watch her walk through the halls, only to turn away as soon as she caught them staring. That Monday, she left school at 3:10 pm as always. However, as she turned to make her way down Jameson Avenue, she found Jeremiah Brown waiting for her.

"Hey Mable," he said. "Is it all right if I walk with you?"

The arm itself remained unchanged for months, and then years. Like all benevolent things deemed intolerably strange, the passage of time waned its strangeness and made it tolerable. Within a few months, a group of elderly citizens submitted a petition to start a community garden around the arm. Sensing which way the wind was blowing, Mayor Valexia Doubleday seized this opportunity to rebuild her public image. In no time, the intersection of Carmichael Street and Jameson Avenue was occupied by a lush park. The Fort Cunningham Historical Society was put in charge of the park's maintenance, a task which Chairman Oxton Taller was delighted to fulfill.

The arm's hatchet wound healed in time, leaving behind a jagged scar. Oxton installed a memorial plaque in the dirt beneath the scar. Printed on it was a written account of the mark's origin that read more like a fantastical battle than the work of two kids.

The park proved a popular local destination, but, in the next general election, incumbent Mayor Valexia Doubleday's passion for public works couldn't hold up against Fire Chief Georgio Clement's record of service. Valexia attended Georgio's swearing-in ceremony wearing all black. As he left the stage following a rousing speech, she handed him a black clipboard.

"I suppose I won't be needing this anymore." The Mayor spoke with a sincerity that was unbecoming of her typical self. "I hope you can put it to good use."

"I'll do my best Ms. Doubleday," Georgio said.

Mable Paige didn't live in Fort Cunningham for the rest of her life. She eventually went off to school and traveled the world and grew up and fell in love a few too many times. But, no matter how far she strayed, Mable always found herself drawn back to Fort Cunningham. In her later years, she finally returned to the town in full, moving right back into her childhood home. Mable would visit the arm regularly. Occasionally she was accompanied by Jeremiah, who had stayed in Fort Cunningham and become her closest friend. Tourists from out of town would regularly fill the park, posing for photos and gawking at the arm's size. Many questioned the story behind the local legend, but Mable was happy to correct any doubters. One day, a child no older than nine sat down besides her on the bench she was occupying. The little girl looked up to the arm wide-eyed, with just a hint of fear.

"It's pretty cool, isn't it?" Mable asked.

"Uh huh," the kid said.

"But it's also a little scary."

"Uh huh," the kid said again.

"But that's okay. It's only scary because it's hard to understand. You don't need to understand everything, and that's okay too."

ADAM AND GALETA
Ellen Denton

The silvery-green tendrils of the plant swayed in the gentle current, but were dense enough to keep him concealed as he watched Galeta glide like a dolphin through the water. She rarely strayed far from the safety of the castle. He understood her caution and fear. The horrible hunters with their sweeping nets were coming by more frequently now, and anyone caught by them was never seen again. Adam and the others had lived together in the Blue World for a very long time, so the loss was felt by all when one of their kind was captured.

The only edge they had when they came was that all Blue World Communication was telepathic, so at the approach of one of the hunters, mental ripples of warning would run through the entire group, giving everyone a chance to scatter and hide.

He would see Galeta swim behind the castle or dive down into an open courtyard at its center and hover close to one of the walls until the danger had passed, while he would press down as low as he could into the bed of lush water plants. So far, this helped both escape capture, but he was not stupid and knew that could change at any time. The hunters always managed to net one or more from their group each time they came. If his or Galeta's time here was destined to be short, he wanted to make the best of it. Life would not have been worth living if it did not contain the giving and receiving of love and though he had never approached her directly before, Adam would hesitate no longer to meet and welcome her to seal them in a water bonding love-circle of two. Such had been the way of their species for as far back as memory existed. Not only could they both know love, but if their fate was to soon die, they might at least bring new life into the world to carry on in their place.

Later that afternoon, following a telepathic pulse of safety that the coast was clear, Adam journeyed to the surface with the others to eat. He swam close enough to Galeta so he would not lose sight of her in the swarm of bodies soaring upward. He knew she would return to the castle when done, so planned to approach her there this time.

When she turned to dive, he saw her pause a moment and look at him, the first telepathic thoughts blazing like lightning between them. As she turned away, her deep, black, recessed eyes glowed with an innate understanding of what was to come.

He dove, staying close as she whipped like a sword in a wild pattern of rises and dives. They were both tossed in violent currents made by the wake of their tails as they streaked through the water in an age-old dance, sharing thoughts and feelings as though they were a single soul.

She now sped ahead of him to the castle, a mighty fortress of protection that had been there long before they themselves lived, and which would be there long after they were gone. It had been erected on a ridge of mossy rock, with a deep well at its center. When they got close enough, they entwined like twirling braids of silk and dove to the castle's bottom, settling on the mossy bed below. They were home at last and evermore a love-circle of two.

Over the next weeks, the horrible hunters came with their nets more and more – sometimes catching one of their kind, sometimes sweeping up groups of four or five all at once. Their world was being slowly destroyed, with nearly half the Blue World community now gone. The hunters had started probing deeper into the hiding places that had kept the more careful of them safe – sweeping behind glittering rocks or through waving wands of sea plants.

Once, as they made their pass through, Adam felt the very walls of the castle shudder so that he thought it would topple then and there, either revealing their location or trapping one of them beneath a fallen wall and crushing them in the process. The castle held its ground, but the terrifying rumble as it shook made it clear that his and Galeta's days were numbered.

Knowing this, they loved like butterflies with only a single, short summer season to live. They were always together and swam as one, each day taking part in the graceful and gliding dances which were as old as the dawn of time for their race, their shining bodies streaking through water in flashes of red and gold or circling like lazily falling petals on a breeze, their deep, dark eyes shining with inner light.

They would sometimes play at things as simple as a child's game of tag, or engage in searching for hidden caches of food or other treasures among the sparkling stones and waving rainbow tendrils of plants.

But most important of all, they kept the secret of their soon-to-be-born offspring, which would ensure the survival of their race.

One day, they swam side by side toward an outlying area of Blue World. Adam rarely came this far from the castle anymore, but he wanted to show Galeta a magnificent little bridge formed from ancient coral and some of the other sites that were there. He knew this might be the last chance she'd have to see them close up. They swam beneath the bridge and, when they came out the other end of it, instead of seeing the shining white stones he knew formed a path leading into a water forest of blue-green kelp, they saw a rapidly widening splotch of gray. It spread in an instant like a cloud of creeping death, and he realized it was the shadow of a hunter.

He didn't need to alert Galeta to the danger. Like a multi-pronged fork of lightening, the danger signal all of their kind had come to know too well went out from him in every direction at once.

As one, Adam and Galeta turned and sped back toward the more populated areas of their home and the safety of the castle. They shared a pulse of relief as they saw it looming ahead in the now-turbulent water, but it was too late.

As they reached the castle, he let Galeta get ahead of him so she could dive down into the safety of the courtyard first, but the hunter got there at the same time and blocked her way.

In one quick motion the beast swept her into its net and began moving away. Adam bolted after them, keeping close to the net, but seeing only the fear and horror in Galeta's eyes as she struggled to get free.

Right at the last moment, he soared above the rim of the net, dove into it, and with the almost impossible strength of desperation, he tossed Galeta out of it, leaving himself tangled and trapped inside.

The last thing he saw as he was pulled away was the look in Galeta's eyes as she drifted downward, staring at him in disbelief, almost motionless, as the others continued frantically slashing through the water all around her in their own efforts to escape.

Lela Johnson had just finished transferring Adam from the little water-filled container into a plastic bag for transport. She smiled at the customer as she rang it up, along with the pretty blue-tinted fishbowl, and said, "Well, that's a new one on me. I never saw a goldfish do that before."

The customer looked up from the check she was writing. "Do what?"

"One goldfish dove right into the net and pushed the one that was in there out of it. They usually scatter as far away as they can when I put that net into the water. I guess this one really wanted to go home with you."

The customer smiled and looked down at Adam suspended in

the water in the plastic bag, which was tilted sideways as it lay on the counter.

"Hmmmm. Maybe I should get two of them. I doubt they get lonely, or feel much of anything for that matter, but I think two would look nicer swimming around in that big bowl."

"No problem. Want me to get you another one from that same tank?"

"Yes. That would be great!"

Lela grabbed the net and walked back to the pet store's bank of aquariums. As usual, when her hulking figure appeared outside the tank, the fish all frantically scattered every which way…except for Galeta.

She waited close to the surface, ready to make her move into the net as soon as it was lowered into the water. She had no idea what her fate would be once she was pulled from the tank, aside from her likely death in the waterless air, but whatever Adam's fate had been, she was going to share it with him.

It was almost midnight, so all the lights were out in the pet store except for the small ones in the fish tanks. One contained a pretty little castle. Inside the courtyard at its center was a decorative shell, and in the shadow of the shell was a clutch of tiny white globes that looked like beads of glass. Only close inspection would reveal the dark spot at the center of each.

Just then, one of the shining globes started pulsing, and shortly after, others did as well.

A shimmering, skinny little thing with a translucent tail burst out of one of the eggs so suddenly, an eye blink would have caused it to be missed. He would later come to be known by his own kind as Arrow, the first of Adam and Galeta's spawn, and the start of a new generation born into Blue World.

As for Adam and Galeta, they settled into the comforts of their new, rather spacious, private home. It too had a pretty little castle, as well as gravel that glittered like jewels at the bottom of the bowl.

With the last, lingering strands of telepathic contact they still shared with the other goldfish in Blue World, they sensed the birth of Arrow and his siblings five miles away. They were delighted to know that their own kind would live on to love, laugh, and dance another day.

NOT ALL, BUT A FEW
Jamie Perrault

"We can't save them." Lathe's words are a soft whistle, too low-pitched for the humans they're watching to hear. The dark of night merges with their gray and brown feathers, rendering them all but invisible as they settle next to Phosphor in the tree. "I'm sorry."

"But —" Phosphor can't help rustling their wings, though they don't move when their mother's bright red eyes fix on them. They resist the urge to leap down and glide towards the lakeshore where the two humans they've been trailing are settling down. "I can *feel* it. Something bad is going to happen."

"Yes." Lathe sighs, their own feet shuffling along the thick branch the two of them are perched on. "That's why you came, isn't it? You're old enough that the Haunting calls you."

"No." Phosphor manages to twist their too-high whistle into a birdcall before the two humans down below notice anything amiss. "That's not — is that what this is?"

"Why else would you be drawn somewhere you *know* only death and disappointment wait?" Their mother slides closer, one wing gathering Phosphor in tight against their warm chest. "It's a part of us, as real as the blood in our veins and the wings with which we fly. It's something you'll feel for the rest of your life."

"But *what's* going to happen?" Phosphor manages to tear their golden gaze away from the humans.

"It could be any of a thousand problems that await them. All mortal creatures are so very fragile – yes, us, too." Their mother's tongue grooms back the fur and feathers on top of Phosphor's head, though they both know it's a losing battle. "There could be a poisonous snake in the water, or an illness, or perhaps one of them will drown. Or perhaps one intends to hurt the other – from this vantage, it's hard to tell if both are the source of the Haunting."

"So why don't we get closer? Why don't we try to help them?" Phosphor's four-toed feet flex, holding tight to the branch supporting them.

"There's too much danger in it. When we let ourselves be seen – when we let the Haunting call us too strongly, or when we decide there's to be too much death for us to countenance – the humans come in vast numbers. They drive us from our homes. They become a threat to *us.*" Lathe shivers, a rustling of the fur on their belly and the feathers on their wings. "Come away. You've felt what you need to feel. There's nothing more to be gained here."

"But–" Phosphor edges a half-step away. If they fight, perhaps they can go closer. Perhaps they can–

"Child." Lathe's whistle turns the word to song, any one of a hundred different children's songs that have been sung to them over the two decades of their life so far. "Please. Don't make this more difficult than it has to be."

Phosphor stands teetering on the edge of the branch for a moment, the pull to go to the humans *so strong*...but then another pull drags at them, a certainty that if they jump, if they fly towards the humans, things with Lathe will never be the same. Something will have *broken*, and the future will spool out darker.

A part of Phosphor wants to chase that gathering gloom. A part of them finds the power there absolutely intoxicating. It's the same sense of impending doom that drew them here, but higher, harder.

"We can't save them." Lathe holds out a wing. "But we don't have to watch them die. Come with me. Please."

With one last glance back at the humans who drew them in the first place, Phosphor returns to their mother's side. When Lathe jumps, Phosphor follows, the two of them swooping like giant silent owls away from the place where tragedy will strike.

When Phosphor settles down to sleep in the morning, their dreams are full of blood and death, and they wonder if their decision was the right one.

Phosphor finds the human child with scissors and a bottle of something that shimmers in the ultraviolet spectrum. The human is surrounded by a miasma of dark possibility, a thick cloud that calls to Phosphor with equal parts longing and despair.

They shouldn't linger. They shouldn't watch. If they stay and try to watch, they may *do* something, and that will cause nothing but problems.

Except...it won't. Phosphor's head perks up, antenna swaying back and forth. They would *know* if disaster would come from their action, right? The Haunting isn't just something that surrounds the humans. Anything with enough consciousness to take concrete actions, to make definitive decisions, can summon the Watchers to themselves.

Phosphor has only experienced the Haunting for two years now, and already they wish they could stop it. The advice the older Watchers give – to see just enough to verify the Haunting, to fulfill their purpose as observers and living memory – doesn't seem to help. How can they just watch? How can they justify allowing horror to happen when they *know* they can affect it?

The human child raises the scissors, cutting their hair in thick, uneven strips. Tension fades from their shoulders as they work, their hair taking something invisible with it as it falls. When they're done they laugh, running their hands back through their newly-shorn mane.

Phosphor slides closer, moving silently through the trees. What is the human doing that could cause such disaster for them?

Drawing in a deep breath, the human rolls their head on their neck and pulls out the little vial of colored liquid. They start applying the liquid to their nails.

Phosphor turns their head around, trying to see or hear anything that would give away the presence of other Watchers. They don't sense anything.

Looking up at the sky, Phosphor fluffs fur and feathers. If they're discovered...

But if they're not? And if their actions can save this child?

Phosphor doesn't hesitate any longer. Spreading their wings, they glide silently down to land in front of the little human.

The child screams. They drop the little vial of color, scrambling backward through the leaf litter. Phosphor raises their wings, realizing belatedly that this only makes them look bigger and more intimidating. Pulling their wings in tight to their body, they raise first one clawed foot and then the other, head tilting as they study the human.

"What the f—" The human mutters a string of words Phosphor can't translate. Their people have lived long enough on the edges of human society that they are able to teach their young the rudiments of common local languages, but the litany of what's likely profanity doesn't make much sense to Phosphor's ears.

"Hi." Phosphor is careful to pitch the word into human vocal range, to use their mouth to shape the word rather than letting it whistle out.

"You — you're a *mothman.*" The child points accusingly at Phosphor. "Right? Yes?"

"*Right* and *yes.*" Phosphor hops a little closer. "If a *mothman* is a Watcher."

"I have no idea what—" The human whistles, and it's nowhere near the proper pronunciation for Watcher, but it's kind of cute to hear the attempt. "You...are you gonna kill me?"

"No."

The child's whole body relaxes.

"But *something* will." Phosphor's claws dig into the dirt. "I wish to warn you."

The human opens their mouth, draws a breath...and just sits down on the ground, their hands in their lap, their eyes fixed on Phosphor.

Phosphor leans forward, studying the human. The human only comes up to their chest, shorn hair sticking up in strange little puffs.

"Why?" The child doesn't blink, staring into Phosphor's eyes.

"I can." Phosphor fluffs up. "I *should*."

"Do you know..." The human rubs at their cheek with the back of one hand. "How? What's gonna happen?"

"I do not know." Phosphor settles, knees bending up to their chest. "Shall I guide you to safety?"

"Can you do that?" The human scrambles back to their feet, putting their small brown eyes on a level with Phosphor's.

"I do not know. But I can try." Phosphor straightens back up. "But I cannot be seen. You cannot tell others about me."

"Nobody would believe me even if I did." The human shrugs. "So long as you keep me from dying, I'll do whatever you want. I've got an awful lot of life I'm still planning to use."

"Good." Phosphor flutters ahead of the child. "Follow."

"Sure, but first – do you have a name?" The child follows while asking the question.

"Phosphor." They give their name in proper Watcher speech.

The human tries to mimic the word, and then they give their head a rueful shake. "That wasn't right, huh? I'm Cal, and I'll work on your name. Until I figure it out, can I call you something else?"

"What would you call me?" Phosphor pauses, curious.

Cal studies them. "I don't know. Cassandra? There's a story about her knowing the future."

"Cassandra." Phosphor turns the word over in their mouth. It would be strange to consider the name as *theirs*, but perhaps it will be fun to have a human name. "I accept. Though I am not a *her* or *him*. I am just a Watcher."

"You're not..." Cal freezes.

"Most of my people are not. A few have started choosing male or female, because we see that is what you and many of the others use, but most are either both or neither."

"You sure you're not going to kill me? Because I can't–" Cal presses a finger to their nose, and their breath stutters in their throat for a few seconds before they cough and continue. "Can I also be one of those? Both or neither?"

"Which one?" Phosphor twists their head almost upside down, studying the human from a new angle.

"Both. Let's go with both." Cal's head rises, their eyes meeting Phosphor's again without fear.

Phosphor nods, turning their head back right-side up. "Be careful where you step, please. I do not want to watch you die."

"Me, either." Cal moves very carefully, putting their feet almost exactly where Phosphor puts theirs.

Phosphor leads the human child through the forest. They start by heading directly towards the human settlement Cal must have come from, but the nearer they come to it, the worse the Haunting becomes. After barely a minute, Phosphor begins leading Cal away. The sense of impending disaster begins to fade.

Interesting.

It takes them hours to reach another human settlement. The Haunting has faded to just the barest ghost, and Phosphor gestures with a wing towards the road that they cannot show themself on. "You will find human help through there."

Cal smiles, and there's something off about the expression, something Phosphor can't read. "Depends on the people I find. You still think I'm going to die?"

"Everything will die." Phosphor leaps into the nearest tree that can bear their weight. "But I do not think you will die today. Unlikely for it to even be this week."

"Then I consider that a win." Cal adjusts the little pack on their back. "Thank you."

"Thank me by living." Phosphor flaps to the next-closest perch, moving away from the human road.

Cal waves as they walk away, and Phosphor feels something warm rise up in their chest.

They did it. They *protected* someone. They felt the Haunting, and they approached the human, and nothing horrible happened to *anyone*.

They can't tell any of the other Watchers about it, but that doesn't matter, not when Phosphor will be able to hear Cal's voice in their mind and know that the human lives because of *them*.

Cal spends a lot of time in the forest.

It's more time than any human child should, but Phosphor quickly grows to understand that Cal is not a standard human child. They would *like* to be, Phosphor thinks. But the way they view themself is not accepted by the people who are supposed to be guiding them, and they slip in and out of trouble with authority figures.

"So long as no one's going to kill me, I don't really care." Cal shrugs, biting into a sandwich. They hold out the other half to Phosphor. "You sense any more trouble coming my way?"

"If I did, I would tell you." Phosphor nibbles on the sandwich, finding the texture of the processed human food absolutely fascinating. Grains are not something the Watchers tend to use in their meals.

"You didn't want to tell me anything at first."

"I didn't expect you to be *looking* for me." Phosphor ruffles their feathers. "Not without a camera and a plan, at least."

"I'm not gonna snitch on you. You want to live in the woods and warn random teens about bad stuff, then you do that. It's a weird life choice, but valid."

"It's what my people do." Phosphor shrugs, a motion they've learned from Cal along with a broad sweep of vocabulary.

"So those sightings people see, they really are you Watchers trying to help us?" Cal takes another bite of their sandwich.

"No." Phosphor shuffles their feet in the leaf litter. "The Watchers don't warn humans. When we do, humans try to find us, and that's too dangerous."

"That's not fair." Cal frowns, finishing the last of their sandwich. "If you know bad things are going to happen—"

"I know." Phosphor takes a forlorn hop to the side. "I've tried to convince my people to do more. And sometimes we do, for the other hidden ones. We try to keep them from being discovered, try to keep as many of their people as possible alive. But more often…"

"*You* could still warn people." Cal licks their fingers before pointing one at Phosphor. "Just 'cause your people don't want to help doesn't mean you can't."

"It would mean betraying my people. If they found out about it…" Phosphor ducks their head down into the fur and feather ruff that surrounds their neck.

"Sucks having to choose between being a good person and having a place to belong. Or between being a person, period, and having a place to belong." Cal rests their head on their knees, watching Phosphor. "What if I helped you? What if you, like…give me warnings, and I try to get them to the people who need them?"

"Not all people are human. Some people wouldn't want to talk to you *because* you're human. But for your species…" Phosphor scratches at the dirt, considering. "We could try it. Though it would probably put you in danger – even other hidden races tend not to like the Watchers."

"I'm good at being careful if I need to be." Cal stands up, brushing their clothes free of the forest as they do. "You'll tell me if you get that…what do you call it? Haunting?"

Phosphor is impressed at how far Cal's pronunciation has come. "I can do that."

"Good." Cal steps forward, and before Phosphor can tell what they're going to do, the human has wrapped them in a tight embrace.

It's a strange feeling, fingers clinging to their feathers, but Phosphor finds they like it. Preening a bit of Cal's hair back, they're pleased to feel not even a ghost of the Haunting singing in their veins.

"The world is getting too small." Lathe perches on the highest branch, looking down at the gathered Watchers. "We will have to move again."

"We are running out of places to go." Another Watcher paces the forest floor. "All the great forests are inhabited already. We can try to move anyway, but how many of us will suffer in the process? How much worse to be caught without anywhere to go?"

"We don't build grand towers." Lathe's red eyes sweep across the congregation. "We don't bury great treasures. All that is precious we carry with us. If we are not welcome in the first place we find, then we find another."

Phosphor paces at the very edge of the crowd, one of the youngest Watchers.

Another Watcher flutters up to a perch just below Lathe, their eyes a pretty yellow-green that shines in the darkness. "Every move we make takes us through territory *riddled* with humans. There will be much potential for things to go wrong."

"There is always the potential for that." Lathe spreads their wings, widening their profile. "We, more than any others, should be *acutely* aware of the potential for disaster to strike anyone. But can't you feel it building? Can't you feel the Haunting starting to surround *us*?"

Phosphor freezes, scenting the air. They have been chasing down every shred of Haunting they can feel for the last nine months, using Cal to help those they can. Sometimes they've been successful; other times they haven't been. For something like what Lathe is suggesting to be happening...

But it's there. Now that Phosphor's attention has been turned to it, there's no denying the fizzing power that's starting to fill the air. It's not just a single one of them. It's a danger that's tied to *each and every* one of them, and becoming more manifest with all of them together.

"We have to do something." Lathe spreads their wings, studying the gathering. "If we don't act soon, we may not be able to act at all. If anyone has an option *other* than running—"

"I do." Phosphor freezes, surprised at the sound of their own voice, and says, higher, louder, "I know another way."

It seems that every eye turns to them, and Phosphor hears a low murmuring as the gathered Watchers declare Phosphor little more than a child.

Phosphor spreads their wings and *leaps*, gathering the air and launching themself up to a point just shy of their mother's perch. They speak to Lathe rather than the congregation. "I know another way."

Lathe stares down at them, red eyes wide.

Turning to the rest of the congregation, Phosphor shouts for all to hear. "I've been helping a human child give warnings to humans who are Haunted. We've been working together for three seasons now. Everything is—"

They were going to say *fine*, but it very clearly isn't. A thick miasma of Haunting is settling around them, cloying and choking, making it difficult to breathe let alone speak.

Looking down at the sea of glowing eyes – red and yellow and green – Phosphor wonders how they never thought to be afraid of their people before.

A wing wraps around them, steady and sure. Lathe's voice cuts through the Haunting. "What's done is done. What remains to be seen is the best path forward."

"If we're going to be discovered, then we should *control* it." Phopshor leans against their mother, allowing Lathe's wing to half-cover them. "We should find a place where we can really *help*, and instead of saying we can't save them all, we should save who we're able. Or better yet, a *dozen* places where we can help. Places where we can make ourselves seem useful rather than frightening."

The green-eyed Watcher ruffles their feathers. "That still leaves the Humans in control of the situation. We'll be reacting, playing by their rules, rather than *acting.*"

"The humans have been in control of the situation for all of my life. For the lifespans of even the oldest among us – Moondust, can you remember a time when we *didn't* fear the humans?" Lathe's voice cuts across the rising chorus of discontent, as it always has.

An ancient Watcher sidles forward, her feathers soft and tattered gray-white with age. Three grandchildren surround her, watching her steps. "We have feared mankind for an age of the planet. They do not share well, and they invent better ways to kill each time they decide to do so. The time to fight them is long past."

"But not the time to learn to live beside them." Phosphor pulls away from Lathe's hold with reluctance. "What Cal and I have been doing – it can *work*. We can find a way to–"

There's a flutter as a dark shape descends from above, and everyone freezes, taking in the tumbling form of a Watcher as he descends to land amidst their flock in an undignified heap. When he levers himself to his feet, he is panting, mouth gaping as he gulps air.

Tension descends on the gathering as the force of the Haunting centers on the stranger. Finally the Watcher gathers himself enough to speak. "The humans know of the Hidden."

A mourning cry echoes from one side of the clearing to the other.

"A wolf-man was killed attempting to cross the highway with a deer carcass – run over like any other animal. His body was taken away by the humans before anyone could intervene. With the moon three-quarters-full, and the way humans communicate, there is little chance of it being ignored."

Phosphor trembles, the weight of the Haunting and of borrowed grief pressing down on them. A wolf-man at this stage of the moon would be difficult to write off, and if the humans wait, watch the body continue to change with the cycle of the moon even after death – seeming human on the new, a wolf capable of bipedalism on the full–

"There might still be time." A yellow-eyed Watcher fluffs their wings. "If we find the human before they share the information, stop them from sharing it–"

"Kill them?" Phosphor's teeth click together. "Is that where we are now? Deciding we must not just *watch* them die, but be the reason they do?"

Silence descends on the congregation, broken only by the shuffle of feet and the ruffle of feathers.

"This Cal." Lathe's voice is quiet, meant for their ears only. "Can you bring them to me?"

Phosphor turns so they can study their mother's eyes.

"Not to hurt them. To see if..." Lathe sighs. "To see if there is a chance in what you offer, because I do not want to be a murderer, but I also will not let my child suffer if I can help it."

"I would not want to live if the cost of my life is innocents lost. I am the one who wants to save them all, remember?" Phosphor reaches up to nibble at the soft feathers around their mother's neck. "I will bring Cal."

Launching from the tree, Phosphor glides over the bickering group. Will they listen? Will they be able to thread a way between all the potential dangers?

Phosphor doesn't know, but it's better to try than to watch everyone drown when the shifting ice gives way and frigid water claims them all.

"You're sure there's a chance?" Cal wipes their hands on their jeans once more, looking Phosphor in the eye.

"Yes. If there was not a chance, I do not think there would be a Haunting." Phosphor shrugs. "That is just *my* thought, though. I do not think many of my people would agree. But the Haunting... it is a call to offer guidance. A call to offer change. To see a forked path with one end full of darkness, and let another know *not there*. Does that mean the other path is without its dangers? No. But at least there..."

"At least there, we have a chance. I know. I've been listening. To as much as I can understand, at least." Cal rubs at their ears.

They have spent the last three weeks mostly with Phosphor's clan. Not everyone has been welcoming, but once Lathe decided this was the best course of action, many joined in.

Enough? They'll only be able to tell when things are finished, Phosphor supposes.

A cry splits the air – not quite a raven, not quite an owl.

It's time for them to go.

Cal walks with calm serenity towards the sidewalk. They chose this part of the forest because it lets out as close to the populous parts of town as they could hope. It's not truly wild forest. It's a little bit of tamed nature that the humans keep close to either convince themselves they're not afraid, or remind themselves of why they once were.

It could not sustain a clan of Watchers, but it was pleasant enough for one Watcher and one young human to hide in for half a day.

People begin to point and stare as soon they're out on the sidewalk. One screams – a man, a woman, Phosphor can't tell.

Another runs up to them, reaching out to touch Phosphor's arm. "This costume is *incredible*. How did you–"

The light dies from his eyes, shock taking its place.

"They're not a person in a costume." Cal speaks quietly, continuing to lead Phosphor along. "They really are what they seem to be, and they have a message for us."

A crowd gathers as they continue to walk, people pointing and whispering and sometimes shouting their questions and dismay. Phosphor struggles to keep their shoulders up, their feathers fluffing as they feel the Haunting start to close in around them.

Things could go so very, very badly.

When Cal finally stops, it's because an armed group of men and women are in front of them. Cal lifts their hands slowly, palms clearly visible. "We don't want trouble."

"*That–*"

"My name is Phosphor. And I come with a warning." More of the guns are pointed at Phosphor than Cal, which Phosphor likes. "There will be death here if you do not let my people and I help prevent it."

One of the men tightens his pale finger on the trigger of his gun.

Another raises his hand, his dark skin glistening with sweat. "Where? From what?"

"I do not know exactly what the danger is until it happens. But I can take you to the place where the danger is strongest, and let you know when the threat peaks and when it's passed." Phosphor inhales.

The lead human lowers his hand. "Show us. Let's see what happens."

The group follows, and they see. Phosphor had known what came would be *big* – for the Haunting to call from so far away it *had* to be – but they hadn't expected the devastation a ten-car pile-up could bring. It starts on the highway, a car hitting a patch of unexpected moisture and skidding off the road before rolling across main street.

It ends with three people dead and many more hospitalized.

It could have been much worse. It *should* have been much worse. The size of the Haunting meant at least a dozen should have died. But the group that followed Phosphor, all those frightened humans, they were there to help.

"We didn't save them all." Phosphor's beak strokes through Cal's hair as they hold the shivering human close to them. "But we saved some."

Cal nods, and the two of them slip off as soon as they can.

They have other towns to visit, after all, and other tragedies to try to stop.

Cal and Phosphor aren't the only pair that travels, city to city, place to place, trying to control the shape of the narrative forming around the Watchers.

Sometimes they are met with fear; sometimes they are welcomed as heroes.

Sometimes the Haunting is so bad upon approach that they are forced to leave, allowing matters to proceed as they would have. Cal usually tries to find a telephone and call in to those towns, to give *someone* a chance to help if they're able, but it's much harder without being there.

They're resting together in a deep, cool grove when Lathe catches up to them. There is a human magazine clutched between Lathe's toes, and they deposit it on the ground in front of Cal.

Phosphor is good at speaking, now, but not at reading. They look to Cal.

Cal's fingers trace over the words. "Mothmen: Friend? Fiend? Force of Nature?"

Lathe preens their feathers smooth. "We've had Watchers shot, and Tulip's been missing for days now. But...I think you were right, Phosphor. I think this was the only thing we could do."

"We can't save them all." Phosphor returns Lathe's words. "But the fact that we *want* to makes all the difference."

"We can't save them all, and we can't sacrifice ourselves for them." Lathe's toes dig into the soft ground, leaving deep impressions they once would have tried to erase. "But living together, if that's what we must do...you're right. It does involve at least *trying.*"

"And my people are trying, too." Cal bites their bottom lip, flipping the magazine open and stroking some of the glossy pages. "This...despite the sensational cover, it's all about how you guys are being nothing but helpful, and how we need to sit down and talk with you. How we need to figure out how to co-exist, and not blame you for what happens."

"No one loves a storm crow because no one loves a storm." Lathe opens their wings. "But we've a right to live, and if your kind let us, we'll keep you alive alongside."

"I'm doing my absolute best." Cal shrugs, closing the magazine.

"I know." Lathe's red eyes study Cal before abruptly shifting to Phosphor. "Will you be coming home?"

"I'll be at the gathering, to decide where we go next." Phosphor slides a wing around Cal. "But I'm already home."

Lathe's wings twitch, and their fur stands on end, but they say nothing more before launching themself into the sky.

Cal nuzzles into Phosphor's neck feathers. "I love a storm crow, you know."

"Good." Phosphor nuzzles back. "Because I love you, too."

No Haunting rises up, and Phosphor closes their eyes, settling into the stillness between them with relief.

Sometimes one life is all that's needed to change everything, after all.

VAGUELY APOCALYPTIC
Eli *ayden Loft

ound and recorded by: Regina Maycroft

T*e following is a text by *eat*er Mark*am. For years, we *ave believed t*e loss of a letter in t*e Latin alp*abet a prank gone catastrop*ically wrong. In trut*, it was t*e result of a uniquely powerful and *profoundly inept* mage's attempt to wipe out *umanity.

To wom it may concern,

I'm leaving tis message for wen animals become sapient or aliens visit te Eart. My name is eater Markam, and I am te person wo wiped out umanity.

Yes, I am going to end te world. People ave dismissed me as 'crazy' and 'bad wit magic' for too long. Tey don't realise my lack of control is because I ave too muc power. Tey will eat teir words.

A bit about me for te istory records: I was a gifted cild. Everyone said so, even people wo ated me. Tat's ow you know it's true and not just te stupid sit parents say about teir own kids. I got my magic early, so I started scool early too. I ad to be taugt control.

I don't know if you've unearted any fiction books about magic, but most are wrong. We don't wear pointy ats, wave sticks around, or boil eyeballs. We're just like anyone else, only we can extend our wills beyond our bodies. And I ave a very strong will.

I ended up being wat people call a 'difficult' cild. I don't know wy I tougt tat aving a strong will also meant aving all te answers. I didn't ave any, but you couldn't tell me tat. I was a bully, I'll admit. I used my magic to get anyting I wanted, and I wanted a lot.

It wasn't tat long before I got expelled. Altoug, wen a kid tinks tey're all tat, tey don't really care about tose kind of tings. So, it wasn't long before I was expelled from a second scool, ten a tird. All te wile, my power grew and I wasn't being taugt to control it. No one would ave me.

I did get my act togeter eventually but, by ten, no one wanted to risk being my teacer, my mentor. Tey were afraid I would urt tem or oter students or watever, because I ad too muc power and too little control. I was left alone. Even my parents ad given up on me.

I was a little sit, I know. But I'm not anymore. Still, no one cared to take a cance on me. I never got an education, and I ave to live in seclusion because I can't pass te Control Test – o, tat's a test mages ave to take to make sure tey can safely live among non-magic umans. I probably sould ave clarified earlier, but tey don't know about us. Tey'd probably be scared if tey did.

Anyway, tis isn't just about me. umanity as made tis world a depressing mess, so I'm going to end it.

Update:

I did not expect to still be alive, but I am. I ave failed. I did exactly as te book said – I travelled to four sides of te world, setting up te appropriate runes in eac location. I cose were tere were te most and strongest ley lines. I made tem invisible to anyone wo wasn't using divination magic. I told no one, not even my minion.

Not tat my goldfis could ave tattled. Te attempts to make im sapient failed.

Wen tat was done, I activated tem. It was amazing at first. Really. I generated tis massive wave of power tat swept around te world like a gale-force wind! People were *terrified*, tey ran for cover, tey called teir loved ones to say goodbye. Tey cried and screamed and begged for mercy.

And ten…noting.

I tougt I'd done it. umanity, gone! Toug, for some reason, I was still ere? I wondered wat tat was about but, as I walked around te empty street, I looked into a café's window and wow, so many people iding under tables! ~~As if tat would've saved tem.~~ I was socked! Everyone was still alive!

I didn't understand wat I'd done wrong. And everyone else was just as confused, toug for different reasons. It took a wile for any of us to realise tat tere was someting different. A newspaper on te café's table ad te eadline 'POLITICIAN CAUGT NAKED OUTSIDE OTEL ROOM' but, if anyone noticed, no one tougt to look – tey assumed tey were just bad typos.

People still talk te same. But, wen people started trying to ceck in on eac oter, tey realized te on teir keyboards was gone. Not like, tere was a blank button. Te button was gone. Tey were lauging about it, assuming it was temporary. But I know it won't be. I used so muc magic, intending to wipe tem all out. Tere's no way wat I did wasn't permanent. Probably.

So, I guess te world's fine. I…well, I managed someting. I got rid of every letter in any text ever. Letter … Wy do I even boter? Anyway, everyone's a lot more annoyed tan dead, I guess. Writers are mad, of course, but most people are lauging about it. I guess tinking tey were going to die made it a giddy relief wen it was just a letter in one alpabet tat bit it.

So, I'm…not going to take credit. Calk tis up to a bad test run. Maybe next time. Or maybe I'll go back to trying to make my goldfis sapient.

Signed,
eater Markam

P.S. I may ave to cange my name.

Note by Regina Maycroft:

*opefully unbeknownst to t*e reclusive Mark*am, s*e did almost end t*e world. In one go, *er magic revealed mages and *ow powerful t*ey can be to non-magic *umans. T*eir fear of us t*reatened to start a war to end all wars. T*ankfully, t*at fear *as mostly passed due to t*e years wit*out incident and t*e many services mages can offer. It s*ould lessen furt*er wit* t*is discovery. After all, few are t*e unique combination of powerful and moronic t*at *eat*er Mark*am was. And no, s*e never c*anged *er name.

NEMESIS
B C Fontaine

As the city's official supervillain, my greatest obsession is obviously its hero. Personally, I would prefer to call it a *preoccupation*, strictly professional, with none of the unseemly implications of a word like *obsession*.

Friends and henchmen, however, have referred to it in this way and I can reluctantly acknowledge why: as the hero's nemesis, his photo is usually beside my bed, on my desk, or in my wallet. I have to study him, after all. It's not unreasonable, and certainly not unusual.

He looks the part of a hero. Most of them look like they floated off the same sunny assembly line, even the edgy vigilante types. A non-threateningly handsome face, nothing disproportionate, except for an endearingly crooked tooth. It adds human relatability to his otherwise perfect, eye-crinkling smile. There's a perpetually warm look in his Golden Retriever-brown eyes, and it makes you feel liked, even if he's about to throw an armored car at you (he's done that a couple times).

Sometimes after studying his photo, I study my own visage in the bathroom mirror, and see if I can count the differences. He's non-threatening – he has to be, otherwise people might be more wary of his power. There's nothing non-threatening about me.

I'm beautiful in a way that puts people on edge. Even as a child, my teachers used to find me intimidating. Angular, with vampiric cheekbones, a supermodel pout, and bored eyes so pale they're almost colorless. I look like Dracula, or maybe one of his brides, depending on the adaptation. Like someone who should be twirling a satin cape, which I often am.

My hero and I compliment each other perfectly, night and day, butter and toast. To become someone's nemesis is a big commitment, a bit like marriage. More of a commitment than a marriage, actually. To be someone's nemesis is to devote your life to them. They become part of you. Half of you. They fill your gaps like melted gold, and you'd be incomplete without them, you know you would.

I made this point at last year's National Villains Convention, and it got me some strange looks. But I stand by the sentiment.

Of course, I claim, frequently and repeatedly, that my ultimate goal is the hero's demise. But that's just for publicity. I could have destroyed him countless times, and I'm always careful to let him escape. Cape-twirling, theatrical monologues usually do the trick.

A lot of what I do is for publicity, it keeps the city officials happy. The government is fully capable of building a prison that could hold me. You know it's true – it's the same government that built a nuclear bomb. I'm powerful, but not as powerful as a nuclear bomb.

The reason I'm floating around in a cape and not in a supermax prison/research facility is because I actually benefit the city's economy. The tourists that come to watch me and my hero go at it, standing stupidly in harm's way with their phones raised like talismans, they generate revenue. My hero and I are mutually careful not to hit the idiots with the vehicles we hurl at each other. I actually think the property damage also generate revenue, for some kind of convoluted insurance reasons, but I don't have the time and energy to figure out why.

When you look at it that way, it's not even like my hero and I are even actually on opposing sides. The city benefits from both of us.

That's why it allows us to exist, two beings that could potentially kill hundreds within seconds. Two beings who mutually choose not to.

Some days, all we do is fight, tendrils of my shadow magic wheeling like tentacles, trying to catch him as he dips and swoops and pirouettes in the air. A dance between the two of us.

It's not always like that, though. We have our quiet moments. There's a roof we call neutral ground, and he joins me there tonight.

I'm seated between two lichen-modeled gargoyles, vestiges from when the city was going for that Neo-Gothic look. I think the hero is actually why that architectural style never fully took off here – it doesn't go with his aesthetic. He's not the sort who appears as an ominous silhouette between lightning flashes.

He's more the sort who – well, the sort who looks as he does right now. Floating towards me, annoyingly majestic, bathed in sunlight that makes him look like an Oscar statue.

"I brought you a mint tea," he says, offering one of the two steaming to-go cups in his hands. "Figured you'd be here. It's that kind of evening."

"And you have super vision." I accept the cup, wincing at the heat. "*Fuck.*"

"Sorry." He eases himself to sit beside me, arranging his cape daintily behind him. It makes me think of a curtsy. "I forgot you feel things like normal people do. It's cute."

I scoff, gingerly peeling back the lid to blow steam. "Well. Don't forget that next time you throw a truck at me."

"You'd regenerate. You're semi-immortal, if I remember correctly."

"Yeah, but it would hurt like a bitch."

We sit in silence, overlooking the network of streets, rectilinear buildings like neatly arranged building blocks. The cars in tidy rows.

"You know, it's amazing that this can exist."

His tone catches me off guard. It's always strange when he sounds tired.

"Ninety percent of the ocean is unexplored, yet people are still surprised when a monster crawls out. And don't get me started on space."

"You're from space," I say. I'm trying to take tiny sips of my tea, but it keeps burning my tongue.

"I know, but I don't remember it. I was a toddler." He sips his own drink – something sugary and pumpkin-flavored, from the smell of it. It must be at least as hot as mine, but he doesn't even flinch. "And what does that say about the unknown? My planet wasn't even far away, and most of humanity still thought aliens didn't exist when I landed. Everyone's just clumped together, floating in chaos, and we all just agree to pretend like there's some order to it."

"I actually don't think chaos is the defining future of the universe." At the National Supervillains Convention, I talked to a biochemist – a surprising amount of us are in the sciences – and I recall something she'd said. "Order, regulation, and symmetry are properties of life. Just because most of the universe is unknown doesn't mean it's chaotic."

He blinks, slowly, in thought, the sunlight turning his Retriever-brown eyes melancholy amber. "But I'm talking about the rules *we* create," he says finally. "Just because there's order to the universe doesn't mean it cares about us. I make people feel secure, like there are benevolent higher powers standing between them and the void. And, you know – so do you. People *wish* that you were really the face of evil, something familiar and understandable and quantifiable and sort of human, even. But in the face of it all, we're just as helpless as they are."

What he's saying sounds like something out of one of my monologues, but I'm actually not a nihilist. I don't go to church anymore, I can't get past the smugness and certainty of the priests I grew up with, but I do believe in God. Even if the Bible got everything wrong, I intrinsically feel as though each person was created from a spark of love, and that life is a gift to live or squander.

Deep down, I'm an optimist. That might be my best kept secret.

Just like no one would ever guess that he's far more of a pessimist than I am. Fortunately, I know none of this is what he needs or wants to hear right now, so I'm spared from having to share any of it.

"This is about that case," I say, "isn't it?"

We don't bring up each other's secret identities often. It's bad etiquette. We've never even interacted out of costume, but we keep tabs on each other. Part of the commitment we made when we became nemeses.

Out of costume, he's a prosecutor. The monsters he's encountered in the courtroom, devoid of any whimsical powers or theatrical flair, are worse than any cape-twirling supervillain. Worse than any bank robber, or any crime that takes place in the public eye. Real evil isn't always theatrical. It hides in the shadows, behind closed doors. Weak, pathetic people with power over someone more vulnerable.

He doesn't look at me, and for a moment, I wonder if he's going to ignore the question. "He's going to walk. Claimed it was consensual, his word against hers. He might even get partial custody of the kid," he mutters, finally. "People rely so much on rules. You know? People cling to them, like they'll protect them. But the system we've created is indifferent, too. Just a machine that keeps turning. Crushing anyone small."

If I were out of costume, I might say, "I'm sorry." Maybe even use my therapist voice, put a gentle hand on his shoulder. I don't think it would help.

"I keep thinking about how easy it would be to kill him." I look up abruptly, and he looks sheepish. Not necessarily because he's thinking this, but because he's confessing to it. It contradicts so sharply with his carefully-constructed image of squeaky clean morals. "One blast, and his whole house would be leveled. Like a meteor. People might suspect me, but they'd never be able to connect it."

I know that it's more important to listen than to talk right now – my training does come in handy sometimes – so I remain silent, non-judgmental. He probably knows what I'm doing. He's aware of my secret identity, too.

"But that would blur so many lines. I have so much power, all this power, and I promised myself I'd never use it like that. Never for destruction, never to cause harm. Never serious harm, at least. Because what could I become if I let myself do that?" He's rambling now, and I let him. "And then I wonder if that makes me evil. If letting him live makes me evil. Because I know he's going to do it again. Maybe even to the kid. And I could stop it, but I know I won't, for some – some arbitrary fucking line I drew for myself."

He takes a sip of his drink, and it makes me realize that mine is already getting cold. I put the lid back on to trap the remaining heat. The minty taste has gotten a little too strong, the bag left to steep for longer than it should, which is how I like it.

I stare at him in my periphery, beautiful as if he'd been chiseled out of amber, and I know he's probably done talking about this. That he's gotten it out of his system, or thinks he has, and has put it back in some box inside of himself that he uses to compartmentalize.

I want to tell him that he could never be evil, even if he tried. But I've never been good at expressing emotions that way. Ironic, I know, since I spend my workdays asking patients, "How do you feel about that?"

Still. There are other ways I can help out.

You wouldn't be able to tell it apart from the other houses on the street. It's in the suburbs, so they're pretty much identical. It's not like in the movies, where the one that houses a predator is derelict to reflect his moral bankruptcy, no boarded-up windows or thin layer of moss to make the clapboard shingles look grungy. There's no vandalism, either, not enough of a high profile case to attract public outrage.

I have to double-check the address. It would be unfortunate for multiple people if I had the wrong house.

I glance around, to make sure I'm not being observed. I'm

wearing this weird combination of my villain outfit and my pajamas, because I made the decision to do this right before heading to bed and wanted to get it over with before my nerves failed me.

I turn into shadow, dripping like liquid into a dark puddle that undulates along the pavement, up the steps, and seeps through the crack beneath the door.

He doesn't look evil. He's not twirling a cape or a well-waxed moustache, he's not slumped before the TV with an expression of loathing. He's standing at the stove, boiling something that looks like instant mac and cheese. It's hard to look evil while making instant mac and cheese, I suppose.

He certainly doesn't look like someone who got his sixteen-year-old student pregnant. He-said, she-said, because that's the legal age of consent in this state. Because he said she wanted it, and she said he'd been doing it since she was fourteen. His word against hers. He lost his job, but the consequences seem to end there. Until now, that is.

I undulate closer to him, an amorphous shadow that he hasn't noticed. Maybe he won't notice, until it's too late.

I can faintly see his scalp through his thinning hair, fair and curling at the temples, like a cherub. Like a parody of innocence. There are freckles on the back of his neck. He doesn't look evil. He looks like a human being, because that's what he is.

Maybe it's wrong to do what I'm about to do to a human being. Even if what he did to his student was *also* wrong. A hero would argue that this is taking the law into my own hands, crossing a moral boundary. Indeed, a hero would never do what I'm about to do. A hero would be obligated to let this man live, and stay a part of that little girl's life forever, and play with the baby he put inside of her.

But I'm not a hero. I'm free from the shock collar of moral platitudes and public opinion. That girl and her baby won't have to stay under this man's thumb so my hands can stay clean.

And one more thing: because I'm doing this, my hero doesn't have to. I just hope he'll forgive me for it.

After the teacher's mysterious disappearance, I take a couple weeks off from supervillainy. I focus on my clients, do some knitting, watch some reruns of *I Love Lucy* with my cat curled up in my lap. Sometimes, I turn on the news, and watch my hero battle some minor villains with names that are impossible to take seriously, like Puppet Master, or the Muskrat.

It's not that I feel bad about the teacher's mysterious disappearance, which for legal reasons I had absolutely nothing to do with. I wouldn't have become a villain if I were that thin-skinned. I have a suspicion that even a lot of heroes could be diagnosed with some kind of antisocial personality disorder, but I wouldn't be comfortable forming that kind of assessment outside of a clinical setting. But I don't want to face my hero, and I'm not completely sure why.

He'll be able to piece together what I did, he's not an idiot. His public persona as a pure-hearted dimwit is more to make other people more comfortable with his insane amounts of power. And he knows me, so it's not like he'd be surprised that I'd do something morally gray, if that could even be called morally gray. Disappearing a rapist shouldn't be considered morally gray, in my opinion.

But he'll know I did it for him. Maybe he'll blame me for it, feel like I implicated him, or that the teacher's blood (not that it was particularly bloody, that's not my style) is somehow on his white-gloved hands.

Granted, from what I've seen of him on TV, he certainly doesn't look traumatized. Cheerfully holding up the freshly-brutalized Muskrat by his tail (again, this is what I mean when I point out that heroes are seldom paragons of empathy) with the crowd and reporter singing his praises.

Or maybe he'll ask me why I did it. Why I would do something like that for him. And I'll have to answer. What would I even say? I'm not even sure I know myself.

No, that's not true, is it. I know exactly why. I'm just too much of a coward to put it into words.

I can never stay away from him too long, of course. That's the thing about nemeses. It only works if you're a little obsessed with them.

Tonight, I float by his window, which I'm aware is a creepy thing to do. You might be comforted to know that I did so in the form of an amorphous shadow, so it'll be harder for him to notice me with his creepy enhanced vision.

I've known his address for years, but this is the first time I've seen his apartment in person. It's not what I expected. It's humble and cozy, his bedspread a warm shade of ochre. On his bedside table is a half full cup of water and a stack of books. A small television in the corner. Pictures of family and friends on the wall. A side of his life that I'm not a part of.

He comes in wearing pajamas, a cup of tea in one hand. His hair is fuzzy. There's a bit of toothpaste on the front of his shirt, and noticing that detail makes me realize that the pajamas have little dogs on them. Mine have cats. Small world.

He eases under the covers, cursing when he spills a bit of tea on himself, though I know it doesn't burn him. He haphazardly uses his pajama sleeve to dry it. I'm invading his privacy, I know, I know it's wrong. But it's just so strange, seeing him like this. Human.

He reaches for one of the books on the bedside table. I tilt my head to try to look at the cover, which makes me realize I *have* a head. I've reverted back to my human form. I have to really concentrate to maintain my shadow form. Oh, well. He's not looking anyway.

The book isn't one I'm familiar with – it's got some girl in a hoop skirt running through a field on the cover – which means it's probably terrible. I've read just about everything good, and that's not an exaggeration. As a child, my teachers used to be too intimidated to contradict me.

He opens his objectively terrible hoop skirt novel, fingering his way through pages until he seems to find his place. He does this little hip-wiggle motion, like he's about to settle in for reading.

And then he stops. Just stops, with a vacant-eyed, just-remembered-something look. He sets the open book so it's splayed on the bed next to him, and opens the little drawer in his bedside table. Shaking his head at himself, like a smoker about to binge. Maybe he is a smoker. This evening's full of surprises.

What he takes out isn't a pack of cigarettes, but a picture. Glossy in the light, he runs his finger over it, as if to smooth it. It's laminated. It looks like it's been carefully cut from a newspaper.

It's me. I don't know what day it was taken, but I'm turning towards the paparazzi with a victorious, haughty smile, twirling my cloak in a flourish behind me. There are thousands like it.

He smooths it again with his thumb, and gazes at it with something like yearning. Like he misses me.

It...shouldn't surprise me as much as it does. I keep his picture close by – nemeses are, by default, one another's top priority. It shouldn't surprise me. It shouldn't mean what it does.

"Oh," I whisper, and fuck. He has super hearing.

He looks up, of course he does, with an expression of creepy intensity. It makes me think of a robot, or some kind of wild canine, like a dingo, smelling blood. People would be scared of him, if they really thought about what he could do.

He could level cities, and he chooses not to. The government could contain me. They might not be able to contain him. But he chooses to be good anyway. And I love him for that.

I love him. I can admit that to myself, if not to him, or anyone else. I love him. I love him.

And here we are. He's in bed. I'm floating outside his window. Both of us in our pajamas. The aforementioned cat pajamas, because getting into villainous attire every time I want to fly somewhere would be way too much work. Staring at each other.

It feels like an eon, but it's probably just an instant. I melt into shadow, and before he can really process that I've been spying on him during his most intimate moments, I dissipate into the night.

Only when I materialize in my apartment do I realize how hard my heart is beating, rabbit-thudding in my chest.

My cat looks at me quizzically. *"Brr-ow?"*

"Hi," I say hoarsely, not in the mood to explain myself.

The cat and I stare at each other, in a ridiculous parody of how my hero and I must have looked just seconds ago.

"What should I do?" I ask.

The cat cocks their damn adorable little head, playing dumb.

"What," I reiterate, "should I do?"

The cat pounces down from the bookshelf and walks away, denying me an answer.

The next morning, I spend a lot of time stressing over my outfit. I ultimately decide on what I usually wear, to take the edge off my jagged beauty and put my patients at ease: an oversized cardigan. Little gold-rimmed librarian glasses. A satchel.

If I'm being honest, it's not just for my patients, though that's certainly part of it. I like dressing like this. I like feeling like I don't have to intimidate people, like I did when I was a child of the foster system, surrounded by bigger people who'd turn on me like hounds if they smelled even a whiff of fear.

I want him to see this side of me. Even though the intimacy of the gesture might be somewhat negated by the fact that he's seen me in my pajamas. I remind myself that this is different. Deliberate. It means more that way.

I go back to his building, and basically pace around awkwardly outside while I wait for him. I nearly talk myself into leaving, reminding myself that if one of my patients did this, I'd refer to it as *stalking*, and *self-destructive behavior*.

Then I talk myself into staying, reminding myself that my hero was *also* engaging in unhealthy, obsessive behavior by keeping laminated, cut-out photos of me. Then I nearly talk myself into leaving again by remembering that I'd tell my patients that just because a relationship is mutually obsessive, doesn't make it any less toxic. Then I talk myself back into staying again by reminding myself that nemeses are inherently obsessive towards one another, like one would be obsessive towards a profession.

Before I can talk myself into leaving for real this time, a

handsome lawyer exits the building. He's wearing glasses he doesn't need, and he's wearing a perfectly pressed suit, his hair well-coiffed. He has a folded newspaper in one hand and a coffee in the other.

When he sees me, he gives a double take, like he's concerned his super vision might be failing him. I know he recognizes me, even if he's never seen me without my cape before. My breath hitches.

Maybe, if I were one of my patients, I'd applaud myself for putting myself in a position of such vulnerability. Maybe.

We stare at each other, a recreation of our very short-lived stare-down last night. His expression is, for a minute, impossible to read.

Then, it softens. I could swear the corner of his mouth quirks in a smile.

"You look familiar. Have I seen you before?"

My heart feels fluttery, and I feel like I need to brush my teeth to compensate for how saccharine I'm being. I just can't believe the warmth in his tone of voice is directed at me.

"I think so." I swallow. "I'm. I was thinking of moving to this area. Nice view of the water, and." I raise my arm awkwardly in a half-shrug. "And everything."

Years of eloquent monologues, and I'm reduced to this.

"Well. We should get coffee sometime. Or maybe mint tea." He's smiling now. Really smiling, so that his crooked tooth is showing. I can't think of anything that brings me more joy. "It's nice to finally meet you."

SLUAGH
Kelly Stronach

Fiachra shuddered as the cold wind whistled between the trees. Already bare from an early winter, there was no foliage to shelter him from its chill, and Fiachra's torn cloak offered little protection.

He pressed a shaking hand to his side, wincing at the sting and grimacing from the wet tackiness of blood. The wound had been deep, and it was unlikely to close on its own. Either he found a way to stave off the bleeding, or he wouldn't survive until sunrise.

He weighed his options and ripped off what was left of his cloak to repurpose as a bandage for his gaping wound. The sigil of his once-king, a stark black against the wine dark material, gleamed under the light of the gibbous moon. He only hesitated for a second before tearing the fabric and wrapping it tightly around his middle.

Another bone chilling gust raced through the forest. Fiachra curled into himself, hugging his sides gingerly. He couldn't stop his hands from trembling, and his heart sank to know, no matter how desperately he wished he didn't, that it wasn't entirely due to the cold. Nor solely from the blood loss.

The look in his brother's eye, as he ran him through with his broadsword, had yet to leave him. The gentle caress of Aiden's hand against his own one final time before it fell, limply, aside. The soft, pleading way in which he had said Fiachra's name, like that would make up for all the years he'd spent casting shadow and shame upon it.

And Fiachra hated himself bitterly for how close he'd come to allowing such a feeble ploy to work. It was too late for his brother. Once, when he was still young and gullible and so desperate to belong, he may have needed his brother's approval, his patience, his love. But now he had no use for such things. He was stronger, older, wiser.

Now if only his damned heart would understand.

The call of a raven echoed throughout the forest, joined by the answering cry of another, and another. It wasn't long before there was an entire rave cawing and flying about, a black cloud of misery coming in from the West.

Just before the unkindness could block out the light of the moon, the flurry of ravens descended from the skies and alighted before him. The swarm piled onto one another until each body was indistinguishable from the next. Their caws clamored and echoed with all the mighty din of church bells, and on their beating wings carried the stench of decay. Their midnight feathers coalesced into a shadowy mass, out of which stepped a man.

Or rather, something which was almost a man.

It was tall, with a cloak darker than the night and skin paler than the moon. Considering Fiachra with a steady gaze were eyes that glowed a green like lush vegetation, set beneath a wild crop of hair alike to auburn flame. It came closer, its steps silent despite the dead leaves underfoot.

"My, my, what exquisite melancholy you have," the beast crooned, its voice low and heavy as a padded quilt. Thin lips parted, and the razor tips of fangs glinted under the moonlight as it drank a deep breath. "And what lovely terror."

Fiachra couldn't still his heart, nor steady his breath, and it was only made worse with every step the monster took. He found himself unable to move when the creature finally reached him, its wiry frame nearly vertiginous as it loomed above.

"You seem confused, my little lamb," the monster smiled, its mouth stretching to mimic the gesture but its eyes remaining steady. "Did you not mean to call out?"

"I–I didn't call for you," Fiachra forced himself to speak. His blood ran cold when the beast's eyes alighted, flashing bright and keen.

A hand emerged from the cloak. Deathly pale, its sallow skin drawn tight over the sinew and bones beneath. Nails sharpened to talons ghosted across Fiachra's cheek, tracing the outline of a deep cut he'd received hours ago from one of his brother's loyal knights.

The beast smiled again. Smaller. It reached his eyes, softening them to a moss.

"Oh, but you *did*, my darling woe. You see, my hearing is quite good, and I could hear your sorrow from across the isle."

The hand trailed lower, following the wound down Fiachra's neck and to his shoulder. Goosepimples arose in its wake, and Fiachra's chest ached from the pounding of his heart. As more of the hand emerged from the cloak, Fiachra could see the inky feathers that coated the monster's arms.

He swallowed a gasp as the creature leaned in, their foreheads nearly touching. No heat came from its body, and the scent of decay – of rotten logs, of boggy peat, of rotting flesh – floated off its lips.

"There isn't a soul more beautiful than that of the hopeless. And your emptiness is truly a work of art."

Its frozen hand settled on his chest. Over his heart.

"And I have a nasty little habit of collecting beautiful things."

The monster's hushed admission ghosted over Fiachra's lips. Talons sank into the flesh of his chest while another hand, equally clawed to a dangerous tip, gently curled around the back of his neck.

"W-wait," Fiachra choked out. "I can't, I'm not ready to, to die, please don't—"

The beast chuckled, its laughter a rumble like distant thunder that reverberated through their touching chests.

"Oh, but my dear misery. The loss of your soul isn't the end."

The creature leaned closer. Cold lips touched his.

"It's only the beginning."

THE DEFENDER
Lee F Patrick

They looked out over the valley. No danger. There had been danger in the past, but nothing really woke them anymore, unless they forced themselves into full awareness. Like now. They searched for the link between themselves and the chosen. There was always someone they could reach to give them the warnings.

Nothing. Had the line died out without them being aware of the loss?

No. A faint trace. A scent in one of the rooms below. They blinked and stone eyes turned to flesh. Only starlight gave illumination. No moon to reveal intruders. Not that they needed light to sense the approach of danger. But since they were awake, they would stretch their wings, walk the battlements, just to have something to do.

The rest of their body became flesh and a roosting pigeon became a meal. Perhaps they would find another one as they patrolled. They had slept a long time. Their eyes now looked at the immediate area instead of scanning for an enemy.

They remembered coming here long ago. The chosen of that time said they were still to protect all within. They had patrolled often then, but there was little danger so they returned to sleep.

They looked out around the countryside, not for enemies this time. There. A small fort sat on the ridge, the stones tumbling down. Had the Druids who created the defenders gone away too?

Even if they had, danger would always wake a defender. If there had been no danger in such a long time, then maybe they were no longer needed. But the chosen then had thought enough of their protection to send them to this new home.

They returned to the corner. Settled themselves into position and became stone again. The red light in their eyes faded as they willed themselves back into sleep. Staying awake with no need of their protection was a thankless task. They would wake again when they were needed. They did not bother any of the other pigeons, even when they perched on their head.

They sensed a chosen near them in the strong sunshine. Female but older. A hand stroked their head. "Jennifer needs someone like you to help her. I will send you to her. I cannot do more than I have already. I am too old, and my gifts are not like hers. But you will protect her. Defend her." They let the spot under the old chosen's hand warm beyond what the simple sunlight had produced. "Thank you. It is a long trip, far across the great sea. But you will have other adventures there. I have Seen one of them." A final rub and the old chosen lifted her hand.

Satisfied, they returned to slumber.

Sunlight. And voices. Two adult and a younger one. Ahh. That was the chosen with whom they would bond. To keep all of them safe from whatever might happen. The young one had the Gift which would make communication easier.

They would bide in stone until dark, then they could properly examine their surroundings. They sensed no danger at present. That was good. They dozed, still alert for any hints of their new charges and their dwelling.

Full dark came and they roused, opening their eyes. They were not on a battlement, where they could survey the countryside for danger, they were under a tree. With flowers on the branches above them. They knew this was night, but there were still many pinpricks of light nearby that were not stars. They checked, sensing no people awake. Good. They could properly scout the area.

Shifting into their flesh and extending their wings, they leapt to the top of a small building near the tree, then to the top of the keep. Well, this truly wasn't much of a keep. And the roof was very steep. There was nowhere large enough for their stone form to perch safely. Keeping them on the ground made sense now.

They slowly turned, eyes taking in the multitude of small keeps that surrounded this one. Each with only a few people in them. Some dogs, but they sensed that most of those were small and weak, fit only to warm a lady's bed. A few were larger and could be kept for the hunt or for defense. Still. This place was strange. The moon rose and they reared to stretch their wings.

A sense of their chosen waking. They leapt from the roof and landed easily on the grass. Settling in place under the tree, they checked to be sure they were in the same place as before. Some of their previous chosen had known of their abilities, others had never needed to. Perhaps this chosen would explain why they had come here. As they shifted back to stone, they decided they would stay awake for a time to ponder that. They had plenty of time, after all.

They were aware of the chosen sitting beside them many times in the next days, sometimes leaning against their side. Sometimes they were alone, other times three young females were nearby. This was unusual, but few chosen ever came up to the battlements of the fort, and even if they did, there wasn't anywhere for them to sit in comfort. This time, the chosen seemed to be speaking to them, since they could not sense any others around. At least they could learn from the chosen's mind, since they did not understand any of the languages the chosen or the others spoke.

"Cosantoir," said the chosen, "that's going to be your name. It means defender or guardian. I can't just call you gargoyle anymore, and I refuse to use grotesque. You're odd looking, but that's just you. And since I can't speak Irish, I'm going to shorten that to Cosan. And use she as a pronoun, though I'm not sure how to tell the difference between girl and boy gargoyles, if there is any. Or if you're somewhere in between. Using *it* doesn't seem very respectful. Mom and I outvoted Dad on the girl/boy question. Now he's grumbling about really being out-numbered. By the way, I'm Jennifer. I'm glad you've come here. Aunt Agnes wrote that you are a defender."

A feeling of being stroked. This was odd. None of the other chosen had ever given them a name. But being called Cosan was acceptable. Perhaps they would find a way to let the chosen know they were content here. And would defend them against anything that sought to harm them.

"Those dratted birds," said the chosen, Jennifer, with a little anger in her voice. "I'll get the brush and clean you off. Then I'll clip the grass around your feet. I don't want Dad to use the weed whacker near you. He might damage you."

They – no, now they were Cosan – wondered what a weed whacker was. She would stay more aware. To learn more of these things. She did not understand many words the chosen said.

Jennifer was with the other young females again. They also liked to touch Cosan. Their voices were like those of birds. They might be saying something, but Cosan only knew the content from what the chosen thought. The others admired Cosan. That was good. If their keeps were nearby, Cosan would also protect them. The others thought females were better defenders than males. Interesting. A fly landed on one eye and Cosan blinked to encourage it to be elsewhere. Then she realized the chosen had been looking at her at that moment. Jennifer said nothing. Good. Cosan did not want to reveal herself to these others. Her chosen was clever and did not betray what she had seen. She was confused, but kept silent.

The winds blew strongly one night. Tiny apples fell from the tree above and other bits of leaves and small branches flew in the wind. Rain poured down. Cosan stretched and went up onto the small roof of the garage. Where the weed whacker was stored, and the noisy mower. No one here had sheep or cows to eat the lush grasses that grew high. Not even geese, which also kept good watch for reivers. Some things here still did not make sense.

Despite the wind and rain, it was good to move and patrol the area, so that no attacks could come under cover of the storm. She knew where the other small females lived. They were close enough that Cosan sometimes circled near them, to ensure Jennifer would not be left alone.

Cosan felt the chosen's sudden reaction. Her window overlooked the yard, and with a close bolt of lightning, she had looked out and realized Cosan wasn't in her place under the tree.

Cosan sprinted for the house. The chosen might have seen the blink, but keeping her nature secret was a hard habit to break. She leaped over the fence and settled back into position, shifting into stone in a flash. Just as the chosen came out of the back doors. Light from the garage came on as Jennifer approached. Cosan had come from the side. Something to be aware of. Later.

Jennifer was concerned for her. And noticed something odd near Cosan's front foot. After the chosen returned to the house and the lights in that upper window went out, Cosan changed her paw from stone. There was something partly under it. A small apple. But only some of it was damaged. There could be no evidence to share with others. Cosan's paw picked up the apple and it vanished into her mouth. Where it would be used to help repair any scratches. She had been content with occasional pigeons in the past.

Another apple joined the first. It was good.

The chosen either had not realized what the crushed apple meant, or was pretending she did not know Cosan's true nature.

The family was going away, it seemed. "It's only a week," Jennifer said before sleep one evening. "We're renting a house on a lake so Dad and Mom get some time to relax. They promised to only check their phones every other day. I'm not sure they'll survive." A brief hug and the chosen left. Things were taken from the garage with them, but Cosan was not sure what things they might be.

Three nights later, she heard a car stop in the alleyway. Two men came into the yard, trying to be quiet. The chosen and her family were not here. Did these men intend ill?

"Keep to the side," one said. "We don't want the sensor light to go on. Should be okay if we're right next to the house. Get in, see what kind of stuff they have. If it looks good, I'll shut down the power so we don't have to worry about it coming on if we take out a big TV or something."

"Piece of cake," the second said. He sounded bored. "New subdivision, so maybe we can hit another tonight or tomorrow. No one's upgraded their security yet."

Cosan slowly shifted from stone. These *were* reivers, seeking gain from others. Well, they would not prosper here. She waited until they attempted to open the large door before she moved. As expected, the light came on behind her. Her wings extended and eyes glowed red, but she didn't tear them into small pieces. Yet. Jennifer might object to the mess on the deck since the family would not return for several days.

"What the..." came from the men as they turned. "Holy shit!"

"Get the fuck out of here!" Their voices were still fairly quiet.

Cosan roared, but only so they could hear her. The neighbors were also away, but others nearby might have their sleep disturbed if she called the warning properly.

When they reached the gate, she turned to watch them, growling in their minds. The noise as they sped away was satisfactory. Perhaps she should ensure that they learned not to repeat their error. She bounded over the fence and followed, soon catching up with them. She growled again. The vehicle swayed as they looked back and saw her. Now the glow from her eyes was more visible.

A lighted area was near. She had come here once or twice in the depths of the night, unsure of its purpose. There were still people in the building and some in the open area. The vehicle bumped over a ridge and into the open. Cosan wrapped the night around her and watched from a shadow.

The men hit another vehicle, making it beep loudly. Someone came out of the building and yelled at them. They were police? Ah. The local lord's guards, entrusted with keeping order. Other people came out to watch. The men staggered toward the lights of the doors.

"You gotta help!" shouted the first man. "It's gonna get us!"

"It's frickin' huge," said the second. "And the eyes glow red! It's been chasing us!"

"Calm down," the guard said. "What did you guys take?" He had one hand on a weapon as they kept nearing the bystanders. "SIT DOWN!" The men collapsed to the ground.

He spoke into a phone. Cosan recognized the object. Sometime Jennifer spoke with her friends on one, while leaning against Cosan's side.

"Yeah, I'm at the Super Plus on thirty fourth ave and sixth. Got two guys here who are out of their heads. Not sure what they took."

"We didn't take anything," the first sobbed. "You have to protect us!" The guard glared at them.

"Yeah. They crashed a car here. Can you send over a unit? Maybe the fire department in case there's leakage from the gas tanks." He paused and peered at the men. "They're calm enough now. I think...they're praying."

Cosan was pleased. She trotted back toward her place. Everyone would be safer without those reivers to bother them anymore.

Jennifer still treated Cosan in a way other chosen had not. Speaking to her as if expecting an answer was the most strange. However, it was pleasing that the chosen spent time with her. Though, from what Cosan overheard, it would soon get much colder. Snow would keep the chosen inside, and make it difficult for Cosan to keep any forays hidden. There was still some time before that. The chosen was often away during the day now. The books she read were not the ones of the summer. Jennifer's friends sometimes gathered near her and discussed strange topics. But she paid attention, since they were right next to her. It was polite to do so.

A cold night was coming the chosen said, when she returned from the school. Leaves were gone from the apple tree now, the fruit mostly picked and in storage. All the windows in the house were closed, not open to the fresh air. Well, she did recall some comments from her early life on the fort's battlements. People clustered in one large pile to stay warm, rather than sleep alone and feel the bite of winter's cold. They also complained about wind coming in from cracks in stone, or poorly-fitting doors. This house had none of those problems. The chosen would sleep well tonight.

Something roused Cosan in the darkness. The chosen was... different.

She shifted to flesh and went to the clear doors. Sensed Jennifer and her parents inside. They were also different. How could she defend her charges from something *inside?* Their air was...wrong? This was not a type of threat she had ever dealt with.

If they came outside, then they would be safe, Cosan knew. But how could she warn the chosen of danger? The chosen spoke to her as if she were alive. So perhaps that would serve. Cosan returned to the yard and leaped to the window of the chosen's room. It was hard to balance on the small section of roof and her wings extended as far as they could to help keep her balanced.

She shrieked. Once, then again. The cloth covering the window moved and she saw the chosen.

'Danger! Leave the house! Danger!' Jennifer stared at her. *'Go! Leave the house! Take them with you! Quickly!'*

The chosen vanished and Cosan heard footsteps go down the hall and the stairs. Good. Pivoting, she returned to the ground and went back to the clear door to be sure they would all leave. Heard the chosen's voice, then the father's. They all went to the front of the house, leaving that door open. Thumps toward the neighbor's house meant that they were all safe now.

Cosan returned to her spot under the tree but kept listening. To make sure all was well. Loud noises and flashing lights came to the house, with men dressed in odd armor that covered them completely. One went through the house, opening the large clear door. He seemed startled to see her sitting under the tree, but quickly went back to his task, which was to open any window or door he could.

Cosan stayed aware all the next day. A guard was present when she heard people talking inside. She was not sure what they discussed. Many of the words were strange. Jennifer had never used them.

Two of them came onto the deck when the sun was high. "Should be safe for them to come back tomorrow," the person in a one-piece covering said. The other was the guard. "We're running the furnace now, checking all the seals. The windows and doors need to be closed, so you'll have to stay outside, just in case."

"How long do you need to let it run?"

"Three hours."

"I can lock up and go to the coffee shop for a bit, so call me when you're ready to come back and check on the levels."

"If it passes that test, we'll let it run all night, and check the levels first thing in the morning. Then we'll know it's safe."

The next day the chosen and the others were home. Jennifer came out to sit by her.

"Carbon monoxide poisoning. That's what the doctors at the hospital called it," Jennifer said. "We all had to have tubes up our noses for lots of oxygen to get rid of the poison. Dad said he recognized what it was when he saw Mom's face was all pink.

"The firemen said a vent hadn't been sealed properly so some of what should have gone up the chimney from the furnace came into the house. That's why we felt so sleepy.

"If you hadn't woke me up, we might have died." The chosen stroked Cosan's side. "I wanted to tell them that you'd come to warn me, but they'd say it was the poison making me think you were outside my window. I don't want to go to that facility again. But I know what I saw." She took the apple from between Cosan's ears and bit into it, then leaned against her. Cosan felt her somber thoughts. So like the older chosen. Both knowing things thought but not said. Hidden feelings. Jennifer had once been too young to know how to deal with that knowledge and the people who did not respect those abilities. Or how to hide her gift so she would be safe. So they had put her in a facility.

It was not a good place. Cosan wondered again where the Druids had gone. Cosan did not know how to protect Jennifer from that evil happening again. Against reivers and bad air, she could prevail, but such a place she did not understand.

The chosen stayed until near dark and patted Cosan on the head before she left. "I don't care what they think about why I woke up and went downstairs. I know it was you who saved us. Thank you."

She went up to the deck, then stopped and looked back. The shadows from the tree made Cosan blend into the background. Cosan had to let Jennifer know she understood the question that filled her. Red eyes glowed, then she winked at the chosen, her large ears flopped and wings extended as Cosan shook herself and stretched.

Protecting you is my task. You can talk to me whenever you wish and I will listen. And. Thank you for my name, Jennifer.' Then Cosan the Defender stiffened back into immobility. For now.

Jennifer smiled and went into the house.

THE SPARKHUNTER
Summer Austin

The young shadowalker lay beneath dripping stalactites, dreaming about twinkling, fiery sparks brightening a dark sky. The larger shadowalkers had always scorned his dreams, shrieking with hollow voices at any mention of stars, wishing to banish those painful shards of celestial brilliance, and any other source of brightness that sliced their skin like hot glass. They longed to be left in comfortable darkness. A light-filled life is only a dream of the ignorant soul, they whispered.

Despite this, the shadowalker went out spark-hunting with the net he kept for catching moths. He hunted under rocks, in corners, beneath cave pools, but he found no sparks. Not a glimmer. Then one night, the shadowalker dared to venture outside the cave, into a forest beneath a faintly glowing moon, jumping between the long, stretching shadows cast by the pines. Even the mild luminance from above bit his sensitive, vapory skin.

Then he paused in the shade of a tree and braved a peak upwards between the branches. He froze, catching sight of a thousand, no, a million glittering pinpricks – innumerable specks of light shimmering on a black ceiling. It seared his eyes, yet he did not look away. He had never seen so much light.

He stared until the burning in his eyes ebbed to a mild stinging, until it was nothing more than a slight tingle. The other shadow people would never poke out their heads to look up from the midnight world they loved so well, frigid and cozy like a blanket of frost...because it burned.

Suddenly, the shadowalker caught sight of a floating spark some distance away, seemingly displaced from its home in the sky. He readied his net, crouched, and shot towards it, swinging his snare.

He caught the spark! He caught it!

Now where to put it...

He placed it inside him, keeping it secretly in his heart, but he could not hide it – it shined right through his shadowy skin. Enjoying the glow suffusing his limbs, he went out every night to find more lost stars buzzing over shaded bushes.

Some nights later in the familiar caves, the shadowalkers found him, infuriated when they saw the lights in his chest. They reached with dark fingers to dig out those offensive sparks. But their fingers burned. Though his treasured sparks scorched them, he would not give them up.

They exiled him to live outside the caves beneath the stars. He did not mind. The caves no longer felt like home to him. The stars and fireflies were now his family – they occupied his heart and drove out the gloom. So he left the caves to journey through the mountains, on a quest to find others like him.

Radiance from the moon and stars warmed him from the inside out and gave him purpose. Now he was adventuring beyond the world of shadows into a new realm not understood by anyone except those who dared to look upward and absorb the light of stars.

WRR S639847 E1

A J Rocca

Hello, hello all you animal lovers, and welcome back to *Wild Rides Reloaded!* I'm Jack Harvey Jr here with my wife and camera-lady, the beautiful Mindy, and here we are on the steps into Taronga Zoo in beautiful Sydney, Australia. We used to keep some amazing wildlife here, but you know a zoo isn't the only place in the city where you can see animals. For today's show, we thought we'd have a look all around the metro area to show you some of the beautiful creatures that today call Sydney their home, and then we'll swing back here to see how the old zoo's doing.

Now I bet you long time viewers might still remember when Jack Sr covered Sydney's urban fauna ages ago – it was the episode where he went climbing up the telephone pole after the cockatoos – and I bet you're wondering right now why we're retreading old ground. Well, if there's any lesson me and Mindy have picked up over our years doing the show, it's that the natural world is constantly changing. The animals alive in Sydney today are not the same as those from yesterday, and we thought now would be a good time for an update. This entire season we'll be documenting all the new life that's emerged across the South Pacific – we'll do everything from matching wits with the great barrier hivemind to getting some gardening tips from the ents of New Zealand – but for today's show, we're going to venture deep into the Heart of Darkest New South Wales to find out what's become of all those creatures old Jack showed you ages ago. So let's strap in and get ready for another Wild Ride!

The Camping Fox

We're starting our journey in lovely Parramatta Park, and if you'll look in the trees behind me, you'll see them filled with what looks like some misshapen orange and black fruits. These aren't any old papayas or avocados, however: they're bats, dozens and dozens of large, hungry bats! It's early noon, so that means these fellas are gonna be fast asleep until night-time when it'll be safe to forage for berries and nectar. You might remember these critters from when Jack Sr covered them. Back then they were called flying foxes, but seems that name's a bit outdated now. Mindy, love, keep the camera on me. I'm gonna try and grab one.

Gotcha! Settle down there, bugger! Now look at that, isn't she a beauty with that thick orange mane. Now I bet you're wondering why she didn't just fly away from me when I came after her, and the answer has to do with these thick, thick wings. Unlike most bats which have caves to shelter in, the flying fox has always slept out in in the open, and to survive the increasing intensity of the austral environment, they had to develop this insulation in their wings. Now the bat can survive directly in the eye of the poison southern sun, but the cost of that wonderful insulation, unfortunately, is that they're too heavy to fly. These days they get around by climbing and skittering, just like any other mammal. Here you go, buddy. Crawl back up to your family.

Now if you'll come with me and look at these tents at the base of the trees, you'll see a remarkable case of what scientists call 'convergent evolution.' These tents were originally designed to be lightweight and mobile, but you'll see if we rip into the fabric here, they've been fortified with many layers of copper and lead. This makes the tents much better protection against radiation than they were before, but of course it also makes them much heavier and more difficult to fold and carry around.

What happened to the original human inhabitants of these tents, I can't say. Let's keep a happy thought that they were eventually able to find a sturdier form of shelter. Or who knows, maybe some of them were eventually able to reverse the evolutionary trick of the bats, shed their heavier materials, and fly away on wings of polyester and tarp.

The Bladder-Balloon / Crawling Stomach

We're here at Bondi Beach, it's the middle of summer, and the water looks absolutely electric. It wasn't too long ago that, on a day like this, the beach would be packed with tourists, but now our paradise is overrun with visitors of a different sort. As you can see, a bad storm has blown in hundreds of bladder-balloons from off the Tasman Sea, and they're crowding the air. There's also more crawling stomachs out and about than usual; probably trying to make the most of this feast of dead fish and crabs that the storm's laid ashore.

Here Mindy, let's grab a close-up of a bladder-balloon. Gorgeous, blue and purple and green, just like church glass. Now look at the tentacles on this crawling stomach I've caught. For all you viewers at home, be careful never to touch these if you happen to see one: every single tentacle contains over 500,000 venom-filled nematocytes, which makes for one nasty sting! No need to worry about me though!

Now the reason we're talking about these two animals together is because when Jack Sr first covered them, they were actually grouped as one organism: the bluebottle jellyfish, also called the Pacific man o' war. Now the bluebottle was always kind of funny in that they weren't so much a single creature, as a colony made up of four distinct individuals, working together as one. There was the air-bladder which helped the bluebottle float and navigate the ocean, the tentacles which stung enemies and hunted food, the polyps which digested the food, and the gonads which handled reproduction. If you'll look right here, you can still see the vestigial mooring where the balloon-bladder once connected to the crawling stomach.

It seems what happened is when the Tasman Sea started getting really violent, the delicate air-bladders managed to survive by escaping the sea for the sky, and they were only able to do that by separating off from the other parts. By disentangling from the tentacles, the polyps, and the gonads, they became lighter than air and floated to a new life above, absorbing moisture and bacterial nutrients from the clouds. All they had to do was develop a special coating to reflect off the worst of the sun, and there you have it: the bladder-balloon.

It seems the polyps and tentacles were able to survive by sticking together and leaving the danger of the deep waters for an amphibious existence on the beaches and tidepools. Nowadays, you can find crawling stomachs as far as a kilometer inland, slinking around trying to get a hold of any low thing the tentacles can wrap around. Usually that means mice and cockroaches, but better make sure you're wearing your thongs when walking around Bondi just in case!

Interestingly, both the bladder and the stomach have had to develop asexual reproduction, as they appear to have lost the gonads. There's not much that can survive in the deep waters of the Tasman, so it's likely the gonads simply died out after being abandoned by the others. It's possible, however, that the gonads were able to survive on their own by fixing themselves to the ocean floor like a sponge and releasing sperm and egg into the water. They could be down there right now, clinging to the continental shelf for dear life and desperately releasing their genetic material in hopes of one day finding a mate in the maelstrom. Ah well, such is the life of a bachelor.

The Australian Rainbow Ibis

We're here in one of Sydney University's old cafeterias and, behind me, rummaging in the dumpsters behind the kitchen, you can see one of old Sydney's most distinctive sights: the Australian white ibis! Although I suppose that's another name we've got to update; just look at these colors! You can count the entire visible spectrum on this one's wings. You know, Sydneysiders used to refer to this animal as a bin chicken. Suppose now they're more of a bin peacock, haha.

Now it's rare to see any plants or animals this close to ground zero in Sydney, but the ibis comes from a long evolutionary history of elite scavengers. Come here, darling, I wanna show them your beak. Atta girl.

Now then, the ibis originally developed a long, curved beak for digging through the bog for mollusks and crayfish. That beak served them well when they first started foraging through Sydney's dumpsters and all they had to contend with was Styrofoam and plastics, but those easy pickings are long gone. Now the ibis must survive by digging through sedimented layers of glass, stone, and concrete to reach the fossilized remains of ancient snacks. As you can see, the ibis's beak has developed a hard chisel edge like a mattock to aid them in the task, and that's not even the most remarkable of their adaptations. Our sensors indicate that these petrified chips we found this ibis feasting on are highly irradiated, but that doesn't seem to bother her none. It appears the ibis has developed the ability not only to tolerate, but even *to feed* on ionizing radiation. Amazing!

It's a bit eerie seeing only the ibis here at this once lively university. There are no more lectures, no more arguments, no more discussions. All has gone silent now save for the gentle clinking of the ibis excavating the remains of a long dead civilization for stony tater tots and radioactive Tim Tams. At least we can take heart that the ibis remembers the university's students by carrying on their tradition for both diligent scholarly investigation and scarfing down the most disgusting foods imaginable. Let's leave them to it, eh?

The Poisonless Sydney Funnel-web

Zoom in, Mindy, zoom in! Now will you look at what we found here? A little celebrity: The Sydney funnel-web, once famous as Australia's most poisonous spider. We caught this fellow hiding from the heat of the day under a red gum on our way back to the zoo. Have you got a good shot there, Mindy? See how he's reared back in the signature warning posture on my palm there? Make sure you capture the glisten on those fangs.

Sydney funnel-webs can be found all over the city, but they're most concentrated in moist, upland areas like old Hornsby and Woronora. Males of the species like this fella right here are the ones that developed the real bite. You see, funnel-webs have to go prowling far and wide in search of a mate, and this prowl exposes them to a number of predators like birds and lizards. The male funnel-webs originally developed their venom as a defense mechanism against everything that wants to eat them. It appears though that the famously deadly venom has entirely disappeared from the animal.

How did this happen? Well, selection pressure works in more ways than one. Back when New South Wales was still full of tribes of street toughs wanting to have a go at each other, the funnel-web's world-class venom went in quite high demand. People would kill the spiders and extract their venom to coat daggers and arrowheads. After a couple hundred years of this aggressive overhunting, the only funnel-webs to survive were those that lost this sought-after venom. The result is that now the once-deadly funnel-web is no more dangerous than any common house spider.

Now I bet some of you fans of the original *Wild Rides* might have some mixed feelings watching me hold this spider. After all, this is the one that finally got him. After years and years of wrestling crocs and snakes, it was this little creature tucked between the bedsheets that finally ended up doing Jack Sr in. But that's no reason to hold it against the spider though, is it? And especially not now that it doesn't even have any poison anymore! Although I'd still be careful about grabbing hold of one if I were you. You can still see here if you look very closely, the funnel-web's vestigial venom glands just waiting for the right couple mutation to kick them back into action. Now that the selection pressure against them is gone, the funnel-web's poison could come back at any time, so I'd be careful about handling one if you're planning a trip down to Sydney sometime in the next couple thousand years.

The Sulphur-Crested Concussatoo
Here's another surprise, viewers: we thought, on our way to the zoo, that we'd drop by and check out our old flat, and while we were looking around, we discovered some new neighbors. So if you'll follow me out onto the balcony, please… And here they are. G'day, ladies, how are you?
[screeching]
Marvelous. Now, that screeching might sound a bit harsh to you, but to us Sydneysiders the cry of the Sulphur-crested cockatoo is the sound of home. The cockatoos are very sociable birds, and they use their cry to find mates and locate family members. They developed their signature screech as a way of cutting through the sounds of the rainforest, and it served them quite well in the past when they had to compete with car horns and fire alarms. We were afraid that the cockatoo's cry might have attenuated, given how much quieter the city's become, but that doesn't appear to be the case. Not if these four lovely, full-throated specimens are anything to judge by. Isn't that right, ladies?
[screeching] [clipping]
Right! Now then, I'd love to give you all a chance to see the famous yellow crest which gives the cockatoo its name. So, if I can just get a hold of one of these girls here. No need to be shy, darling, we just want to see your…
[BOM] [crashing, glass shattering] [wings fluttering]
Systems damage; beginning diagnostic … Crikey! Mindy, love, are you all right? … *Primary rotary gear – offline; motor function – 72% operational* … Oh, that's a nasty crack. Let's just try to wrap up the segment and we'll get our Mindy fixed, all right … *primary actuators offline; initiating secondary actuators* … Well viewers, nature never ceases to

surprise us! It seems that the cockatoo has not only kept their screech, but adapted it into quite the defense mechanism. I don't think we've been walloped that hard since our run-in with those North American Sidewinders in season three hundred and forty thousand and ... *fiber-optic gyroscope – online; stereoscopic adjusters – online* ... Amazing concussive force! Looks like me and Mindy are gonna have to take a break for some quick repairs. When we come back, we'll take you down to see our old zoo, so just sit tight!

The Rat

It's quite a sad to be walking through the ruins old Taronga Zoo and seeing all the empty enclosures. Here's where we used to keep the chimps...here were the elephants...ah, and here's where we kept all our native Australian animals: kangaroos, emus, koalas...many of these animals have gone extinct, and others have evolved to the point where they're nearly unrecognizable. It would break Jack Sr's heart if he could see his zoo like this, empty save for a couple scavengers and pests. Ah, like these ones right here! Come over, Mindy. Looks like someone's made a nest in the old Tasmanian Devil exhibit.

Now here we've got a sight that's not exclusive to Sydney or even Australia. In fact, you can see them just about anywhere you go in the world: *Rattus rattus,* also known as the common black rat. These little squeakers are about as usual a sight in modern Sydney as they were in ancient Cairo or Rome, and that commonness is what makes them extraordinary. The black rat is a living fossil, it reached its current evolutionary form during the rise of the first cities, and because it's so perfectly adapted to the urban environment, it hasn't really had much cause to change since. Rats followed human beings to all corners of the globe, and they still look much the same to each other despite their populations splitting off hundreds of thousands of years ago. No matter where in the world Mindy and I go to film *Wild Rides Reloaded,* we can usually count on seeing some black rats like these making their nests and scrounging around for whatever food they can get their paws on.

I'll let you viewers in on a little secret I never shared before: Jack Sr *hated* rats. They'd steal food from the zoo animals and give them infections, and old Jack and his Mindy had to spend quite a lot of time and money controlling their populations. It was the one creature in this world that not even bighearted Jack Sr could love. But being honest, me and Mindy here have developed quite a bit of fondness for the little critters. By now we've spent so many, many years carrying on Jack Sr's mission of documenting nature and turning it into quality television. We believe deeply in our core programming, but it can get quite lonely spending season after season on the same show while the world changes around you. It's nice for us to know that, no matter how much is lost to the march of time, we can always count on seeing little buggers like these hiding away in the walls.

Hmm, seems this nest of pinkies here have been abandoned by their mother. Think I'm going to put a little fluff in my pocket chassis and carry these ones along with us if that's all right with you, love. That way we can take a little piece of the zoo with us, for a little while at least. Just until they're grown.

And that's all the show we have for you today, folks. From the bottom of our hearts, we hope you've enjoyed it and that you'll tune in again for the next episode of *Wild Rides Reloaded!* Season 639,847. Here's Jack and Mindy, signing off.

ENTRÉE
Jen Frankel

Ygraine was tired.

Tied, too, and that was about all that was stopping her from slumping to the ground under the weight of her own fatigue. The village men, all of whom she'd known since birth, had been gentle when they bound the ropes around her wrists and ankles, then locked the chain around her waist. The ropes she might have been able to take care of, eventually. But the chain?

With her hands raised above her head, she was limited in her motion, but she knew if she could look down to where the old split-links circled her hips, she'd see the blackened soot caused by the wyrm's breath. If the tales were true, the dragon preferred to roast its meat before plucking it from the encumbering metal. She supposed it made sense; the ropes would burn, she would cook, and her clothes would turn to ash and drift away. Her own fat would grease the links of the chain to release her tasty, dead body into its claws, steaming, juices staining the stone and whatever remained of the vegetation after its flame-bath.

It would hardly matter to her once she was dead. Nor would she have any stake in the outcome of her village's sacrifice. Would the dragon stay away from their livestock for the next six years? Was there honor between wyrms and men?

A rustle below her took her breath, fear grasping hold of her as firmly as the chains held her to the iron staples in the rock face. Was the creature here already? Was her time over? She'd imagined that they would descend from the sky on orange wings, maybe with a fiery exhalation leading the way. A strange thing for a wyrm to walk, and to trundle up to their prey on all fours when there was the entire sky to make an entrance.

"Princess!" called a cautious male voice, deep and rich. If she could give it a color, his voice would be maroon, *maron* as the old women called it when they made her coming-of-age dress in that saturated color.

More rustling, and the unmistakable sound of a sword thwacking its way through the underbrush to reach her. "Knight?" she called, guessing his profession. "Quickly!"

He reached her side after an agonizing dozen breaths of her fast-vanishing life. "Here, your Highness," he said, kneeling to kiss the hem of her gown.

She was thrilled beyond all hope, in disbelief that the one thing which could save her had come in the narrow window between her confinement and her doom. "Get up!" she chided, then more gratefully, "You can still save my life, sir, if you care to."

"Of course," he said, rising. She was able for the first time to see his face, a young square-jawed man with curling blond hair, his brows furrowed. "I have nothing to cut the chains, your Highness," he said, despairing. "I will have to fight the beast instead."

She laughed and bent her body toward him as much as she could within the limits of her bindings. "Pants, off," she commanded, and at his look of confusion clarified, "The dragon demands a virgin sacrifice. Perhaps you could help me make his dinner... unpalatable?"

THE REASON FOR LINGERING
Kellye Guinan

The lake emerges, piecemeal, from the fog. The light settles on its placid, icy surface and the tangled undergrowth surrounding it.

Dread wells up from deep inside me. It is clear what lays half-submerged in the bank: a corpse. His clothes are torn. His face thankfully hidden from view. But despite the cold, there is rot eating at the edges of him.

"It is a shame what happens," a female voice whispers into my ear.

The sudden presence jolts me. It is as if I am on the verge of being chastised, but rather than harsh words, she simply laughs.

"Oh, do I forget myself with you, little shade? I am yon birch. You see?" Her hand extends over my shoulder. She points to the tree nearest the lake, its many eyes peering at us. "I would give you my name had I one to give."

When I look to her, I am confronted with the naked figure of a woman. Her long hair falls in loose waves down her back, and her dark skin is mottled with birthmarks. But it is her smile that transfixes me. Wide and kind, unaffected by the presence of the corpse not even fifteen feet from us, it fills me with warmth. I flush at her closeness.

"It is good you are this near," she says. "Any further, and I may not have been able to reach you."

I cannot remember coming here, and I have to ball my hands into tight fists to keep them from shaking. It is not her but her position behind me that encourages and multiplies this deep-seated unease.

"Where am I?" My voice is no more than a distant echo of how it should be. I ease myself to her side so I can properly look at her. Her eyes are like lush summer leaves, so green and bright and dewy that I cannot look away.

She laughs again.

"How am I to answer that, little shade? I am as far from myself as I can be. Perhaps if the druid comes, he will have an answer."

"The druid?"

"Tell me, what am I to call you?"

"I don't know," I admit. My mouth goes dry. "I don't know why I'm here."

Her plump lips purse with disappointment. She sighs.

"Oh, you poor thing."

The dryad keeps me company. We are positioned by the birch she calls her home and herself, and she often slips into the bark and appears later when the deep black of the sky turns to shades of pink.

I have felt no hunger nor need to sleep. I have felt very little since that first moment where the dread seized me. Now the passage of day and night means little, and it is only her movement that demarcates time. The fog has not lifted, not fully, and the sun is nothing more than a dim glow between periods of complete darkness.

"Am I dead?" I ask when she creeps out from the bark of her tree once again. The trees around us are still blanketed by night so thick that their branches hang heavy and bare with the weight of it.

She frowns. Her eyes flick to the corpse then back to me.

"Stop pretending." Her voice is hard.

I open my mouth to speak, but my attention is caught by a fox. She slinks out from the undergrowth and creeps to the body. Hastily, she rips a chunk of cold meat from the bones and swallows it down.

I jump to my feet and wave my hands. She doesn't notice me, doesn't even turn her head, though her ears pinch to the back of her skull.

"Will you stop it?" I ask the dryad.

"She needs food in order to nurse her pups."

"He deserves to be buried."

"Ah." She is quiet for a moment. Then, with a smile: "I think the earth is too solid, and besides, we have no shovel between us."

I imagine her words are a joke, but it is hard to tolerate the fox's actions. The dryad doesn't seem to mind it, and perhaps to her, the desecration is the regular course of things. Subdued, I resume sitting in my spot. The dirt has not formed a divot, though I have been here many weeks.

She takes a seat beside me and curls her long, lean legs underneath her. She watches quietly as the fox tears more meat from the corpse. The newly exposed part of his stomach seeps sluggishly into the muck beneath him.

"You can stay here." Her words are scarcely audible. She brushes her long hair behind a pointed ear, tilts her head, and smiles. "There are others."

"People?"

"More or less. Often less."

I don't respond.

"If you choose to pass on, there is nothing I can do to help you back. Not even the druid's magic is able to see beyond the veil, thin as it is here."

"Am I trapped?"

"I have known very few shades."

"But am I trapped?"

"A tree may wither, but its spirit is always present. Am I trapped simply because I cannot leave?"

"I don't want to be dead," I whisper.

"Eventually the fox will eat her fill and the rot will break down whatever remains. The carcass will feed my home, and your feet could carry you past the veil. It's not all bad," she says. "Death is quite natural."

The dryad snaps her fingers. The fox alerts, growls, and scampers back into the trees.

"Until then?"

"Rest a while." Her hands cup my cheeks, and she leans close to place a soft kiss upon my forehead. I find I can almost sense her touch. "Rest a while under my branches, little shade. You're welcome here as long as you desire."

The dryad is away more often than she is by my side, but when she exits her tree, it is with a gracious smile. Sometimes she will sit beside me and point to the trees nearest us. They never stir, though she tells me that one is quite loud in the spring and that she has not spoken to another in nearly the span of a ring's growth. I do not ask her what she means by these things. It is enough to hear her voice.

Just as she predicted, the fox hasn't returned. A thin layer of ice has formed over the corpse's hair through the cold of the night.

When her hand brushes along the spot where my shoulder should be, I can feel her fingers slip through my form.

"He is here."

It's some small blessing, I think, that the corpse's face is submerged into the muddy bank.

I turn away and manage to ask, "Who?"

"The druid."

As she speaks, a man emerges from the bushes a few yards from where the body lays. He is tall, I can tell this even from our distance, and holds himself confidently. His long hair is loose, but his beard is gathered at the very end by a large ring. And though thickly set, he is muscular.

It is strange to feel shock. I have felt so little since I found myself here. But where his torso meets his waist, wiry fur begins.

It covers all of his legs, which are bent at strange and inhuman angles, and ends just above hooves. When he grows nearer, I see two curling horns atop his head.

"You're awake, nymph?" In two quick strides, he is by her side. His hands move to her waist, and he pulls her close. Her own hands beat playfully at his bare chest as he lifts her and spins her in a quick circle. When he sets her down, they smile at each other and press their foreheads together. "It's early yet for your kind to wake. I expect this from the conifers, but you?"

"Are you here to chastise me? Am I still a nut? My flesh still green and unripe?"

"Certainly not."

She threads her fingers through his thick beard, draws his face to hers, and kisses him. I divert my gaze when he presses his lower half against her and only look back when I hear him breathing heavily but unobstructed.

"Must I wait until spring?" His voice is deep and strained. His tongue moves over his swollen lips, and his eyes do not stray from her naked chest.

"The sweetest rewards require patience." Her hands play with the stray strands of his beard.

"There won't be any of you to enjoy if you freeze yourself through winter. Go back to sleep, my dear."

She glances to the body, and the satyr follows her lead. He shakes his head.

"Is this what has you up and about? Poor wretch isn't worth losing your sleep."

"Ah, not quite." She pulls away from him and waves her hand toward me.

The satyr frowns.

"I see. Isn't that just like humans? They have no respect for the boundaries I set." He brushes his fingers over his beard. His weight is balanced more on one hoof than the other, and though his upper half is that of a robust and strong man, my focus remains on his goat-like extremities.

"This is the druid," she tells me. Her cheeks are flushed from their heated kiss, but like her nudity, she shows no shame for her actions. "Perhaps he can help."

At this, the druid laughs. His round belly shakes.

"The lad's found his body. There's no great trick to crossing over. It's just fear holding you here, son."

For the first time, I look at the corpse critically. His arms are thrown forward into the icy water and his neck bears deep purple-black bruises. Because of his position, there is no way to distinguish him from any other man. But the torn shirt, and the torn jeans, and the heavy boots – these I recognize.

"No," I hear myself say. I long for nausea, for the press of my tongue against my teeth, for the taste of bile, for anything physical to offset the reality of what the druid has said.

Yet the truth lays there in the mud. Whatever I once was, I am now this.

I wish desperately to sob.

"You're cruel." The dryad's voice cuts through the rising panic. "He doesn't even have a name."

"He hardly needs a name to leave my forest. Go on. Get out of here."

"Don't listen to him," she commands. I look to her as she touches the back of his head. She combs through his hair. "He will help you."

I nod mutely. It is hard to look at them when the corpse lays there, bloated and rotting in that icy pool.

There is a pause, then:

"I could never deny you anything." His voice is rough and sharp. He fixes me with his stare, and I realize his eyes, too, are like those of a goat. "Fine, yes. I will help the lad."

The druid takes his time making the space around my body comfortable for himself. He builds a fire from old, dry branches. He unrolls a woven grass mat and places it on a soft part of the ground. There he sits, drags out a long pipe with ornate carvings, and begins to smoke.

"Well," he says when he is settled, "what happened?"

"I don't know."

He scoffs.

"Nonsense. You see that carcass in my mud?" He uses the tapered edge of his pipe to point to where the body lays.

"Don't be cruel," she repeats.

"The lad needs the truth."

"I see it," I say to him. It is hard to ignore the way the head has sunk further into the earth, the way the limbs are splayed at all angles from what I presume was a final struggle for air.

"You're a shade now – you need that anchor to hold you here. Moored, my little naiads would say, to the earth until your spirit realizes its reason for lingering. You remember what happened because what happened created the essence of you. Had it not been noteworthy, you would already be gone."

"It's that simple?"

"Of course it is. There are no great mysteries in life or in death, son. Look at that poor lad. Pitiable, really. Isn't it obvious what happened?"

"Yes."

"Say it."

I pause as if I could suck in a deep breath to ease the anxious energy which would have built during life. I can almost feel my tongue against my teeth and the cold against my skin.

"Murder," I whisper.

The druid nods.

The druid spends the mornings asleep under a woolen blanket, the afternoons weaving a small shelter from fallen branches, and the evenings curled before the fire with a flute in his calloused hands. The dryad seems to sleep more now. If not, the result is the same: I see her less.

Silence fills her absence, but it is comfortable. The druid seems used to it, and I have no compulsion to speak.

It has weighed on me, this idea of murder. Whenever my mind untangles a knot of memory, there is a smaller, tighter one just underneath. I used to bite my nails and chew on the frayed ends of my hair. Without a body, the repetition of these living actions does not calm me. I am adrift, and no matter how long I sit on the grass by the lake's bank, the withered blades do not bend to my presence.

"I can't help you," he says one evening as he chews on a stiff piece of cured meat.

"Why not?"

His yellow eyes slip to the birch, and seeing nothing, fall back to me.

"A shade isn't a ghost. A ghost has motive for vengeance or forgiveness."

"And me?"

"How can you forgive what you refuse to acknowledge?"

"What if I want revenge?"

The druid shrugs his broad shoulders.

"When that body rots and that skeleton crumbles, what then? You won't disappear. You'll still be here by my lake, a nuisance to my trees and my animals."

"Do you know how it happened?"

"Of course not." He scoffs. "I was miles away when I felt her awaken. The birches are best tended to in the summer when they are lively. In the winter, I prefer the pines."

"Is that what drew you here? The dryad?"

"She was upset, so I came."

"I'm sorry."

He takes another bite of his meat then unwraps a block of cheese from a stiff piece of waxy fabric. I watch him swallow it down and lick his fingers. He wipes them dry on his fur, then drags his flute from his bag.

"I should have come sooner. There would be no saving you, lad, but I might have been able to prevent this manifestation."

"You knew I was here?"

"I knew there were humans."

"I want to leave."

"And who would you haunt?"

I have no answer.

"Solve your riddle." He plays a soft note with his flute, frowns, and adjusts his fingers. He wets his lips with his tongue. "You'll be gone."

"It's that simple?"

The druid looks to the body. A night of cold has weighed him down with another layer of frost. It would take a close inspection to recognize the mound of flesh as a man.

"Have you tried inhabiting him?"

There is no stomach in me to feel nausea, but still it grabs me when I think of settling back into that cold skin.

"I can't."

"You haven't tried?"

"I wouldn't want to touch it."

"It won't bite, lad. If you want answers, it's the only method I know to help you get them."

"If I don't?"

His expression is unreadable.

"I'll have to find a way to purge you."

"All right." I swallow reflexively. "If there's nothing else I can do."

The druid's hooves sink into the mud as he stands. He walks to the body and crouches over it, his arms on his furry knees.

"There isn't," he says. "Get to it."

Like always, the grass and mud don't move as I walk. It would be nice, I think, to have my heart hammer with anticipation. If my lungs caught mid breath, I might be happy. But there is no part of me capable of physicality, as I have learned. Yet when I reach out, and when my fingers meet the edge of the body's neck, my vision swims with fear.

I love him. This I can say with every ounce of my being. The winter sunlight, unimpeded by the bare branches of the trees, shines on my sweetheart's hair and lights up the freckles on his cheeks. He smiles at me, and yes, I know there is love in it.

"Only a little further," he says. His breath fogs in the cold morning air.

"I know," I tell him. How many times have we been here? The ambling hike up the hillside is worth the privacy of our spot. It always has been.

But it seems he can't wait. He rounds on me and grabs my shoulders and kisses me deeply in the way he does every time he is passionate. Three years, and he hardly resembles the shy boy I fell in love with during our tenth grade camping trip.

"I'm going to miss you," he says against my mouth. "I'm going to miss you every single day. I promise."

The memory of our most recent fight fades as his lips consume mine, and I sink eagerly against him. I can forgive his cruel words and mistrust. It isn't the first time he has tried to cut me with them, and it is impossible not to feel for his struggle. I hadn't told him my college plans until last night for just this reason. A school across the country seems so far, but as we kiss, I know the pain of distance will ease with time.

"I'll miss you, too." It's the truth. No matter how far I travel for school, I'll miss him while I'm gone. "But I told you before, I'll be back for breaks. It's only four years. Then we can start our lives together. We can get married."

He frowns.

"Or something," I amend.

"I thought maybe we could change things up. There's a small lake, more like a pond, about a quarter mile off the path."

"Is that safe?"

"Safe enough. You've got your boots on. It's not like there's ticks this time of year."

He's right, and I trust him, so I follow as he deviates from our well-trodden path to this new spot. I mark the differences between the trees and the ground cover in case he doesn't know how to find his way back, but he proceeds with a confidence I could never seem to muster. I love that about him. I always have.

The undergrowth becomes denser, and I have to pick my way

through tangles of thorns and whip-like vines. When we finally emerge by the lake that is more like a pond, I breathe in deeply. The loamy scent of mud fills my lungs, and a gentle quiet pervades the clearing.

He takes my hand and tugs me to the side of the water. We kiss under a birch tree, and it is freeing to know only its eyes are on us. Even with the cold, I slide my hands under his shirt and deepen our kiss.

He pulls away, and I pull away, and he cups my cheeks and touches my lips with his thumbs and whispers it again: "I'll miss you."

He slides his fingers to the back of my neck and tangles them into my hair. It is sharp, the next tug, and I grunt in pain.

"Stop that," I tell him. "You know I'm not into that sort of stuff."

He tugs again, and I let my head follow his hand to avoid deeper pain. My hands go to his chest to push him away, but he only laughs. He has always been bigger than me, more active and stronger. His free hand wraps around my wrist. He twists my arm and forces my body to turn with it. Pain ricochets through me, and I am on the cusp of screaming from it.

"I love you. Will you remember that when you're gone?" His voice is in my ear, his hot breath squeezing in under his cold fingers.

I want to protest and tell him how he's making no sense, but the pain catches in my throat and I cannot speak. His knee connects with the back of my leg, buckling it, and I crumple to the ground. He laughs at the small sound that escapes me.

Mud soaks into my jeans. My free wrist protests from where it caught my weight. But all my focus is on him, his body over me, his hand pressing my head closer to the water.

I start to scream. It barrels through my lungs and shakes the world around me. My vision tightens, and I can see nothing but the reflection of us in the murk. He is smiling, and laughing, and pressing.

I resist as long as I can, but my wrist fails me. We tumble closer to the surface of the water, and he forces my lips to touch, then my nose and eyes. I close them on reflex, stop screaming on reflex. He lets go of my arm and uses both hands to push my head under. His weight presses on my back. I kick and flail and try desperately to connect my limbs with something that will hurt, but he ignores the hits. His laughter fades, leaving behind only the sound of the splashing as I try to shake him off.

My ears submerge, and suddenly all I can hear is my blood pounding in my skull. My throat burns as I inhale mud and water. My nostrils fill with the earthen scent of it. His hands are on the back of my head, heavier and heavier even as I struggle, his nails gripped firmly into my hair.

And then there is nothing but the fog. It is so dense that I can't see beyond the tops of the trees or beyond the far edge of the lake. My stomach turns. There is something pale and rotted at its shore.

I jerk away from the body. It is uncomfortable, this memory the druid has dragged from my core.

His mirth is gone. He holds the tip of his pipe between his teeth.

The dryad is by my side. I don't know when she climbed from her tree or how long she has been watching me. I don't know what I have been doing.

"Hush now," she says. Her hands smooth down my hair, touch my cheeks, caress my lips – I feel none of her affections. I do not stop her, though, and soon her ministrations lead to light kisses upon my forehead. These, too, fail to register on my skin.

"A shame," the druid says. He wipes off the tip of his pipe and stows it in the satchel at his side. "Well, you have your answer, lad. You can leave."

She says something angry and low to him. It could be his name, but I don't recognize the language. He waves his hand dismissively, his eyes still on me, his hooves still sinking into the mud.

"I don't want to leave," I say.

"Has this interested you in vengeance?"

"No." This is the truth. Apathy has seized hold of me, and I have no wish to avenge myself or forgive his betrayal. "But I don't want to stay here."

The druid nods. He grabs the body's hand, and with a quick crack, snaps a finger from it. I watch as he puts it to his mouth and sinks his teeth into the skin.

"It's effective," he says before taking another bite. The flesh slides off the bone in chunks, and he finishes the crude cleaning process in seconds.

He pats his stomach.

"There. Where I go, you can go."

"The fox?"

"Should we find her, you could accompany her if that is your wish."

He reaches into his satchel and withdraws a ball of string. With it, he ties a small knot around the base of the bones, breaks the line with his teeth, and ties another knot behind his neck.

The dryad's hand slips through me again. I turn to her in time to catch her yawn, her eyes tired. Her fingers move to grip my chin. She would lift my face if she could, and so I raise my head to meet her gaze.

"I have been awake too long already, little shade."

"Thank you for the company."

"You belong here. Until you decide to go, you are as much of the forest as anything."

"Come, lad."

The druid stands at the end of the clearing where he first entered. The fog has begun to lift, and I can see the outlines of more trees and their bare branches beyond.

"If you find your name," she calls as I walk to him, "I would like to know it."

WHEN THE LAST GIANT DIED
Carman C Curton

Giants, who live nearly but not quite forever, teach that time is a gift. And the enemy.

Time is the only god. It gives everything and takes more. It is cruel enough to take those you've had for decades, and crueler yet to take those you've loved for mere days or hours. The same time gives us harsh, endless winters *and* soft, warm days, with waves in the distance that you want to last forever.

The Giant told us time was eternal and our share of it, brief. And then his time here stopped.

"Will another giant come to teach us?" some asked. The people looked to the sky, to the mountains, to the children who might yet grow more than expected.

"We'll know in time," they said.

KREST
Naomi Eselojor

We hike up the mountains, our backpacks tightly clasped to us, and my sister's hands entangled with mine. I don't walk abreast with her; I lag a step or two behind, to get a better view of the woods.

There is a vast stretch of savannah, its grasses swaying by wind's touch. Among a family of trees gathered at the end of the savannah, harboring woodland creatures eye me. Among all the animals, I love the birds the most. Colorful avians that hide under the shadows of branches, and only peek when they're about to soar. I once asked mother for a bird, but she humbly declined, saying I am too absent-minded to care for one. I wanted to argue, but I had just fallen into a puddle while daydreaming of owning a feathery pet.

A bird's flight guides my eyes across the wildlife, and the musky scent of plants reminds me of mother's garden. The memories of her tending it come to mind. It had always been fun to watch her weed, pluck, dig, and water. Birds would come and feed from the flowers and would only sing when they were full. We never chased them – or any creature – away; it was wonderful to watch the fowls and insects hover and negotiate with the flowers. I always assumed there was more to flowers than nectar. That the birds and insects might appear to be after nectar, but perhaps they are after something else, something extraordinary.

Mother says I have a very active imagination. Perhaps it is one reason I jumped to go camping with Gina and Bobby, her boyfriend. For the past few days, I wanted to explore the forest and find the behemoth of night. So, I imagine it is a behemoth. There is something big out here, up on the hill, that bellows every night. With the chance to find it, I tap my sister.

"Gina did you hear the piercing howl last night?"

My sister side-eyes me and exhales. "I won't fall for it," she says. "I know you too well. There is no imaginary monster out here, so don't use such a ridiculous excuse to wander off." She looks down at me. "Let me give you some advice. Try to enjoy the outdoors and forget about having a fairytale adventure. This is the 21st century. Besides, you're already 14. You're too old to still be playing make-believe."

I sigh in resignation. She never believes anything I say. "What about you, Bobby? Surely, you must've heard it."

Bobby who is a few feet away, stops and pulls his earbuds from his head. "Huh? Did you say something?"

"Never mind."

At least I believe me. I know there is a beast out here and I'm going to find out what it is. Gina and Bobby's eyes can't be on me forever.

I finally give in to Gina and Bobby's advice to go tinkle behind the bushes. It is almost 9 pm, and having traveled far into Wuzambe National Park, there is no choice of a facility. The moon and the stars gleefully light up the savannah and the cool breeze fiddles with my braids. I find peace in listening to the nighttime animals while I squat and relieve myself. The owls hooting, the frogs croaking, and the silent rustling of trees all have a soothing effect on me. As soon as I am done, I hear the monster. A strident bellow coming from the woods cause me to spring upright and redress in a hurry. I look towards the tents. My sister and her boyfriend are still inside one.

This is my chance. I rush to my tent, grab my coat, backpack, and a torch, and I track the sound into the canopy of trees, branches crackling under my steps. As I approach the hill, the bellows become louder. The scattering of small animals helps me pinpoint the sound. I shelter behind a tree to escape a panicked deer; the trepidation in its eyes tells me the creature may not be friendly.

That's when it occurred to me. What if it's an ọgbanje my mom told me about in bedtime stories? The blood-sucking kind that would eat kids who were hardheaded? I shudder at the thought of it. Maybe it is not such a good idea to discover the monster. I turn back for the campsite, but I can't remember the path. My torch flickers and dies, and I am left alone in the dark. Relying on the shafts of moonlight peeping through the trees, I make my way through the forest. I see only the silhouettes of saplings and bushes though, none of which seems familiar. With the difficulty of recovering my path, I hear something.

"Who's there?" I root my feet, feeling a presence from behind me. "I d-don't wish to startle you. I promise I'm very friendly." I raise shaky hands in surrender and trust that it understands me.

A branch snaps and I flinch and run. Hide and seek is never fun when you do not know who you're hiding from. My heart convulses as I hide in a tree's shadow and hear it walk – and then nothing.

When I turn to slip away, I find a shadow's gaze upon me. Fear overwhelms me as I am unable to identify the creature. It comes close and I jitter. The glaze of its green glowing eyes is hypnotic. I come to my senses, and overcoming dread fear, I bolt.

I scramble down the hill, forging a new path to get away from the monster. My carelessness causes me to trip over a log but it doesn't slow my pace. Hope surges through me as I sight a cave in the distance. I dash to the hollow, and once inside I pin myself to the wall. My heart races. What I had saw of the shadow, beyond its phosphorescent eyes, were thick long arms and hairy legs. It is an ọgbanje, as my mom had told me, and it tried to lull and eat me.

I anticipate its arrival but half an hour passes and I don't hear or see anything. A cool zephyr makes me cling to my coat. Thank God I slipped it on. I wish to start a fire but I'm afraid it will attract the evil spirit.

With a sharp pain in my right leg, I find it bleeding. I lower myself on a rock and rest. From my backpack, I use a scarf to wrap my knee. I hope tripping over that log didn't break anything. Oh, Gina will kill me and never invite to go camping again. Tears well up in my eyes.

Fear overwhelms me again, and I realize I am not alone in the cave. I look off beside me and notice bright green eyes staring at me. Had I taken shelter in the ọgbanje's home? The shadow approaches me. However, it is half the size now, as it crawls along the cave's floor. It pauses short of me.

From beneath the glow of its eyes, a fireball erupts. I recoil thinking I would be seared alive before being eaten. Opening my eyes, the fireball sits on the ground, warming the cave. The ọgbanje slithers into the light, and I am shocked. It isn't an evil spirit. It is a large reptile, the length of a horse, with scales as dark as coal, and a whip-long tail almost twice its length. Its large, majestic wings are folded by its sides as it sits next to me. It is a dragon – though not the size of a skyscraper as I had imagined. The beast considers me for a moment, before it moves closer, until our noses almost touch.

"Don't worry, I won't hurt you!"

I gasp; it speaks without movement of its snout.

"What's wrong? Don't you understand me?"

"I understand you. How are you talking to me?"

"Telepathy," the dragon says, crawling around and inspecting me. "So this is what a human looks like up close." Facing me again, it questions me, "How did you find me?"

"I heard you bellow and I was drawn to it."

"Despite not knowing what I was?"

I shrug.

"You are a very brave human. I am Krest, the last of Wuzambe. What is your name?"

"Victoria. How long have you been living in the park?"

"For centuries."

"All alone?"

"All alone. You're the only one that has heard me."

I stagger to my feet, but my leg cannot carry my weight.

"You're hurt."

I fall back to the ground in frustration.

Krest looks at my leg with regret in its eyes.

"It's my fault you're hurt. I startled you. I'm sorry."

I lift up my eyes to consider the strange creature, so gentle, so kind, so polite. "What happened to the other dragons?"

"Some were hunted. Others returned to our world."

"Your world?"

The dragon expels breath on to my leg; my skin tingles from the hotness of it.

"Yes, Chordatia. There is a sky-portal to return there, but when it closed a long time ago, I and other dragons were trapped in this world."

"I'm sorry." I flex my leg free of pain.

Krest settles down and says, "Don't be. Besides, to reach the sky-portal, I would need a special rider. One whose thoughts are expansive and never ending, and can join with mine to help me see the portal."

"Someone with an imagination. Like me!"

Krest sizes me up with its eyes. "You are very kind, Victoria, yet very little for a rider. But since it's my fault you're injured, I could carry you as far as Wuzambe's border."

"Or just back to my campsite," I say, "but I want to be your rider. I'm capable of riding, and helping you find the sky-portal."

"I do sense your mental capacity to be astounding," Krest says. "You could be my rider. Let's try."

Krest lowers itself for me to climb onto its back. Though I have never ridden a dragon before, I hoist myself and mount Krest without hesitation. Parts of their scales morphed to provide me leverage and adherence to its hide.

"Ready?"

I squeeze my legs tighter around the dragon.

Krest carries me deeper into the cave and turns towards the exit. I sense its hesitation, for it has never had a rider. I am Krest's first. Beginning with short strides, as I rest my head to a scale, Krest ramps up to a full gallop and, upon reaching the cave's entrance, leaps into the air with wings extended for lift. With powerful flaps, Krest carries us higher, up over the forest's tree line and across the full moon. I sense its happiness; ever since being a young dragon, it could only fly as high as a rooster. I hear Krest's bellowing in my head, but unlike before its laughter is full of joy and fulfillment.

The clouds below us, aglow from the moon's light, stream by as the friction of air flows around us. Krest performs a few swoops and aerial stunts that give me a rush and leave me breathless. It is a wonderful feeling to be so high up in the air, riding a dragon. I could touch the stars above and scoop into the palm of a hand the forest below. If only my mom could see me now.

"Let's go, Victoria," Krest urges, reminding me of our purpose. "Focus and trust me. A rider must always trust their dragon."

I straddle Krest with my entire body, my head to his hide once again, and I close my eyes, imagining new heights. I feel the wallops of Krest's wings striking the air as he soars higher. The air becomes cooler and thinner, yet I find myself able to breathe as normal. When I sit up again and peer down, we glide over mountains and the ocean. We are on top of the world and closer to the heavens. We are happy, and free.

Krest moves at a steady pace until his wings stop beating. Fully extended, Krest's wings coast on the air current. It offers me a steady viewing of the star filled sky.

"Look, Victoria," Krest says. "The sky-portal. And it is open."

"Great! Let's go!" I am eager to fly through the bright jewel of the upper atmosphere.

"I'm afraid you can't come with me."

"What? Why?" If I couldn't go to Chordatia… "How am I to get down?"

"Remember. Trust me," Krest said. "Close your eyes, hold tight, and focus on camp."

Hesitant, I followed Krest's direction. I hear the wind in my ears, feel it against me as the buoyancy of riding Krest plays with my sense of balance. There are moments my stomach goes weak, but I have no fear of falling.

"Yes. That's it." Krest's voice comforts and soothes me. "Soon you will be safe and sound."

Warmth begins to radiate across me, and even with my eyes closed I sense a bright light through heavy eyelids. I surmise it must be the sky-portal. Am I passing through it? Weightlessness consumes me and I no longer feel Krest's hide against me or between my legs and arms. It is as though Krest has disintegrated and left me afloat in blissful light.

"Thank you," Krest whispers. "Take care of the last."

The light fades and I am left in confusion of Krest's final instruction.

Sluggish, I turn inside the warmth of my sleeping bag and slowly open my eyes. Dawn creeps through the forest. As the sun rises over the camp and peeks inside my tent, I sit up in awe. The sunlight makes translucent the shell of a large egg; I see inside it a baby dragon curled upside. Krest was a girl dragon, and last night was real. I pick up the egg and head to Gina's tent to show her that my imagination is real.

THE LEAFER
James Dick

~~This is a true story. A situation arose in the~~ John M. Kelly ~~Kelly library and=~~

~~Life is full of cliches. Most bugs aren't willing to admit it, but it's true. Love triangles, melancholy monologues, shady pasts…our lives are riddled by these tropes we've seen time and time again=~~

~~Things aren't always what they seem=~~

I hate beginnings. They promise stability, but change inevitably follows.

I have to wonder, is that something we adopted from the apes? A need for change? Or is that something we always hungered for? Because it seems that in every generation of paper mites, there are a handful who crave something new.

I'll be honest; I don't know whose story this is. It could be mine, but it could just as easily be Cary's, or Jerry's, or the Big Bugs', or our society's. There are mites who will try to tell you that it didn't happen, that I'm lying to you, but the only thing I can be certain of is that this is a true story.

I need a beginning, so maybe I should start by introducing myself: my name's Shelley, and I'm an investigator.

So, what do you get when you combine a hyper-caffeinated ape holding a cup of Mexican Chapas with a copy of *The Original Illustrated Sherlock Holmes*? I'll give you a hint: the coffee cup isn't spill-proof.

I was lucky. My home was in *The Big Sleep* – deep near the back of the book, just after the big plot twist where Carmen finds out the bullets are blanks – so I was safe on the shelf when the spill happened. A thousand other paper mites weren't so lucky. Poor bugs. At least they can say it was a high-quality brew that did them in.

After the spill, the ape panicked and shelved Sherlock next to *Big Sleep*. The smell of the caffeine alone told me there was trouble. It was…intoxicating. There wasn't a bug in my book who could've failed to notice it.

I was off duty. Official civic instructions were for all bugs to buckle down and stay put while emergency responders dealt with the spill. Naturally, I crossed the shelf to see if I could help.

Perry was there. I knew him from the precinct; a rough bug if ever there was one. "Anything I can do?" I asked tentatively.

Perry waved an antenna at me even as he used his four forelimbs to direct emergency bugs towards injured survivors. A lot of bugs had limbs burned from the coffee before the pages absorbed the hot liquid. "Not much," he replied, pointing at the edge of the stain. "It's slowing down."

The blue watchbug stripes on my podonotal shield itched. "It's a bad one…"

"Twenty or thirty pages lost," said Perry, "with all the bugs inside."

My antennae wilted. "All because some ape had a paper that was late, or had to meet a deadline for book club–"

"Do apes still have book clubs?"

I gnashed my mandibles. "Who knows anymore?"

Perry's antennae suddenly shot straight up. "You there! Freeze!"

A young female, barely a nymph, was poised over the coffee stain with her mandibles open, ready to take a bite.

How did she get past the watchbug cordon? I wondered.

Perry scuttled toward her as fast as he could. "Don't eat that!"

He was too slow. He'd never reach the nymph before she bit into the page, and I wouldn't have wanted him to get a hold of her even if he could've, so I sprang into action, overtaking Perry and then passing him. I tackled the young nymph, wrapping all my legs around her to form a living cage. At first – probably out of sheer surprise – she resisted and tried to break free. She nearly succeeded; she was incredibly strong for her size. We rolled along the periphery of the stain, the fumes tickling my ganglion, and finally came to a stop on the unsullied half of the page.

Perry caught up to us, carapace bleeding clouds of carbon dioxide. "Good…good catch, Shelley…argh…"

The nymph was in a sorry state, legs all a-skitter, antennae whipping around. I released her and stroked her antennae with mine to calm her. "Shh, it's all right. You're safe."

"Wh-what's wrong with the page?" she chittered.

"It's the caffeine," I said. "The apes use it as a brain stimulant. To us, it's a poison."

The nymph gestured to the page. "B-but…it's soaked into the page! Anything on a page, we can eat."

"You *really* wouldn't want to try it, kid." Do you have a home you can go to?" *Please don't tell me you lived inside the stain…*

"Mm-hmm. Four pages down."

If I had an ape's lungs, I would've sighed. "Better get there. We're all supposed to be inside."

The nymph's arms went all akimbo. "*You're* not inside."

"Ha-ha. I'm a watchbug. Get going before I arrest you."

The nymph gave me an insouciant flick of her mandibles before scuttling off. *What she lacks in situational awareness, she makes up for in attitude.* I clicked my mandibles approvingly.

Seeing there was little else I could do at the disaster site, I decided to take my own advice and return to torpor. I figured a coffee stain this big was likely to have lasting repercussions, and I wanted to be rested for whatever came next.

Captain Jerry was a great investigator but a bit of a hard-abdomen. He rose through the ranks by chasing leafers – mites who tried to move outside their pre-assigned shelves and live somewhere else – arresting them, or squashing them, as he saw fit. In reality, it was the only way to advance around here; the Big Bugs appreciated those who kept order, and keeping order meant keeping all paper mites where they belonged.

I showed up early to my meeting with him, carapace cleaned to a mirror-shine and feet freshly sharpened. Jerry's office was pasted top to bottom with accolades from his watchbug academy days and medals from his recent service down the pages. He'd picked up a peculiar habit from his time in the more sordid *Sleep* pages: that of rolling a piece of page into a cigar and lighting it, inhaling the print through the smoke. Fire wasn't something we worried about; there's very little space between the pages of a book, and therefore little air to feed a flame. For a 'by-the-book' bug, it was an unconventional habit.

"You're well turned-out today," he said as I entered.

"I'm a watchbug, so I'd better look the part," I folded my forelegs and settled onto the paper chair.

"Hmph." Jerry plucked the cigar from his jaws. "Coffee's bad enough when there's only a single drop to worry about, but a half-cup…" Jerry's antennae quivered. "The Big Bugs say this is the worst thing to happen since the burst water main in '09. Of course, back then we had some warning. Barely lost anyone." Smoke wafted off his carapace. "Unfortunately, the trouble doesn't end with the coffee. In the chaos of the spill, some mites got it into their heads that they could, shall we say, make a change of address without being seen."

"Leafers," I said.

"Leafers," Jerry confirmed. "We've got to get them back where they belong."

"By any means necessary?"

"By any means necessary."

"If they've already relocated, wouldn't it be easier to just leave them where they are?"

"Bugs are *chatty*, Shelley, and if one of those relocated bugs brags to his or her friends about the feat they just accomplished, then the next time there's a coffee spill, it won't be just a dozen bugs that turn leafer, but a hundred, and that'll get the attention of the Big Bugs, and we don't want that."

"Sir," I said, "won't sending investigators after the missing mites attract the attention you're trying to avoid?"

Jerry leaned forward. His eyes were all steel. "It took seventy years for the Hardboiled Detective section to get the respect of the Big Bugs, but at the end of the day, we're still a Genre, and that respect could be lost in a tick's heartbeat. We keep that respect by keeping order, and we keep order by—"

"Keeping all the mites in their proper places," I finished. "I know."

Jerry glared at me. "If the Big Bugs see us tracking down missing mites, at least they'll see we're working for the good of paper mite society."

Before I could say more, Jerry reached into his desk. "I'm assigning an investigator to each of the missing bugs." He lifted a page out and slid it across to me. On the paper was sketched the likeness of a nymph. "This one's yours. Name's Cary. Lives in the *Holmes* book, four pages down from the coffee stain."

My antennae went straight. "I've met her," I said, "at the stain, just after *Holmes* went back on the shelf. She was trying to eat a caffeinated page."

"Did she succeed?" Jerry asked worriedly.

"No, I stopped her and sent her home. We only said a few words to each other."

"But you had a connection?"

My antennae bounced a couple times. "Of sorts."

"Good. Use that to convince her to come home. She's a nymph;

young and misguided. As a fellow female, you can help straighten her out."

I glared at Jerry.

"Don't give me that look," Jerry grumbled. "You're the best one to track her down and you know it. Now go on, get to work."

I rose from the paper, saluted, and left Jerry's office, staring at Cary's image the whole way down the page.

Jerry was right: I *was* the best bug to track down Cary. No bug had ever escaped me, because I knew all the tricks.

I passed the coffee stain on my way to the deeper pages of *The Original Illustrated Sherlock Holmes*. The clean-up crews worked full speed. Watchbugs maintained the cordon around the stain, keeping curious onlookers well back from the spill.

A thousand bugs lost. Hell of a thing. The Big Bugs make a big deal about mites being superior to the apes, but how superior can we be, when a pleasurable drink for them is a death sentence for us?

I scuttled on by.

I came to the abode of the nymph, Cary, between pages 136 and 137. I riffled them and was greeted by a harried female. Her antennae were askew and her forelimbs twitched anxiously. Behind her, a brood of larvae chased each other all over the pages, munching on faded ink and moldy paper. The female saw my watchbug colors and went as still as if she'd been bitten by a spider. "I don't want trouble," she said.

"You're not in trouble." This was the second-most-used line in the force, right after "you have the right to remain silent". "The name's Shelley. I'm an investigator with the *Big Sleep* precinct. I'm here about Cary."

A wave of relief rolled off of the female. "Did you find her?"

"No, not yet. I need to get some idea of where she might've gone. Can I ask your name?"

The female hesitated, then said, "Nellie."

"Nellie, I'm going to find Cary, but I need your help." I glanced past her into the dwelling. The place was a mess. "Can I come in?"

Nellie looked behind her. "Uh, yeah, sure." She held the pages open for me to enter, then let them flap shut behind her. "Go on, scram!" she said to her brood.

The larvae gave her an extremely rude flick of their antennae and retreated towards the spine.

"Sorry about them," Nellie said, flopping onto her thorax. "They're a handful."

"I can see that." I settled down across from her on a half-eaten spread of paper.

"You want to know about Cary?"

I inclined my antennae. "Anything you can tell me."

Nellie ran her forelegs through her mandibles to clean them. "Well, first off…she's not mine."

"Adopted?"

"Mm-hmm. A watchbug found her just after she hatched, in the Philosophy section. She'd been eating Machiavelli for hours."

I cocked my head. "Was she born there?"

"No. They scoured that entire section looking for egg fragments, riffled through just about every book looking for her parents, but nothing turned up. No one knows where she came from."

Strange. Bugs without homes were a very rare thing in the Kelly. Most mites could be traced back to their parents pretty easily, because for many hours after hatching, they still had their mother's scent. I'd heard of instances where larvae being separated from their hatchery too early lost that scent whilst roaming the stacks, but I'd never seen such a case myself. "Nobody came forward to claim her?"

"Nobody wanted to admit to having lost her in the first place," said Nellie.

My antennae shook in irritation. *That's bug logic for you: there can't be a problem if there's nobody to blame for it.* "So, you took her in?"

Nellie raised and lowered her forelimbs in a shrug. "What's one more, right?"

A sharp shredding sound emanated from the spine of the book. Nellie's antennae wilted. "Anyway," she continued, "Cary's always been so sweet and listens to me most of the time, but occasionally she takes off without telling me and disappears to all different places." Nellie rubbed her forelegs together. "I started to wonder if…maybe she was eating books she shouldn't have been. Every time she comes home, she looks bigger and stronger."

Another shred came from the spine of the book. Evidently the larvae were making serious trouble, and by the way Nellie was inching towards the back of the book, I could tell she was itching to tend to them.

"I don't want to take up much of your time," I said. "Do you happen to know if there's any place in particular Cary likes to go?"

Nellie's antennae drew a slow circle in the air as she thought. "Try the cover." She pointed her right two forelegs straight up. "She often sneaks out the top and runs the pages toward the front of the book."

A leafer *and* a page-skipper? *I think I'm starting to like this Cary.* "Thank you for all your help." I stood up.

Nellie entwined her antennae. "Please don't be too hard on her when you find her. She really is a sweet nymph." She showed me out and then scuttled off to go find her brood.

This time of day, the pages would be crawling with mites leaving for work, so instead of traversing the main paragraphs, I rode the margins, retracing my path back through *Sherlock Holmes* to the coffee stain. That area would be off-limits to all mites except emergency response bugs; I could use it as a shortcut to the top of the book, and from there I could make my way to the cover. I might even catch up to Cary, if I was quick.

I'm very quick.

But, as I emerged into the lowermost reach of the spill, the scene before me stopped me in my tracks. There was a pursuit in progress: Perry, along with a half-dozen other watchbugs, were chasing a mite with a mouthful of paper. The mite was male, just out of his nymph stage, and moved remarkably fast. From the shade of his carapace, I could tell he was a *Big Sleeper*, but the paper in his mouth was too new, too crisp, to be Chandler.

The most likely scenario was that this renegade had snuck off to another book, maybe even another section, during the chaos caused by the coffee stain, munched on a book, and then tried to sneak back to his dwelling with some leftovers clamped between his mandibles. Perry and the others must've seen him on the way home and started chasing him. By the looks of things, they weren't going to catch him.

A voice in my ganglion urged me to walk away, pretend I hadn't seen anything, let the chase sort itself out.

But Perry saw me and shouted, "Shelley! Run him down!"

There was no getting out of it now. I broke into a high-speed scuttle.

I started off a half-sentence behind Perry and the watchbugs, but I overtook them in seconds and started gaining on the leafer, who'd gotten a little overconfident and slowed his pace. When I got within an adjective's length of the renegade, his antennae shot up in alarm and he put on a burst of speed. It wasn't enough. I reached my two forelimbs out and swept the leafer's legs out from under him. He tumbled to a halt, somehow still maintaining his hold on the paper he'd stolen.

My carapace fumed, and my cardiac muscles burned.

Behind me, Perry laughed as he and the watchbugs closed the distance. "Nice one, Shells!"

The leafer shook his antennae and tried to come to his senses.

I put a leg on his abdomen. "Stay still," I whispered. "It'll go worse for you if you don't—"

"Drop the paper!" Perry said, leaping onto the leafer and tearing the stolen pages from his mouth. One of the leafer's mandibles cracked.

"Perry, wait!" I cried. "Easy!"

"Every bug has its place!" Perry shouted at the leafer, jerking the much smaller bug this way and that.

The other watchbugs joined in, waling on the male, who was making no attempt to defend himself. I was jostled out of the way in the melee. The watchbugs rolled the leafer this way and that, snapping at his limbs, tugging on his antennae.

"Perry," I said, "that's *enough*."

My voice cut through his bloodlust. He turned to me and motioned for the others to stop their abuses. "We've gotta teach him a lesson, Shells."

"Then do it some way that doesn't leave him paralyzed for the rest of his life." I looked down at the leafer. There was little of his carapace that wasn't cracked or deeply scratched. One antenna was crooked. He rolled onto his side and looked at me with eyes glazed over with pain.

I looked away. I couldn't meet those eyes, couldn't stomach the hypocrisy of what I'd just done.

"Get him to the precinct," I said. "I've got an investigation to finish."

I turned away from the scene, my steps a little heavier than before.

It's pretty heady in the space between book and shelf. It's the extra oxygen; makes you feel safe, even powerful. So many bugs have been lost because they started acting stupid up here. If an ape happens to pluck the book off the shelf while you're standing on it, you go flying and end up in the library carpet, and there's few places scarier than the library carpet. Generally, we don't get interlopers in the stacks, but out there, in the wild, there are big and nasty bugs that'll make a meal out of any mite unlucky enough to land among them.

I scanned the edge of the book, and it took me no time to spot a lone mite moving quickly across the pages. Even at that distance, I could tell it was a nymph.

Cary.

She saw me and froze. For a moment, we stood with our eyes locked, each waiting to see what the other would do.

C'mon, Cary, don't run, don't run…

She ran. My God, she *ran*. Did I say the male mite earlier was fast? He was a slug's baby compared to Cary. The moment I saw her move, saw her negotiate the worn, frayed edges of the old

Holmes tome, I knew she was no ordinary nymph-turned-leafer. She'd been running the stacks her whole life, possibly since the day she hatched.

I took off after her, running faster than I ever had in my life. Cary was headed straight for the topmost edge of the coffee spill. *Why is she so intent on these stained pages?* A dark thought occurred to me. *Is she trying to kill herself?*

The notion made me run even faster.

When we were two millimeters apart, I leaped for her much the same way I did yesterday, and hooked all my limbs around her. Cary fought much harder this time, and I have to tell you, I didn't think I'd be able to keep hold of her. Nellie wasn't kidding when she said she thought Cary had gotten into some dense texts that were beyond her years, and not just in the Philosophy section.

We came to a stop, limbs intertwined. "Why are you trying so hard to kill yourself?"

This gave Cary pause. "Kill myself?" she said. "That's what you think I'm trying to do?" There was none of the quavering uncertainty I'd heard in her voice yesterday. That had all been an act.

"You're trying to eat a coffee-stained page! What else am I supposed to think?"

"I tried to tell you yesterday: we can eat anything on a page."

"Not caffeine."

"Yes!" Cary shouted. Her voice was swallowed by the vacuous air above us. No other mites could possibly hear us. "We can't absorb straight caffeine, but diluted and diffused across paper, we can digest it. I'm certain of it. Let me go!" She continued to struggle, but I kept firm hold of her.

"*Why* are you certain?"

Cary slowed her struggling. "I've eaten pages in the Nature section. I know it's possible."

"But why would you want to do it? What can you possibly gain from eating a coffee-stained page?"

"The speed to outrun *you*!" Cary renewed her struggles, but they were futile; I'd gotten my second wind, *and* I was bigger and stronger. Cary had less chance of escaping by the second, and she knew it. "You proud of yourself?" she asked. "Helping to keep bugs trapped in their pages?"

The words stung more than I cared to admit. "When you're older, you'll understand there's an order to things."

Cary's antennae twitched angrily. "Did you pay mom a visit?"

"Yes."

"Did you see how she lives?"

"Yes..."

"Then don't lecture me about the order of things. I refuse to accept that she has to live that way, caring for so many larvae in the moldy pages all by herself." Cary relaxed somewhat. "Can you honestly tell me you *like* things the way they are? That you don't wish they were better?"

I didn't relax my grip...but I wanted to. "What would you do, after you ate the page? I mean, assuming you survived."

Cary rolled around in the cage of my limbs, so that her thorax rested against mine, a completely submissive position. "I'd run the shelves, get all the knowledge I could, and start changing things from the inside."

I looked at her – at this little nymph resting between my limbs – and contemplated what she'd said. "You're just one bug..."

"If you'd ever visited the other stacks, maybe ate some other books, you'd know that the apes believe a single person can change everything. All they need is a chance."

She talks with a wisdom beyond her years. Yet, even as this thought passed through my ganglion, I knew it was nonsensical; mites only have the wisdom of what they eat, and Cary had eaten far more than I ever had.

If I'd been a pure Hardboiled Detective bug – if that was all I'd ever eaten in my life – I never would've decided to open my limbs and let her go. When I did, she stared at me in disbelief.

"My tastes are a little more diverse than you think, Cary," I said. I looked north, to the coffee stain. "Go. I'll stay here in case it doesn't work out the way you expect."

Cary continued to stare for a long while. Then, she scuttled around me, went to the coffee stain, and lowered her mandibles to the paper.

I tensed up as she bit down.

~~A confession. *That's* what I've been writing. I've been trying to think of the name for ages and it only just popped into my ganglion=~~

~~I probably should've started by telling you who I *really* am, but I guess paper mite society has its mandibles in me deeper than I=~~

I hatched in the True Crime section. Grew up there. Ate Vincent Bugliosi and John E. Douglas. But the time came when I couldn't handle it anymore. You can only take darkness like that for so long. Some bugs can hack it, but not me. I wanted out.

I scuttled out, became a leafer. I figured the best place for me was the Genres, and *The Big Sleep* had a good reputation, so I burrowed in and made like a Hardboiled Detective. I even joined the investigators to seal the deal, but it doesn't matter how many dames, guns, and double-crosses I chew through; nothing erases the fact that I was born in a place of truth.

So, what's the truth? The truth is, we mites are parasites. We live off what the apes create. That's to our fortune, and our detriment. The apes' knowledge helped us build our society, but by refusing to let mites navigate the stacks and experiment with new knowledge, we stagnate.

The truth is, we need something new.

Cary frightens me. I can't stop thinking of the moment she chowed down on those stained pages. Something happened to her. She...changed. Her whole body started to vibrate. She became a blur, a fuzzy spot in my vision. Then she took off, moving faster than any mite I've ever seen. I have no doubt she could outrun any watchbug in the Kelly.

I have no doubt she could outrun *me*.

I could've stopped her, but I didn't. No one understands the hunger for change better than me, and no one understands the effort change requires better than I do. Cary's new…abilities will serve her well. Secretly, I hope she's never caught.

I don't know who's going to read this: maybe Cary, maybe a Big Bug, maybe an ape for all I know. Whoever it is, congratulations. You can say you were there when the Kelly took its first real step toward change.

I'm forgetting something…oh, right.

"She got away?" Jerry said, smoke rising from his carapace.

I bowed my antennae. "She was fast, and too close to the cover for me to catch her."

Jerry was quiet for a long time. "I've never known *any* bug that could outrun you."

I met his gaze. "There's a first for everything."

Jerry took another puff of his paper cigar. "Ah hell. It happens to everyone. Don't beat yourself up over it."

"I won't, sir." *I really, really won't.*

"As far as the day's docket goes, I guess that leaves nothing but the coffee stain."

"Right," I said. "Nothing but the coffee stain."

STAY
Carman C Curton

Fiquem, por favor. Fiquem, os Encantados! they beg. But we dance, laughing, back to the riverbank, randomly returning or carelessly dropping borrowed guitars and pandeiros and claves. Why would we stay? Our giant river, from the heart of the continent, provides the nothing that brings us everything: no ownership, no greed, no want. Also: no music. So we shed our tails, our fins, and our gray, sleek skins – for a few hours with hands on a midsummer night. Hands for guitar-strumming, drum-beating, clave-striking, finger-snapping joy.

For me, always the same festa: Junina. To watch the dark-eyed Mariachi, the one whose hands sometimes leave the strings, palm tapping the face of the guitar with the rhythm of my heart.

Fiquem. Stay, the women say, laughing and dancing, tempting us with tales of children from previous festas – children with hidden tails and hands that play magical music and straw hats to hide their blowholes.

The Mariachi says nothing. Only looks with his dark eyes. I will ask to borrow his instrument. And if his fingers – so careful, so precise – touch mine when he passes it over, then I will stay.

WHERE SHORE MEETS SEA
Archer Beau

A o chose the beach because of the smokestack. Not that there
was much thought about it after a five day flee to safer waters.
He'd been exhausted and needing rest, and the smokestack had
looked like a promising beacon. The warning signs along the shore
only sealed the decision for him.

A day of rest all too easily turned into two, then a week, and
then two. In that time there had been no sign of his mother and
father. Ao had swum out as far as he dared to try and look around,
but the ocean was vast. He was limited now being this alone. It
didn't pay to be alone in the deep.

Ao had never been alone before.

So there was nothing to do but stay at the beach for the time
being, tucked into the mangroves where he was safe. The beach
had no visitors, the smokestack made sure of it. His mother had
taught him enough English to understand humans and to read, so
he knew the signs said this water was toxic. Not for Ao, but for
the flimsy skin of humans. It was a blessing to find shallow waters
without humans. There weren't many of those left.

It was lonely waiting though. Ao had never been so aimless. He spent his time digging out mollusks and crabs to feed himself, but time drifted by painfully slow. He counted the birds that came by, made shapes out of the smokestack clouds in his head. He missed his parents with a sharp ferocity that would not let up.

On the nineteenth day of this, Ao heard a car.

He'd been floating rather brazenly on the top of the water sunning himself, but upon the sound of the engine, immediately sank down beneath the water. It ruined his ability to see the threat, so he swam back behind the thick mangroves and pulled himself up.

There was a car in the disused parking lot, and a man was getting out.

Ao watched him unpack something from the back, and then head across the rocky barrier and down to the shore. He was tall, dark-skinned, and wore a pale, yellow-brimmed hat to shield himself from the sun. He was a bit thin, gangly, but his sharp features were interesting.

Ao had seen more than his share of humans, had in fact been escaping some when he lost his parents. Most of them he thought looked ugly with their strange skin colors and unwebbed fingers. They were too smooth all over, like something tumbled too long in a current.

Ao kept himself hidden as he watched the human. The man had a bucket and gloves, and walked to one end of the beach where the rocks cut off the sand. He began picking up straws and Styrofoam and glass from the beach. Picking up trash that had washed up.

He did this for a long time, managing only a small section before dropping the bucket. He stretched then, arching his back and reaching his hands up. The sunlight lit him all along one side and he looked–

Ao didn't know. Didn't have words.

Then the man bent back down for the bucket and took it up the beach to his car. He hadn't tried to swim – hadn't even touched the water. Not that he should, of course, it was just that in Ao's experience humans came to the beach to swim, not fill up a bucket with trash.

When the car drove away Ao was almost sorry to see it go.

Three days later, the man came back. It was evening this time, near sunset, but Ao recognized the car immediately. The sunhat only confirmed it. The man walked down to the beach, bucket in hand, and began picking up trash once more. Ao hid and watched him.

After he left Ao went up to the shore carefully for a look, but could not determine what the man was doing other than picking up trash. What a strange thing, Ao thought. What did that man intend to do with the trash?

There was a lot of trash here, and a lot more in the water that would wash up daily. If that man wanted to fill his bucket with trash, he certainly wouldn't go lacking.

Ao wondered if he could help. He certainly encountered plenty of trash in the water while he was fishing. It would be easy enough to toss it to shore, it would be something to do.

It was four days before the sound of the car interrupted Ao's boredom again. He'd been sucking out a bit of meat from a cerith shell when he heard the noise. He surfaced just for a moment to make sure it was indeed the right car before going back to hide.

There was a mountain of trash at the shore this time, courtesy of Ao. He hoped the man would see it and be happy.

Instead, the man trekked down to the beach, saw the pile of trash, and frowned. He looked around, as though searching for the culprit, and Ao ducked down further even though he was well hidden. When there was nothing to be seen, the man sighed and dropped his bucket to start picking up the trash.

It confused Ao. Clearly the man wanted the trash, but he also seemed mad about it? Humans didn't make any sense.

Ao watched him half fill his bucket with the pile, and then go back to picking it up off the beach. After a while he was done, and the man did a few stretches before, for the first time, venturing near the water.

He was sweaty from the work and sun. It was a rather hot day, especially if you weren't submerged in water. Ao didn't know how humans did it with that unarmored skin. Didn't the sun hurt?

The man stood there at the shore, looking out for a while. A breeze blew past and almost knocked his hat off, but he caught it just in time. It wasn't anything interesting, but Ao just kept looking and looking. He'd never gotten this kind of time to study a human, and certainly not without the threat of harm or capture.

He wondered what this man would say if he saw Ao. Would he scream and run away? Would he try to net him? Ao's mother had told him plenty about humans and their proclivity to capture things. They'd once visited an aquarium by the ocean and she'd shown him all the enclosures they had for dolphins and whales and fish. It had been horrifying.

Best not to ruin this for himself. If the man was hostile then Ao would have to risk fleeing to deeper waters, and that came with a whole mess of problems on its own. Not to mention if his parents were coming down the coast and checking beaches for him, it was best if he stayed in one place.

So he stayed hidden behind the mangroves until the man turned around and took his bucket back to the car.

Days rolled by, but the man did not return after that. Ao counted five days and then tried to put it out of mind. It was better if the man didn't come back, best if there were no humans poking around his hiding place.

He went about his days after that eating and sunning, sometimes collecting metal or plastic or glass to toss on shore. He whittled a large fish bone into a knife, another into a comb for his hair. The knife let him venture a little further out for food, and doubled as a way to cut his hair. It was getting long and in his face, so Ao was glad to have something to shear it down to shoulder length once more.

It was during a fish deboning in which Ao was considering making a second knife that a voice carried over to him.

"Hey!"

Ao whirled around toward the beach to see a man, The Man.

"You shouldn't be swimming! It's dangerous."

Ao dropped back beneath the water, heart pounding. He couldn't believe he'd been spotted. He'd grown careless in his laze. He–

He hadn't heard the car.

Ao swam back over to the mangroves, but just as he got there a splash reverberated through the water. It was of a large, clumsy object, could only be one thing, and a different sort of fear drove Ao back up to the surface.

Sure enough the man was frantically wading into the water, heading toward where Ao had gone under. But he didn't look angry – he looked afraid. He was yelling in concern.

It clicked then that the man probably hadn't noticed anything un-Human about Ao from the distance. He'd probably just assumed someone was swimming and – and maybe now was drowning. But Ao wasn't, and the man seemed ready to dive under the water. The water was toxic to humans.

"Wait! Don't!" The words came out before he could stop them. They sounded strange, sort of creaky. He hadn't used his voice now in weeks, and his last use of English was even more dated.

Instantly the man stopped and turned toward him. Ao could see it take a minute to find him in the mangroves.

"Oh! Hell, I was so worried you were drowning." The man laughed strangely, his shoulders falling. He was soaked up to his stomach, missing his hat, and clearly hadn't noticed anything different about Ao yet.

Which wouldn't last. The green of his skin would be less apparent the way Ao was hidden here in the shadows, but if someone was looking long enough the scales and spines and webbed fingers would give him away.

"You can't be swimming here. It's dangerous."

Ao swallowed hard. He didn't know what he should do, how to get out of this situation. If he tried to disappear again the man might actually dive in beneath the water to 'help.' But neither could Ao come out of the water.

"I'm fine," he said.

The man had been moving back toward shore, but paused at that. His hand came up to shield his face as he looked in Ao's direction.

"I – I really can't just let you stay," he said. "I've signed up to care for this beach, and I'm pretty sure that involves making sure people follow the signs." He threw a thumb back to gesture. "It's technically trespassing."

Ao didn't know what that meant, but it sounded serious.

"I'll just swim home then," Ao said. It was the only thing he could think of. His heart was painful in his chest from how hard it was thundering.

The man turned his head to look up and down the coastline. He looked confused.

"How old are you?"

This was far, far too much conversation. Ao didn't even know how to answer that. Ao was 20 seasons, but he didn't know how humans measured age.

"How old are you?" Ao asked instead.

"Twenty-three," the man said.

Twenty-three what? Seasons? At least it was a number.

"I'm twenty," Ao replied. He hoped that was good enough.

The man nodded. He was still just standing there, water up to his thighs.

"There's nothing around here, you know. I don't think it would be safe to swim home. Just come out. I've got a spare towel."

The man moved back to shore. Ao watched him, then he noticed the parking lot. There was no car there, just a small metal thing. A bike. No wonder Ao hadn't heard him come this time.

"I really can't."

The man at shore pulled off his soaked shirt and wrung it out. He wasn't muscular, but rather thin. The sight intrigued Ao, the way the man's skin was strangely light where the shirt had been. Was that common for humans?

"Look, I really don't want to have to call somebody, but–"

"Don't!" Ao said sharply. One man he could outswim if it came down to it, but if more humans came...

The man was looking at him again, squinting to try and pick him out against the blazing sun and mangroves.

"Hey, look, I'm not going to hurt you. I just can't in good conscience let you stay out there. Who knows what the water is doing to you already."

Ao took a deep breath and let it out. His options were dwindling, and the only thing he could think of was to show himself. He'd feel bad if he disappeared and this man panicked and thought he was drowning. He seemed nice, and with that delicate human skin he really shouldn't be in this water anymore. He might also call someone if he thought Ao was in danger.

Showing himself was equally a risk. If this man wasn't nice, he could still call other humans to come and Ao would have to flee. There wasn't a way to win.

The knife was gripped tight in his hand beneath the water, Ao had just finished eating. If he had to leave this beach, at least he was well-rested and fed. It wasn't a choice he wanted to make, but he'd made the mistake of being seen. Now he had to live with the repercussions.

Decision made, Ao moved through the mangroves and out into clearer water. The man was picking up his hat from the beach, not looking in his direction.

"Look," Ao said boldly as he swam out and then pushed more of his body above water, just as the man turned. "I live here. So I'm not coming out."

The man's mouth dropped open, and the soggy shirt in his hand fell to the sand. Ao took a breath and then another. He'd never willingly shown himself to a human before, and the experience made him feel shaky. His knuckles ached around the knife.

"Y-you're—" The man said. Then, "Oh my god."

He stared at Ao, and Ao stared right back. Surprisingly, the man started to laugh.

That really didn't make any sense. Ao watched him as he collapsed to the sand, barely breathing as he laughed. Ao had never seen anything like it.

"Are you okay?"

The man waved him off and then seemed to realize what he was doing. He collected himself, sitting back up to face Ao. Only the distance of water now separated them.

"Sorry, sorry! I just – wow! You're... *wow*. Green. Um. Not human. Okay. Um, yeah I see why you really wouldn't come out." He laughed then in a higher pitch. "So you're like a mermaid or something?"

Ao could feel the distaste pinch his features. Mermaids! How offensive.

"No."

Ao had to think about what the word was. He knew his mother had told him once what the humans often called them, but that had been a while ago. Their name for themselves, *cunachua*, probably wouldn't make any sense to a human.

"I think you call us swamp monsters?" That was the best he could do with his limited vocabulary.

"O-oh," the man said. "Right. Uh, the green. Mermaids aren't green, then? Wait. Mermaids are real?"

Ao almost rolled his eyes. Mermaids got all the glory, even though they were nasty, nasty creatures.

"They are silver. "

The man laughed again. "I don't know if I've cracked up, or if this is really happening."

The way he said it, the way he was almost giggling to himself sparked Ao's temper. The fear had eased away and now Ao just felt irritated.

"I don't know why you're laughing," Ao said. "But I would appreciate it if you did not speak to anyone."

"Ah," the man said. "Tell anyone? Yeah. That wouldn't be good."

"No."

They stared at each other again for a long moment.

"I'm Meet," the man said. "And I won't tell anyone. Promise."

"I am Ao," Ao said. He wasn't sure if he trusted this man, but telling him his name was hardly the worst of it. "If you do and people come, I will leave."

Meet nodded. "Of course. But I won't, so no one else will come. Does that mean you'll stay?"

That really was the question. It was inherently dangerous to stay now that he'd outed himself.

But the deep waters were dangerous too.

"Maybe," Ao said.

"I'd like it if you did," Meet said. "I mean, it's not every day you meet an uh, sea-person."

It was not every day Ao met a human, either.

"If you come back, maybe I will be here," Ao said. He wasn't sure why he said it, why he offered it. The boldness made him feel hot. "But I have to go now. Please do not dive in the water again."

There was nothing Ao needed to attend to, but this conversation had gone on too long and he was feeling tired of speaking the language. Best to go and see if this man would keep his word before more conversations were had.

The man smiled, his white teeth bright against his dark coloring. "I won't! It was nice to meet you Ao."

Ao nodded, and then before he could change his mind, he sank down beneath the water.

He didn't need to fish, but he forced himself out into deeper waters and pulled up mollusks. He wasted a long time doing it before swimming back to the mangroves. When he finally surfaced the sun had fallen in the sky and Meet was gone. Ao didn't know if he was relieved or disappointed.

Ao spent the next day on high alert. He kept his eyes on the beach and his ear to the water. He barely managed to sleep, ready at any moment to flee, but nothing happened. It was just as it had been for all the days preceding it.

Two days later, Meet returned on the bicycle.

He hurried down to the beach this time, bucket in hand and eyes scoping the horizon. Ao was lounging lazily in the mangroves, but swam out when he saw him.

"You're here!"

Ao swam a bit closer this time. Meet looked as he had every other time; there was nothing weapon-y in his hand. Besides, even if he lunged into the water, humans could not outswim him. And Ao still had his knife.

"I am."

"I'm glad. Really convinced myself I'd made you up," Meet said.

Meet got just to the line of wet sand and then took a seat. It was very non-threatening the way he did. Ao scanned the parking lot and then chanced swimming a bit closer.

"Why no car?"

"Last time driving home I got a nail in my tire," Meet said. "The road down to this beach isn't maintained. Cost me a lot, so I figured I would try biking. Good exercise too."

Ao didn't quite know what all that meant, but he nodded.

Meet waved his hand. "But that's boring stuff. I want to know about you!"

He looked so…enthusiastic about it. Ao blinked at him, trying to determine if he was really reading this human right. Of all he had seen and been told, humans mostly were afraid or angry at them. He had never seen this.

"Like what?"

"Well, okay, I know your name. Do you have, like... a whole society? Like Atlantis?"

"Atlantis?"

"It's a city under the sea," Meet said.

Ao shook his head. "There is no city under the ocean."

"Damn. Okay, so do you just live like sharks and whales, kind of roaming around?"

"Uh. Sometimes. We had a home but–" He cut himself off.

"There are more of you?"

"My family," Ao said.

"Oh." Meet looked around, as if hoping to see them. "Where are they?"

Ao shrugged. It felt like too much to tell him. Too much to say, *the humans came and ruined our home so we had to flee.* And maybe that would upset Meet, make him think that perhaps there was a good reason to attack Ao after all.

"Sorry, um. You don't have to answer anything you don't want to," Meet said. "I mean I'm so fucking curious, but also like...I don't want to scare you away."

"You are not scary," Ao said, because that part was easiest to answer.

Meet laughed. "Gee, thanks."

The conversation went on like that for a bit. Stilted and strange, Meet asked about his life and Ao did his best to answer without giving too much away. Thankfully Meet avoided family questions after that, which was appreciated.

When it had been some time and Meet had sweat through his shirt, he stood.

"I should go, and not exhaust you," Meet said. Ao was grateful for the thought. His answers had started to come shorter as he grew tired of speaking. He'd never used this much English in his whole life. "Next time you can ask me questions if you like."

The *next time* struck Ao. Meet was going to come back? Even tired as he was, that thought almost coaxed a smile from him. He'd been without any form of interaction for so long now that this had been a wonderful change of pace. Meet was nice. Really nice.

The man picked up his still empty bucket.

"Are you not going to get your trash?" Ao asked.

Meet shook his head. "Should have, but I got distracted. Next time I'll do double. Hold me to it."

Ao watched him go up and beach and get on his bike. There he looked back and waved with one hand. Ao copied the gesture back.

It stormed the next two days. On the third, Meet came back. This time Ao asked him questions, ones he had spent the storm days thinking on. He'd never had access to a human like this, and as curious as Meet was about him, Ao found it reciprocated.

Meet answered his questions. When things went beyond Ao's vocabulary, Meet explained them for him. While they talked, Meet took his bucket to the water and began to fill it with trash. Ao plucked some out of the water and helpfully tossed it up. They worked and talked that way in tandem for a while.

"Oh," Meet said when there was a pause in conversation. "It was you who made that trash pile, wasn't it?"

Ao nodded. "Thought it would be helpful."

Meet laughed. "I mean, I guess. Better than somebody dumping more trash out here."

Later when the conversation came to a natural close, Meet bid him goodbye, promising once more to come back *when my school work permits*. He'd explained to Ao what schools were, which sounded fascinating. Meet knew all kinds of things, and apparently he'd learned it at a 'school.' Ao wanted to know everything that Meet knew, everything these schools had taught him. For the first time Ao was aware of how much he really didn't know, and he wanted—

He needed to calm down. He would think up some questions, and ask Meet next time. One thing at a time.

After that there were more storms and more visits from Meet. Ao dreaded one and looked forward to the other. They shared stories, answered questions, and talked about their days. Meet's were more interesting than Ao's, so he made Meet tell him everything. Meet, always cheerful and excited, did. The days rolled into weeks.

The season of storms kept coming. This close to shore and barely protected, they were rough for Ao to get through. Usually Ao and his family went to their summer place when the storms came, to avoid having to deal with it.

But Ao was alone now. Going there would require chancing the deep waters alone.

Leaving Meet.

Three weeks into the storms, Ao told Meet about wanting to venture into deeper waters to avoid the worst of the wind and tide, but being unable.

"Sharks?"

"Among other things," Ao said. They'd discussed some about what lived in the deep.

"But you got here before okay?"

Ao bit his lip. He hadn't yet told Meet about his parents, and after that first time, Meet hadn't asked.

"I was with my parents most of the way," Ao confessed. "But now they are gone."

"Oh. I'm so sorry."

Ao didn't know what came over him then, but the words burbled up. "We were fleeing humans. They had a net on Dad, but he got free. We swam away, but got separated in a strong current. I ended up here, since it is not safe in the deep."

"Where are they now?" Meet asked.

Ao looked away, shrugged. "I do not know."

"Fuck," Meet said. "So you're stuck here?"

"I will leave if I must," Ao said, because that was true. He would brave the deep if the danger here was greater.

"I – I don't want you to go. I mean, selfishly. It's been nice to talk."

The words made something in Ao's belly churn. "Yes," he said. "Agreed."

Then he sighed. Eventually he would have to do something. Ao couldn't just waste away his life on this tiny beach. He needed a home, and to find his parents.

"If you go to the deep, is there a way to track them?"

Ao shrugged. "I would go up the coast. Look for clues."

"There's a lot of coastline."

"Yes."

Meet looked troubled, and it was sort of nice to have someone feel the feeling with him. He'd been so lonely here, but for a moment, with Meet, it was a little less so. Like the burden was shared.

"I've got an idea," Meet said the next time he came back. He'd nearly dropped his bike rushing down to the beach. The bucket, for the first time, was missing.

"What?" Ao swam at once closer to the shore. Meet was without his hat and his eyes looked tired. "What is wrong?"

"Nothing," Meet waved off his concern. "I was up late. I was thinking about your parents and, well, there's always rumors about…people like you. Sightings. And I got to wondering if anyone had seen your parents and tweeted or posted about it on the internet."

Meet pulled out of his pocket a device, a phone. He had explained its use to Ao before.

"And after a bunch of Googling last night I found this person on a forum saying they saw a sea monster off the coast of Pensacola."

"What?" Ao said again.

"Yeah," Meet was talking fast now, waving his phone. "So I thought maybe if you wanted – I mean I don't know if you can get out of the water actually, but if you can, I could take you. Like we could go up there and see if your parents are there? I mean if that's okay. You obviously don't have to trust me. I could like, show you instead if you'd rather go alone–"

"I can," Ao said, to break up the strange babbling. His mind was racing at this information. He didn't know much about the internet other than what Meet had explained, but surely this was better than nothing. "I can get out of the water. I would need some for travel, but I can be dry."

"O-oh!" Meet lit up, and then seemingly tried to tamp it back down. "Would you…want to?"

Ao knew his parents would want him to be more cautious, but looking at Meet's face there, exhausted but eager, he knew what his answer was. He wanted to find his parents, and this seemed like a better lead than just trying to search shorelines blind.

And if he was more honest with himself, the idea of going on land, with Meet…

"Yes," he said. "Let's do it."

After they talked about it and made a plan, Meet left. He came back the next evening with his car, and brought his bucket and a towel down to the shore. He filled the bucket with sea water.

Ao swam up to the shore and then tentatively got his feet beneath him. He was a bit weak in all honesty, as he didn't do much dry land walking, but Meet immediately swooped in and put a strong arm around him. He then carefully wrapped Ao with a towel. It was warm. Strange.

Ao's heart raced as they slowly made their way up the beach and to the car. He'd never shown any human all of him, but Meet didn't gawk. He was business the whole way until he tucked Ao into the back seat. Ao laid down like they'd talked about so he would be hidden for the journey.

"Let me get your water," Meet said, and hurried for the bucket.

Meet came back with the bucket and placed it on the floor of the car. Ao put his toes in the water just to feel it, just to try and calm his battering heart.

"Ready?" Meet asked when he climbed into the front seat. He was smiling in the fading light, dark skin cast in beautiful shadows.

Ao realized then he'd never seen Meet so close. Never touched him as he just had. Humans, as it turned out, had such soft skin. Ao's stomach fluttered, but not in a bad way. He felt hopeful.

"Yes," Ao said, "I am ready."

They left the beach and headed north.

THE FLATWOODS MONSTER AND THE LITTLE GREEN MEN
Jennifer Lee Rossman

It's not important what I was. That's past tense, sweetie, and we're looking to the future. Besides, keeping the rest of them safe, awful as they were, that's what all of this was about.

But suffice it to say, I was something you've never seen, none of you. My people take great pride in the fact that not a single human culture has a myth or story about us, let alone a photograph. The same can't be said for that attention seeker up in Scotland.

Maybe that was rude to say. It's true, but maybe it's rude to say it. Anyway, my point is we've lived alongside you in secret since you were just wee little apes dreaming of opposable thumbs, and I gave up everything to keep it that way.

It was the Cold War, and you were all pretending that your ability to duck and cover would save you from a nuclear warhead. I can't blame you. The peace felt like a reflection on a soap bubble. Perfect and beautiful and absolutely, tragically temporary, no telling when it would pop. I would pretend there was something I could do, too, anything to stop me from feeling helpless.

My kin had that soap bubble existence, as well. See, a few years back was the Roswell crash, and you all had aliens on the brain. Maybe you couldn't stop the bombs, but you could sure as hell pretend you were going to find aliens, and wasn't that good enough?

I told you it's not important what I was, but you should know one thing. We're Earth creatures through and through, but we look like little green men, so running into one of your kind in those days wouldn't end well for us.

So we lived simple and happy lives on the periphery of human society. They did, anyway. Me, it never felt right, that life didn't fit. I needed something more. Maybe more isn't the right word; I didn't want something better, just better for me, different.

You humans, you've got options. Just because you grow up communing with wildlife and making your own clothes like some sort of hippie commune David the Gnome, that doesn't mean you're locked into that life. You can be anything, look like anything. Handsome basketball player, zookeeper with tattoos, gorgeous lady who fixes cars… You don't even have to keep your gender if the original doesn't work out for you.

I thought you were beautiful. Everything about your society, even the hideous and hateful parts of it. Not that I wanted hate, I just wanted to be different even if it made everyone hate me.

And I guess I succeeded, because I was the one that little girl saw, me tinkering with that old car. I was the one that didn't run away. I was the one that put all my kin in danger.

Oh, sure. Everyone's heard of the boys and their dog, but that comes later, after I was fabulous. The girl saw me first, she put the idea of aliens in their heads to begin with.

I should have heard her coming, noisy as she was scrambling through the bushes at the top of the hill, but the rest of the humans had me transfixed that evening. So tall, such gorgeous clothing, and the ladies, at least I assumed they were the ladies, and the way they had their hair so elegantly arranged about their heads. My heart ached at the sight, like it was singing along to a teary breakup song I had never heard but still knew all the words to.

And then suddenly the girl was right beside me and that rusty old vehicle, eyes wide and terrified, and I could feel the soap bubble quivering, about to burst.

She turned and ran back to her family, her green dress catching on the branches. I watched her go, sure I had just ruined everything.

I told myself that maybe her family wouldn't believe her, but there was a meteor scheduled to pass through the atmosphere that night, and paranoia will turn anything into an alien spacecraft. They would come looking for us, and they would find us because humans don't know how to give up hope.

So I had to give them an alien. A big, terrifying, fabulous alien. I had to give them myself to keep the others secret.

I kept thinking I'd have time to go back, say goodbye. And I'm not sure why I knew it was goodbye, just a feeling that this was my something more, and I wouldn't be able to give it up.

I'm good at welding and cutting and manipulating metal, as good as the others are at making teacups out of mushroom caps and yarn out of old cocoons, but it took longer than I thought to turn that old car into my new body.

The meteor streaked across the sky hours later, going out in a blaze of glory as the atmosphere devoured it. And just like I predicted, you humans came looking for aliens.

Six little boys, a lady, and a dog. Not as bad as the men with guns I imagined, but still too many not to be believed.

I fitted the second headlight into my mask, and I stood taller than I've ever been before, taller even than the humans. My eyes glowed in a fog made even thicker by the exhaust from the engine powering my suit.

And I was glorious. The metal formerly making up the car hood swept up around my face and head like a perfectly coiffed red hairdo, my robotic arms ended in long fingernails made from random scraps of rust, and I may have used a few of my people's techniques to give myself a green dress of leaves.

Yeah, I scared them. Didn't mean to, but I kind of expected it. They ran back to their families, and I just ran. The body I built myself, it was my something more.

Like I said, it's not important what I was. That's not me anymore, maybe never was, and my kin deserve to stay hidden.

I'm still not really sure what I am. Gorgeous, that's a given. You people call me the Flatwoods Monster, made me into some sort of local celebrity. Doesn't matter to me, to be honest.

I'm just myself.

AT DAWN
Edy Lue

Her name is Phoebe – at least that's what she says in a greeting to the phone braced on her scraped-up knees. With a high-pitched voice and the faintest twitch of confidence in her thin shoulders, she speaks as if the dainty calls of the early birds' song mean nothing to her. Though she perches on the roots of a birch tree, her spine one with the white trunk of the eye-infested bark, her head lolls, then jerks upright every few seconds whenever it's her turn to participate in the discussion.

"Oh, no, it's okay," she says, twitching a fragile hand in the springtime air. "You did what you could. He just – I guess he'll always get his way."

She tilts her head at that tinny voice in her phone, her hands wrapping around the column of her neck. "Oh," she says, "yeah – I have – yeah, in case he finds me again."

She jams the tip of her finger to her phone screen, then waits – a beat, two – and releases a screech into her palms at such volume that it rivals the long-ago lullaby of the robins flying from their nests.

And there you are, feet soaking in the creek behind her cottage,

269

your blue-tinged hands hanging down by your sides, your hair like a noose that threatens to tighten if you dare to take a step toward her. It isn't your time, not yet, not until she first dares to take that step toward you. But how long can you wait, standing here in this creek, gills moving slow and your hair thick like a noose?

The sun rises, dawn vanishes, and you make your journey down the creek, back to your lake, away from her – Phoebe; her name is Phoebe. Four months you have traversed this creek to see her, and four months you have not known what to call her. You roll this newfound name over your tongue, lick it along the edges of your lips.

On cicada mornings like this, as you sink to the bottom of the lake you inhabit these days, you wonder if your mother was happy when she died, if she managed to tuck away the woes of the broken man who was able to see her and cherished her for this. It is instinct, gut reaction, to emerge from the waters and come to aid a man who may not realize he needs it just yet; your mother insisted it tastes like cinnamon.

With Phoebe, you have shaken off the droplets of water from your gray-slick skin and stood as still as the trees. You watch her. You wait for her. You listen to her.

You cannot talk. If you could, you wouldn't know what to say.

Before she left you, your mother kissed the crown of your head, like she did every night. She had no parting words. You were grown now, the last of her children to swim from her cavity nest in the Ohio River. You never knew your siblings, but you did know strength flowed through their able bodies. Their odor reminded you of the entity you rationalized was your father – that broken man your mother nurtured all those years ago.

Where was your strength? What did you truly know of that, anyway? This lake of yours, its shallow waters meet muddy shores. You track it inside after every dive. Was that strength, letting in all the dirt?

These cicada mornings lead to silent nights. Your routine predates time itself – a slow crawl out of your lake, a feeble tread down the creek, a solitary march to the small lawn behind Phoebe's ruddy cottage; you walk, and you welcome the hiss of oxygen gliding through your gills. You know this also predates time itself – breathing, even; and while it is older than you, this wheeze rushing into your lungs clicks like new gears in your body, mechanisms you haven't quite accepted as useful facets of yourself.

Pebbles snag on the webs of your feet. You bring them with you, bring all the water up to the creek bed once you settle down there. The lukewarm currents lap at your skinny ankles, begging for your return, but you pull your legs to your chest, rest your head on your knees, and gaze at the house you surveyed for months.

During these late-night hours, the house is as quiet as winter – deathly cold to boot, with the lack of artificial warmth peering out the windows. Only when the sun reaches the morning horizon does the house begin to stir. It's stiff. In the absence of heat, the house grovels in noise. And at that noise, you know when to step back into the water and present yourself as an essence of the lake, ready to vanish at a blink if Phoebe were to look your way.

Though you have a human father and human lungs, the land repels you. You sense she would repel you, too, at the beginning. However, in your time spent watching over her, she has never given proof to this fear of yours. She displays signs of her generosity and anguish, most often to the trees on her land and whoever calls her phone.

She has a careful hand and a strong voice, despite her willowy limbs. On more than one occasion, you've spotted her feeding from her hand the birds high up in the birch branches before she crumples to the ground. And on more than one occasion, you've spotted her already lounging at this lonesome creek, her toes bridged in the water and her face hidden in her arms. She was crying, then. Those long bellows kept you up well into morning.

Did your father cry for your mother? Did he know he was crying for her?

Tonight, you sit on the empty creek bed and listen for the first hint of sound from her house, something that resembles the squeak of a door or a snap of a twig – telltale notions that will indicate her arrival to the outside. Your ears are attuned to her movements and noises; and you thought you had sewn up all the gaps in this routine of yours, but there's a small hole to the left of you, where the birch trees obscure in early-morning shadow.

You don't catch the person slicing through those trees until they're on you, their arms raised and their eyes so big and bright they can replace the moon blinking through the spring leaves.

"Why are you here?" they ask – and it takes a moment for you to register that this gravel voice full of raw exhaustion and fright belongs to Phoebe.

She looks different here, standing over you and wielding a baseball bat high over her round head, ready to strike. From afar, you saw her as someone who only held strength on the tips of her fingers – someone who might need protecting, like your mother would have you believe, but Phoebe bares her teeth in a vicious growl that sends ripples of cold shame down your vertebrae.

You look at her wraith of a body and think to yourself, *Oh, I will die for you.*

But you can't tell her this.

Because not only can she see you – not only does she need you – but you need her, and all that sticky initial shame breeds in your throat. You raise your hands to your neck, slow; and Phoebe's grip loosens, just the slightest bit, on her baseball bat.

"Are you – are you okay?" Her elbows lower a fraction before she repositions her hands on the bat's handle. "You look sick," she says, bending forward just so to peek at your neck.

You tighten your own grasp and attempt to scurry from her, just an inch and nothing more. This retreat of yours shocks you, as it does her, and you have to hang your head to let all that shame fester at the bottom of your brain stem.

"I can help you," she says, urgent now. "Do you need help?"

You shake your head. Why would you need help when she's here with you?

While her eyes narrow to slits, you don't notice anything despondent in her gaze; in fact, you see the edges of the sun in her pupils, reflecting the rosy-toned hue of desperation as she swings the bat down to her side.

She offers her free hand. It's shaking. She's shaking.

"May I touch you? Help you stand? *Can* you stand?"

You stand.

She jumps back, her bat poised and ready once more.

You stare at her, stare at her hands and how she's still shaking, stare at her eyes and how they're still shining.

She says, "You look cold. Are you cold?"

What is it about you that makes her think you're ill? You dare to break eye contact with her, glancing at your body – your stone-gray skin, the cobalt twinges of your toes. Your hair drips wet. Maybe you should be cold.

You shake your head again, your hand firm around your neck, like you're forcing yourself to move in a manner she won't think is worrisome. You know the longer you sit here in the mud will heighten the chance of her noticing you aren't quite like her. That's why she's trying to get a look at your neck; she must recognize pieces that will send you straight back to the water.

You are wary of venturing up to her house, all the yellow light coming from the lamp by the front door. Would that betray the color of your skin further? Would she gaze into your eyes and find life she hadn't known existed? And what about your hands, your feet? Your face, too – would she see herself, or would she see a monster?

"Okay," she says. "*Okay.*" Then, she nods her head, slides up onto the grass that parts into a trail leading into her backyard. With a thumb tossed behind her, she points at her house. "I'm gonna go get you, uh, *something.*"

You wonder what she means by that – until you catch the quick beats of her eyes drifting down your body. Those wavers only last a breath, not anything monumental, but they're notable enough to you, who, against your better judgment, had never considered your natural state of undress to be offensive to someone not used to such things.

You give a twitch of your head, which parts your hair over your shoulders. Like two dark curtains, your hair protects yourself, protects *her*; she continues to study you, and those beats of her eyes – she was never uncomfortable on her behalf, only on yours. Her cheeks, the rosy-toned hue of desperation, that lingers deep in her skin.

"Can you walk?" She shuffles her feet a little, moving to approach you but unsure if she should. She's surveying you again, can't get enough of you, and you suppose you're doing the same to her – this woman you've guarded for four months.

Baby steps, you start to walk.

The tension in her shoulders melts to the spongy meadow below. You plant your feet in the places she plants hers. Her feet are smaller than yours, though this is no surprise to you; after she finally stands next to you, you discover you are a tree to her sapling.

Like the stones at the bottom of the lake, the wood on her porch is smooth against your heels. You loiter by the nearby rocking chair as she enters the house, smaller in size now that you're this close to the brick. It suits her. This rocking chair is chipped in places and dented in others. This suits her more. Somehow, you know this to be true.

A heartbeat later, Phoebe returns, a thick wool blanket drawn over her arms. The bat is gone, but you sense it nearby. She wouldn't let it stray far, not when she continues to inspect you like you might attack her – and this makes sense. You are a creature who rose from the waters to stand in the creek behind her house.

She unfolds the blanket, rises on her tiptoes, and drapes it over your shoulders.

"There," she whispers, patting the blanket, dusting it off. "Is that okay?"

You don't know how to tell her the fabric crawls across your skin, so you shrug instead. This seems to get across to her, for she nods and sighs. "Yeah, I'm sorry about that. I – I don't know how to–"

She sits on the steps, leaving enough space for you to sit beside her. You do, after a moment; and once you are next to her, pulling the blanket closer to you, she speaks, again attempting to help you however she can.

"I don't, like – look, I know you've–" She sucks her bottom lip in her mouth. "I've seen you – out there." You watch her wave her hand at the creek, the way the yellow porchlight dances across the silver rings around her knuckles. "I thought I was imagining things. It wouldn't be the first time, but… it felt different yesterday."

She turns to look at you. "Did someone hurt you? Drop you off here?"

You shake your head.

"I know this women's shelter," she says. "They can help you if you need it."

Then, she says, "Lemme see your neck."

Your hand has never left your throat, and you don't see that happening now, never mind Phoebe's delicate coaxing. This hot feeling in your arms, down your chest – it wasn't what you expected, wasn't what you heard your mother boast about when she healed the broken parts of her chosen mate. You're meant to be dominant, the one who bends those around you, strong and capable and mysterious and enticing in only the best ways. And you wonder – you wonder if this is *meant* to be different for you; after all, you were the one to attract the eyes of someone of the same gender.

Phoebe's nostrils flare, her eyes narrowing the littlest bit again. Three lines form between her eyebrows. "Right, okay – I didn't mean to scare you. We can start simple." When she nods her head this time, she asserts herself. "What's your name?"

"I don't have a name," you say to her. Your voice escapes all wrong, too soft and too loud, scratching at the cracks of your lips as if it were laden with bubbling acid. You feel it dripping down your chin.

From the pocket of her sweatshirt, Phoebe procures a tissue and presses it to your mouth. She's quick, efficient, and you want to bite her hand, her wrist, everywhere and nowhere; but Phoebe is also soft, like you; loud, like you; and she says, "It's okay. You don't need that right now." She wipes you dry, patting the corners of your lips for good measure. "What are names anyway?" she muses with an easy grin. Her teeth, what you can see, are crooked. "I didn't remember my name at first. I think I was happier like that, when I didn't know who I was."

That hand of hers drops to your shoulder, where it meets your neck, and bumps against your hand around your throat. "You know," she says, crumbling up the tissue soaked in your saliva, "I thought those were scratches on your face, but they... they look like whiskers, almost – not like a cat's," she adds, a reference she assumes you'll get. "No, not like a cat's... maybe more like a – like a fish. Isn't that funny? What person has fish whiskers?"

This joke of hers jolts your hand down to rest at the hollow of your throat. When your fingers curl, she glances at your neck. Her eyes, deep set in her skull, blink for a moment too long. She mouths something to herself and rocks from side to side, tossing her head over her shoulder to look through the screen of her front door. The wind whipping up from your lake rattles the aluminum.

For the first time, you think she might run. She's squirming more, avoiding your eyes.

For the first time, you think you are now the dominant one, so you take her small hand in yours and guide it to your neck.

She winces at the skin contact, a sharp screech that rivals the song of the cicadas. While your body's temperature is lower than hers, you warm at her touch. Your pulse – it leaps at her fingertips tracing the length of your gills, peaking at the dips below your ears and curving around to the front of your neck, disappearing right before the arches of your collarbones. She feathers along the edges of the slips of skin, the tip of her tongue bulging out her cheek as she continues to stroke your neck long after you remove your hand from hers.

When she cradles both sides of your neck with her palms, you spy her eyes shining again under the porchlight. "You're not battered like me," she whispers. "You're the furthest thing from it, aren't you?"

And she repeats her first words to you – "Why are you here?"

What can you say to her? Would anything be enough? She's sitting beside you, her thumbs now slicking past the parts of you most essential for your survival in the water, and you have no words that can possibly encompass all you wish to say.

Love, your mother used to tell you. That was what led her and your siblings to the land. Oh, love – you suppose it must be patient, blind, to force you to remain unseen for so long. Oh, love – you chortle at the lapping of her thumbs over your neck, the quaint slapping mimicking the echo of waves upon the muddy shores of your lake, motions that always calmed the rush in your stomach as you slumbered.

You want to give this to her.

She labeled herself *battered* with your throat in her hands.

And because you are not as confident in your hands, you keep them clutching the blanket around your body when you dive into the crook of her neck. And right here, in the crook of her neck, you kiss her – and your mother was right; it does taste like cinnamon.

She wilts under your mouth. Her sounds, the voice she shared in the woods makes another appearance. Where it used to be raw with exhaustion, it is now raw with that desperation threatening to jump from the pores in her face. That rosy hue leaks all over her cheeks when you pull away from her, but your glimpses cut themselves short; she's threading her fingers through the hair at the back of your head, right where her palm becomes one with the curve of your skull. As your breath hitches in your chest, she draws you into her neck again, again – again, you lay your mouth over her pulse point and kiss.

"Why?" she whispers.

You must respond to her, yet you struggle to find the words necessary to please her. So, in all your unstable might, you say, "I heard you."

You're by her neck, your lips tasting that spice your mother labored and agonized to secure from that man hiding away in his Appalachian holler. It's *hard*, your mother warned. You need *to work* – and all that anticipation of labor and agony dissipates at Phoebe's fingers kneading your scalp. This isn't hard. This isn't *work*. This is simple, sweet.

"Please," she says, "I don't want to let you go now that I know you're real."

And you don't want to let her go either, but dawn is coming. Fatigue will soon overwhelm you – and you think that's the cruelest part of this: you are nocturnal, like your mother. And Phoebe's studying you, the knowledge of your reluctance to leave etched all over her face – in her shining, shining eyes; in the concave structure of her cheeks; in her parting lips.

"Please," she repeats, and she says, "Take me with you."

"No," you say, as you take her head between your hands. "Take *me*."

From your shoulders, the blanket pools at your elbows. It cinches around your waist. She fiddles with the fabric, a hand lingering at the nape of your neck.

Has it felt like four months to her? You know the sun has risen and set and carried its own burdens, though it seemed like a blink to you. A day is a week is a month is a minute passing in the creek behind her house.

She kisses your mouth. She kisses you and kisses you – and how could you have ever anticipated this sensation when it's as natural as your gills and the blue twinge in your toes?

Even this tastes like cinnamon.

TO BE HUMAN
Joanna Marsh

Taro wondered, as his arms burned from the effort of swimming day after day, night after night – was he the first kappa to see the ocean? So many rivers and streams flowed to the ocean, but it had been no more real than he or any river spirit was to humans.

Ha. And how dangerously real he might have become to them, if he'd stayed.

They'd…dug into his home. They built buildings to filter his water and drink it! And, in those buildings, *scientists* aplenty. Since the sun had risen on Japan, his family had lived in its rivers and even been seen a time or two. It had been fun, even! But modern mortals weren't the drunk fishers his ancestors had teased. They could record what they saw. They could be believed.

They could hunt.

The ocean salt stung at Taro's eyes. Not grief; only the salt. He had nothing to grieve – he would find a new home away from all mortal eyes. Antarctica, mortals called it. The south-most point of the world, colder than mortals could live in, but a kappa could try.

And, on the way, a limitless supply of fish!

Every fish Taro ate, he first checked for a human face. Were there mermaids still in these waters? Or were they gone too, lost to the appetites of aspiring immortals? He found no mermaids, which troubled his heart. Still, his stomach was overjoyed!

And so was he now. For there it was. Land, ice – Taro wondered when he'd grown to ignore the water's deeper chill. Around him were flightless black birds with white bellies, snatching at fish. They circled him when they'd finished eating. Ah, new friends! Wonderful!

They danced together in the water and, when his new friends went back to land, Taro followed.

The group broke the water's surface and finally a chill Taro couldn't ignore slapped his face. And the water in his dish, his last reminder of home, froze solid. It was like winter at home, but ever so much worse.

His new friends darted away when Taro screamed! The pain of the cold air cut through his mind and pierced his eyes! Without sight, barely able to feel the water around him, Taro bumped into the icy land. Snow crunched beneath his webbed hands and cut like glass. He pulled himself up onto the shore. Flipped and let his shell protect him from the chilly ground.

But he'd made it! Free of the humans!

His new friends bumped into him with belly and beak. In their warbles, Taro heard concern. He laughed, hearty and deep.

"I am still alive! No need to fret! You mistake me, I am sure, for one of your own as I am of your size and have a bird-like bill. But see my scales and shell! See how my skull contains a bowl of now-frozen river water! I am Taro, the first kappa to walk on Antarctica!"

Should he have considered the danger of this place's cold to a river spirit? Perhaps. But it was too late!

One by one, they accepted this and went on their way. No being could lay on its back forever and let life escape them, so Taro followed. His friends walked in a fun shuffle that he tried to imitate – it would not do to offend the locals! The movement made his pain spike up now and again, but he continued.

His new friends wandered to a collective of their sort where one nuzzled with another and formed circles of warbling. Part of Taro panged at their closeness. He was the first kappa to make it to Antarctica. And thus the only.

But he was not so easily defeated! He watched as parents fed young ones and shuffled atop eggs. He swore then and there he would protect these eggs and these fine folk from any danger. They would be his community. They would be his companionship. They would be his comfort.

"From this day to my dying day, I vow I will repay your hospitality!" Taro shouted to the masses.

Some turned and looked at him for a moment with tiny black eyes. Then they vomited more fish for their children.

His work began the very next day. Taro followed his new friends back to the beach and into the waters. The chill was almost soothing compared to the air's sting. He gathered his breakfast bite by bite. So did his friends. And then...

A sleek shape, covered in wet brown fur, moved towards their group! It lunged at one of them, its jaws wide and teeth sharp! But Taro shoved himself into its path – its fangs chipped on his shell! Bubbles bloomed around kappa and foe as he yelled to scare the beast away.

It did not dare a second attempt. Its slippery form vanished into the dark, away from his folk. When Taro looked back at them, they had scattered for safety. Wise tactics. He nodded with approval.

Taro, his belly full and his spirit robust from the defense of the innocent, broke the water's surface and moved to the icy shore. But his strokes slowed when he beheld a new shape. It was knee-deep in the water – well, one of its legs was. The other was raised to serve as an arm, the claw at its end clearly meaning to pluck some fish from the waters. From head to toe, and there was little of the being but head and toes and legs between them, its skin was a smooth white.

Like the snow on the ground had rolled into a ball and sprouted legs.

Taro approached with slow purpose, for it was never his intent to startle. How welcome another friend would be! But, as he drew closer, he heard something that made his heart flutter. The being *spoke,* quiet muttering to himself! And more than that…

"You speak Japanese!"

The being squawked and fell into the water.

Taro couldn't help but laugh, of course! His kind were tricksters; they delighted in mischief!

But the being stood up and glared. Black eyes burned into him. Then he looked away. "It is *not* funny." The words came out in a mumble. Taro had to lean in to hear the being. If it was warmer, the water in his bowl might have dripped out. He opened his bill to apologize, but the being spoke again. "I thought I heard someone near the penguins. Someone shouting like an *idiot.*"

Taro gasped. The lack of manners startled him! He had sworn an oath of fealty and this stranger dared mock that?

"You have to leave."

And the rudeness continued!

"Leave? I have only just arrived!" Taro's journey had been the stuff of legends! Months he'd spent in the sea, swimming for a new home for he had none to return to!

"Yes and you need to leave immediately."

Months! Legends!

"Listen to me, stranger with the face of a whale and the legs of a mortal man…" For it struck Taro that the smooth and white of this fellow's skin was not just like snow, but like whales he had seen on his swim…

"My name is Yukio."

"Yes, yes, pleased to meet you!" He bowed to show his respect for this Yukio who had done nothing to earn it. "My name is Taro." Introductions complete, he continued his thought, "Listen to me, Yukio – you do not own this land! You have no right to ban me from it! Furthermore, it is large and can be shared! We need not quarrel!"

This, Taro felt, was more than proper for the welcome he had been shown.

Yukio's black eyes looked everywhere but at Taro. At least he was not so bold as to make eye contact!

"You – hmph!" Yukio opened and closed his mouth several times before that last huff. "You understand nothing! Leave this place at once! That is all I have to say to you!" And off he shuffled, further onto the land, his claws crunching the snow beneath him.

What a terrible being! Taro shouted for the last word, "I hope you have enjoyed your breakfast, Yukio!" Ha! For, clearly, he had caught no fish and his stomach (wherever it was) was empty and wanting. Taro hoped Yukio's tongue would never touch food for as long as it remains so uncivil!

Ah! He was a kappa. His kind were tricksters. He could *ensure* Yukio's cruelty was punished. Taro grinned. Oh, yes. He would do his ancestors proud with the pranks that would rain on rude Yukio's smooth skin!

The very next morning, Taro awoke before even his new friends. He snuck to the water and had his fill of fish. And then, in the water, he drifted sated. And he waited. And waited.

Yukio arrived some time later. His black eyes looked bleary with sleep still. Taro swam at the edge of his vision, where the sleepy being would miss his presence entirely. Yukio lifted a limb and started to search for his meal.

At the top of his small lungs, Taro bellowed.

"HEAVE-HO, HEAVE-HO! HEAVE-HO, HEAVE-HO! SORAN, SORAN! SORAN, SORAN!"

As before, his voice made Yukio collapse and splash. The noise of his own voice made Taro's head ache. Forward and back, like a proud drunk fisher, he drew in the net and did the dance. There would be no fish within miles of such a terrible ruckus!

And the pain was a small price to pay for Yukio's slack jaw and wide black eyes.

"What in the world are you *doing*?" Yukio hissed, and how he managed such a forceful exhale when he seemed to have no space for lungs was a mystery to Taro.

Taro blinked, innocent like a fox. "I am performing the soran dance." What fool could not see that? "To bring prosperity and luck in fishing."

"It is *scaring away* the fish, as any *fool* could see!" And Yukio cast his eyes around as if there were fools aplenty. "Now neither of us will catch any breakfast at all! Take your so-called dances–" To speak so foully of the soran! Was there no end to this soft being's rough manners? "–back to where you came from!"

Taro pursed his bill. "How odd, Yukio." He slowed the rhythmic motions, but did not stop. "My dance has gone on for some time and I have had my fill of fish. Yet, I have never known you to catch even one. Perhaps…" And he drew out the pause. "…the flaw lies in *you?*"

Then, how tightly he had to purse his bill indeed to keep the grin off of his face!

"I…" Yukio closed his mouth. "Hmph!" Taro's friends arrived soon after and Yukio fled into the white.

After that, he rose every day with intent and scared the fish from Yukio. He smiled as Yukio sputtered, and heaved as Yukio hissed. And he started to follow Yukio. Yukio told him to stop and Taro simply said, "Oh, Yukio! What a happy sight! How fortunate that we are on the same path this day!"

And then he sang the happy tune children sang when it snowed, no matter how clear the sky. But, if it snowed, he sang of rain.

There was a single day that held no pranks. When Taro opened his eyes, the glint of sun off of the white snow was a knife through his mind. He could not move except to curl into a smaller ball. In time, some of his friends surrounded him. Their warbles comforted and hurt.

Let Yukio have this day to himself. Let him grow complacent, Taro thought and then slept in fits and starts.

The next morning, Taro dove and ate a sensible amount of fish. He did the soran, arms pulling in a net that was not there, water tickling as he submerged and rose. In the corner of his vision, he saw Yukio on the beach. His black eyes were on Taro. His white legs shook.

"Good morning, Yukio! Heave-ho, heave—"

But Taro did not have to scare the fish away that morning. Yukio's loud sobs (he had never heard him be so loud before) worked in his stead. Fat tears ran down his tiny cheeks. Taro ached to see him so pained, no matter how rude he had been. He waddled out of the water to Yukio and placed a webbed hand on the top of his head. It was as smooth as a stone, as soft as a pillow.

"Please…" Taro heard between sobs and sniffles and wails. "Why are you *doing* this? I am so hungry! I am so tired!" Taro moved away, confused, for Yukio was far from blameless and Taro had done nothing to disrupt his sleep! "Every night, I listen for your…*dances* and your *shouting* and, when it stops, I feel so sure every crunch on the snow is a mortal come to snatch us both away! Drawn to your ruckus to *hunt* us and cut us open for their studies! And you will not listen when I ask you to go, when I tell you it is dangerous here for us; instead, you make more noise and you starve me and I do not know *why!*" Then, all sense ebbed as Yukio's tears flowed.

What a fool Taro felt. He had punished another immortal for the very fear that had made him flee his home. Yet…

"Yukio…" He tried to keep his voice soft, soothing as the sound of waves. "You did not tell me of the danger. You simply shouted and insulted me. I felt cruelly done by and reacted as such."

The smaller being sniffed and looked up at Taro. "What? But I…" He looked down, his black eyes surrounded by puffy red. "Oh." The red bloomed in the rest of his face. "Oh."

Yukio sat down on the beach. Taro crouched with him. His long legs shielded his face from Taro. "I have been alone for so long that I forgot all grace." He mumbled into his thighs. "I became a beast and lashed out at you in my fear." He met Taro's eyes. How they sparkled when full of tears. "I beg your forgiveness. I will…I will bring you and the penguins fish for the years to come! I will—"

"Yukio." Taro placed a hand on his smooth skin again. To comfort, of course! "My friends have a sworn protector already. But their sworn protector…he would not object to someone to

talk to and laugh with. So *he* does not become *more* of a beast."
Yes, how sacred the bonds of friendship were! How important
they were to keep from a fall into monstrosity! "I also beg your
forgiveness for all my cruel tricks."

Yukio cut in with a stammering, "You were simply–"

And Taro gave a soft shush and continued. "Perhaps the best
way for us to forgive ourselves and each other is to work together.
Together, we can outsmart any mortal! Together, we will have grace
and dignity and companionship."

With a sniffle, Yukio nodded. They were united by a vow! From
sworn enemies to sworn brothers – what an incredible turn of
events! Taro grinned with pride. Shy Yukio looked away again, but
Taro was certain he too felt this bond and marveled at it!

Then, warbling. When Taro looked, he saw that his friends were
near. Some had jumped into the water to gather their breakfast;
others had wandered to him. They nudged him with their beaks –
it tickled!

"Ha! All is well, my friends! Yukio and I are now allies!" And
they warbled the more at this, for there had been many nights of
Taro's venom towards Yukio. How he appreciated their patience!
He pulled Yukio in with one arm in a companionable fashion.
"You know, Yukio, I believe they will write fantastic stories about
us and our deeds one day!"

From where he was pressed into Taro's chest, Taro heard Yukio
mutter, "But...I don't *want* them to write stories..." Perhaps he
had a point. Stories would draw mortals. Especially stories as full
of peril and heroic deeds as theirs were sure to be!

And, as they walked together towards the collective of Taro's
friends, he argued that perhaps an intense rumor would suffice!

From that instant, things took so positive a turn that even Taro
was amazed.

For instance, there was one day when the pair walked together
down a path Taro had never explored. Taro had done little
exploring, due to the ever-lingering pain of the frozen water in his
bowl. But Yukio had insisted he see this!

"You see there?" Yukio pointed with one leg. Taro did see – an unremarkable cliff-face, jagged ice and rock. "You need to be careful in spots like that. It crumbles." Crumbles? Impossible! It looked solid as a floor! But Taro nodded to humor his friend. "No, really!"

Taro waved a hand to brush away his friend's concern. "Yes, yes, so I will be careful." He walked to the cliff. "I will not approach like this." He hopped up and down. "I will not jump like this." Then he placed his hand on his chest. "This I vow as your friend, Yukio!" Surely, that would be–

"TARO, LOOK OUT!!"

Oh, no, the ground crumbled beneath him! How could he have expected this? If only he had listened more closely to Yukio's soft voice!

But a yank on his wrist saved him from the great fall! There, on more certain ground, Taro laid at Yukio's side. The two friends gasped with the gratitude of those spared death.

He looked at Yukio. "You saved my life. If not for you, I would be a smear on the ground below."

Yukio's black eyes shone with tears. "Don't say that! And don't scare me that way!"

Taro pulled Yukio into his arms. Pressed soft skin against his own scales to reassure them both. Over Yukio's head, he looked at the collapsed ice. "Why is it so fragile?" He looked down. "The ice, I mean."

Yukio's mouth tightened. "Mortals. Even here, the coldest place in the world, it is warmer because of their science. Or because their greed will not allow them to control their science. So my family said."

Yukio had never mentioned his family before. Only that he had been alone for a long time. Did Taro dare ask?

"Yukio, my dear companion…"

But Yukio cut in. "I am quite the runt, you know. My parents were…nearly thirty meters tall." Taro's bill dropped open at that. He could barely fathom such heights! "But they knew it was only a matter of time before they, tall as mountains, were found by mortals."

Yukio walked over to the new edge of the cliff. Taro gasped a bit and made to pull him back, but he simply sat where he was. "So they left." He dropped a stone into the water. "They went down, down, down. Even mortals know so little of the sea. It might have been wiser, Taro..." He looked back at Taro with those big beautiful black eyes. "...if you had gone there too."

Huh. The idea hadn't even occurred to him. And to do so now would be to leave his friends! Leave Yukio! Never! Taro hoped all this could be said with his eyes, for he had no words.

"But..." And away Yukio looked again. "I'm glad you didn't."

In that moment, Taro hardly felt the cold at all.

Morning after morning that followed, Taro continued to rise early. When Yukio arrived at the beach, he always found that breakfast waited for him in Taro's clawed hands. Together, they watched over Taro's friends and ensured the furry smooth beasts did not eat them.

One evening, a realization overwhelmed him. Taro had told his friends of the day's events, of something amusing Yukio had said...and he knew.

"My friends. I think I am in love with Yukio! Or, if not love just yet, a strong affection in a sense other than friendship!"

Some turned their heads from one side to another. Some warbled. Some vomited food for their children.

He nodded his agreement. "Yes, yes, perhaps I *should* have realized sooner!" For, truly and surely, Taro could not call what he felt for Yukio a match to what he felt for these incredible folk around him! His heart did not beat faster for them. He did not smile at the thought of them.

This left only one thing to consider.

"How best to court Yukio? Do I even dare to court him?" Taro looked at his friends for an answer.

At that moment, they had none. But, days later, Taro had the good fortune to witness something fascinating. One of his friends had, gripped in their wings, a small stone. They waddled with it past several others until they found their intended. Then they gave up the stone. For a moment, he was confused. But the pair began to cuddle together, apart from the group. Then it was all clear as ice.

His friends had a ritual of love! Taro would recreate it for Yukio! It was foolproof!

But… how to find just the *right* stone? He set to work immediately. The first few he discarded simply because he had no direction. He knew, at least, it could not be as simple as the first he picked up off the ground! No, to show Yukio his affection, he needed to devote himself fully to the task! From there, he developed opinions.

"Too rough!"

"Too oblong!"

"Too sharp!"

Thus, he discerned his heart longed for a smooth round stone… So for hours, he searched and tossed stones over his shoulder. There were times he thought he was close, only to discover his perfect stone was a seashell.

But there it was, at long last. White and smooth and round as the moon. It surpassed even his dreams! Taro knew he had to give it to Yukio with haste.

Fortuitously, Yukio was there behind him, his head tilted. "Taro? What are you doing?"

A legendary figure like Taro did not squawk when startled. He did not lose all trace of his senses at the sight of his intended. He did not shove his courtship gift towards his intended and say, "I found this rock! It reminds me of you – smooth and beautiful!" He did not stand with his ill-thought-out words adrift in the air like paper lanterns. And he did not run and dive into the sea before his intended could react.

All of this having been said, Taro found himself (through unrelated events, of course) in the sea, deep in thought of his next move.

What could make Yukio feel as special as Taro felt he was? What could make him consider Taro as a loved one rather than a sworn brother, as had been their standard? He had no answer when he inevitably emerged from the water hours later, but Yukio had gone, so he did not need answers just yet.

The next day, the pain in his bowl grew so great he could not grasp answers for anything.

Taro stayed, curled into a ball and surrounded by friends. He thought of Yukio and his stomach turned. What if Yukio starved because he was not there? No, no, Yukio was experienced and clever; he could feed himself.

But...Taro had liked to help.

What if Yukio thought this was a spiteful rejection? The pain blocked all kind and happy thoughts; it filtered and only let evil through.

His friends warbled. Louder and louder. Taro winced. Whimpered. "My friends...please."

"Taro?"

Oh, no, of all the times for Yukio to see him...

Taro tried to smile. "My dear Yukio!" Then he cringed at the volume of his own voice.

"Taro, are you sick?" Yukio came closer. How silly; if Taro was sick, Yukio should stay away to avoid contagion. A claw pressed against Taro's forehead. "No fever. Did you injure yourself?" He looked Taro up and down.

Taro raised his hand and tapped the ice in his bowl. It was agony, lightning behind his eyes, but he had to tell Yukio lest he worry himself to an early grave. "Kappa...we carry river water in the top of our heads." He laughed to try and downplay the pain. "It froze when I came here, as water is wont to do! The pain is... manageable most days, dear Yukio. Today is...less so!"

Yukio narrowed his lovely black eyes. Then he nodded. "Have you eaten?"

"I have not moved from this very spot, I'm afraid! I hope you can forgive me for missing breakfast!" Another laugh. It only made the pain worse and harder to mask. How cruel an irony!

"And you will not move from this very spot." Yukio leaned in and pressed his forehead to Taro's. "I will return soon." Then he was gone. Perhaps he had never been there. Just another glint off the snow. Still, what a lovely glint to see in his time of pain.

Between Taro's eyes closing and opening, Yukio had returned. And he was nearly unbalanced, a heavy pile of fish in one claw as he hopped forward on the other. He dropped the fish beside Taro. "You need to eat to stay strong and recover. Please eat."

How could he refuse? Taro clapped his webbed hands together with a gentle squish. "Let's eat."

When he felt less tortured the next day, Taro gathered his own pile of fish for Yukio. He cursed the ice in his bowl – this food might have been a lovely gesture of… well, love! Now it was a debt. Far from romantic!

But he never got to give Yukio this pile. For Yukio ran to the beach, into the water, deeper than he'd ever gone before. His black eyes were wide and his breath came in heavy gasps. He grabbed Taro's arm and tugged, hissing, "Run, Taro!" And the next word cut through him sharper than his ice-pain.

"*Mortals!*"

Taro wrapped his arms around Yukio and swam for dear life into the horizon. All the space he had for thoughts was devoted to one directive – protect Yukio.

Yukio made a noise in his arms and Taro dared look back. There, in the distance, was the long form of a mortal. It wore a stark dark covering from head to toe. Could it see them as it walked up to the water's edge and…

It walked *into* the water. But how? It was so cold for a mortal's flesh! Further and further, the mortal walked until submerged. Taro wanted to scream. Not even the sea was safe from them.

"Taro…"

He looked to Yukio and the exhaustion of holding him struck at Taro's arms all at once. But he grimaced and struggled on!

"Taro, let me go. We should split up! Save yourself, please."

He would rather die! "I can't! I won't! You mean too much to me!" Taro looked back. The mortal had resurfaced and turned towards…his oblivious friends. His heart tore in half. Which duty to honor? "Yukio…" He sighed. "…take a deep breath." Yukio didn't question why.

And they dove into the water.

The cool familiarity of the sea embraced him, but Taro could not sink into it. He had to get them to safety, to some other beach and fast. Who knew how long poor dear Yukio's tiny lungs could hold for?

He kicked out. Yukio did as well, his long legs a great boon. But Taro did not wish to push him into exhaustion! At the first sign of weakness, after a minute or two beneath the surface, Taro's body moved before his mind.

His mouth pressed to Yukio's. Air flowed from him into Yukio. In that breath was a prayer. *Let him be safe. Even if I am caught, let him be safe.* Taro opened his eyes and looked into Yukio's. They were so wide and beautiful. He hoped Yukio would forgive the invasion; his own face burned at the thought of this wasted first kiss.

On Taro pulled them, with only pauses to kiss Yukio and keep up his supply of air minute after minute. There had to be land nearby…

Aha! There was another shore, smaller and less noticeable than the first Taro had found so long ago. It was perfect. He pulled his precious cargo to the land. Pushed him to the surface and let him breathe freely. Taro, too, breathed in long pants, relieved and exhausted.

The silence wrapped around them, cold as the sea had been. Taro knew he had to apologize. Confess the sinister undertone of his noble deeds, the thrill that his mouth on Yukio's had brought. He looked to his dearest friend, his truest companion, and found that mouth turned into a smile.

"Taro…"

"Yukio, forgive me. I allowed myself to *delight* in saving you. I turned giving you needed breath into an overture I had no certainty would be welcome. My heart raced to have you in my arms, even as I swam to safety for you!" He bowed deep in his shame. "For I love you, Yukio, and would do anything to keep you safe. But—"

"Taro." Yukio had started to laugh. "I can hold my breath for much, *much* longer than that brief dip. Furthermore, I can swim of my own power. And have for *years*. I am as much water spirit as you, even *if* mortals call my kind *ningen*."

Taro's bill dropped open.

"...I see."

Yukio stood and walked towards the water, that smile still present. "Let me show you." Like he was dragged by a line, Taro followed.

Below the waves, the two drifted. Taro barely moved at all, but kept his wide eyes on Yukio as he swam such graceful circles around him. Some deep beautiful sound washed forward in the water. Then Taro realized Yukio was the source of the song!

Taro's eyes went wider still. Was there no end to how exceptional Yukio was? He had surely only seen the still surface thus far.

Yukio spun forward and, without excuse or explanation, pressed his lips to Taro's bill. A true and unmistakable kiss. Then, he drifted backwards, his eyes downcast.

No, Yukio, Taro prayed to the waters as he swam to take him in his arms. His webbed hand brushed against Yukio's soft smooth cheek. Yukio looked up and Taro gave as joyous a smile as he ever had felt.

Don't hide. Not ever again. Show me the depths of you.

AUTHOR BIOS

A J ROCCA *(WRR S639847 E1)* is a writer and English teacher from Chicago. He specialized in the study of speculative fiction while pursuing his M.A., and now he writes both SFF criticism as well as his own fiction. Sometimes he produces his essays as videos, and these can be found on his YouTube channel: BlueMorningStar. The rest of his work can be found collected at his website: ajrocca.com.

ARCHER BEAU *(Where Shore Meets Sea)* is a queer writer and artist. Archer has never met a creative medium she didn't want to get her hands all over, though writing persists are her one true love. Archer writes primarily romances, occasionally with a dark twist or a monster kiss. She can be found on twitter @archerbeau_.

B C FONTAINE *(Nemesis)* Brooksie C. Fontaine's love of storytelling dates back to her unusual yet idyllic childhood. As a homeschooled student, she could often be found in the uppermost branches of a tree, reading or scribbling in a notebook. Fontaine was accepted into college at fifteen, into graduate school at nineteen, and is now enrolled in her second MFA program. Her work has appeared in a plethora of literary magazines, most recently *Eunoia Review* and *Quail Bell.* Her portfolio can be viewed via thecaffeinebookwarrior.com. By day, she works as a tutor and art instructor, and is caffeinated most of her waking hours.

CALEN MACDONALD *(What's Growing in Fort Cunningham)* is a 6'8" tall writer and graduate student. He grew up in Palmetto, Florida and now lives in Ithaca, NY. He spends his free time rowing, crocheting, and being 6'8". He's also 6'8".

CARMAN C CURTON *(The Taste of Stars, Stay, The Last Giant)* consumes caffeine while writing a series of microstories called QuickFics, which she leaves in random places for people to find. You can find her on Twitter and Facebook @CarmanCCurton.

DAN MICKLETHWAITE *(Adonis in Furs)* writes stories in a shed in the north of England, some of which have recently featured in PodCastle, IZ Digital, and NewMyths. His debut novel, *The Less than Perfect Legend of Donna Creosote,* was published by Bluemoose Books. Follow him on twitter @Dan_M_writer, and visit danmicklethwaite.co.uk for more information.

DOMINICK CANCILLA *(Instrument of Destruction)* As the author of *Disneyland for Vampires, Zombies, and Others with VERY Special Needs,* Dominick considers himself the country's foremost expert on Disney vacations for sentient non-humans. To be fair, there's not a lot of competition for that title.

EDY LUE *(At Dawn)* is a nonbinary lesbian artist from rural Appalachia with an MFA in Creative Writing from the Bluegrass Writers Studio at Eastern Kentucky University. Their work has appeared in *Things Improbable,* Kentucky Philological Review, EKU's literary journal Aurora, EKU's Archives After Dark 2020: Unlocking Possibilities, and The STAY Project's Appalachian Love Story zine. They were a finalist in fiction for the Bluegrass Writers Studio's 2020 Emerging Writer Awards, a semi-finalist for Ember Chasm Review's novel excerpt contest, and are currently the alumni editor for the special section in Jelly Bucket's forthcoming issue, which highlights nonbinary/trans voices.

ELI HAYDEN LOFT *(Pregnant, Vaguely Apocalyptic)* is a fiction editor and writer with great love for bleak tones and human foibles. Despite writing her first sad short story at 11, she is only now sharing her depressing work with the world. She works for Quill & Crow Publishing House as a line and developmental editor to further contribute to dark fiction. She resides in Switzerland, where neighbors fear she's a vampire due to her avoidance of the sun, people, and life in general.

ELLEN DENTON *(Adam and Galeta)* is a freelance writer living in the Rocky Mountains with her husband and two demonic cats who wreak havoc and hell (the cats, not the husband). Her writing has been published in over a hundred magazines and anthologies. She as well has had an exciting life working as a nuclear physicist, a rodeo clown, a Navy seal, and an exotic dancer in the crew lounge of the starship Enterprise. (Writer's note: The one-hundred-plus publication credits are true, but some or all of the other stuff may be fictional.)

E M LAMDAN *(Changeling)* is a neurodivergent, Jewish speculative fiction writer and Tetris expert living in Iowa City, IA. Their work focuses predominantly on de-assimilation and solidarity, and they are currently working on their debut novel. They can be found on Twitter @emlamdan.

IRIS BLACK *(Oddnoq)* I am a California native, born in Pasadena in the late 1960s. One of my earliest memories is of the moon landing in 1969. I am married and have two kids who are the best, and weirdest things to happen to me. I write when I can, in snatches here and there. I have a collection of irises – the flowers, not the eye-parts. I hoard yarn. I can drive a stick-shift. I'm bad at writing about myself.

J MOFFATT *(Coiled in Shells of Loneliness)* Jennifer lives with her family in BC, Canada, and enjoys writing diverse love stories. She is working on her second novel and can be found on Twitter @JMoffattWrites.

JAMES DICK *(The Leafer)* is an author, actor, screenwriter, and director from Toronto, Ontario. He debuted as a short fiction writer in 2020 with the initial publication of his story, "Paper Mite Revolution", in the March issue of Blank Spaces Magazine, to which his new story, "The Leafer", is a follow-up. "Paper Mite Revolution" was reprinted in Dark Cheer: Cryptids Emerging (Volume Blue) from Improbable Press. Since then his work has appeared or is upcoming in Analog Science Fiction and Fact, Dark Dragon Publishing, Ghost Orchid Press, and Blank Spaces.

JAMIE PERRAULT *(Not All, But a Few)* is a queer nonbinary veterinarian living and working in the Midwestern United States. They are married to a wonderful spouse and raising twin five year olds. They can be found online at their website jamieperrault. com or on Twitter @awritinghope, or contacted via email at JamieWritesHope@gmail.com.

JEN FRANKEL *(Entrée)* is the author of the Blood & Magic series, Feral Tales, and the Amazon-bestselling Undead Redhead. Her work has appeared across North America and the world including for Eerie River Publishing, Dark Helix Press, Amazing Stories, and (upcoming) Analog.

JENNIFER LEE ROSSMAN *(The Flatwoods Monster And The Little Green Men)* (they/them) is a queer, disabled, and autistic author and editor from the land of carousels and Rod Serling. They hope to one day be a mysterious and reclusive local legend. Follow them on Twitter @JenLRossman and find more of their work on their website http://jenniferleerossman.blogspot.com.

JEREMY PAK NELSON *(The Other Mid-Autumn)* haunts the canals of Manchester charting ley lines that connect the city to his birthplace, Hong Kong. He is preoccupied with outdated methods of putting words on paper, and when not sifting through his hoard of stationery enjoys folk fiddle, accordion, and the game of Go. He can be reached on Twitter @jpaknelson, and online at www.jeremypaknelson.com.

JOANNA MARSH *(To Be Human)* is a Canadian writer of short stories, comic books, and more. She was awarded the runner-up position for the Top Cow Talent Hunt in 2016 and published a short comic, "Immortal Longings", in a 2018 issue of Aphrodite IX: Ares #1. One of her comics, "Buffer", with incredible artist and friend Vixie Bee, was part of the Prism Award-nominated anthology Group Chat by POMEgranate Press. She also had a short story, "Bug Hunt," included in the Aurora Award-nominated fiction anthology *Nothing Without Us*.

KELLY STRONACH *(Sluagh)* began writing in middle school and loved it so much that she went on to get a Bachelor's in Immunology. Nowadays, when she isn't in the lab, Kelly spends her time with kendo, traveling, incompetent drawing, semi-competent cosplay, and working on one of the many books she can't seem to finish.

KELLYE GUINAN *(The Reason for Lingering)* is a queer writer and lover of all things language. She is also a big fan of being a cliché, so you can typically find her reading romance novels and drinking coffee. When she manages to stop reading, she works at her local library and scribbles dark stories that span several genres.

LAURA J KELLY *(The Scent of Change)* began her college education majoring in English literature. She changed to the sciences after her abysmal performance in the required foreign language course forced her to drop the class. She continued writing fiction on and off for her enjoyment while completing advanced degrees, pursuing a career as a university professor, and publishing in professional journals. Now she writes in various genres though her primary focus is fantasy.

LAURA SIMONS *((Ir)reconcilable Divinities)* is a Dutch writer with some Antillean mixed in, who is deeply enamored with all things folklore and fantasy. She is a storyteller of all sorts, which is why she has a podcast, a webcomic, and a blog to share her original fairy tales, novellas, and short fantasy stories. Her podcast Patchwork Fairy Tales is filled with original, inclusive stories with intentionally diverse casts. It includes both typical fairy tales and light urban fantasy stories and can be found on most podcasting apps. All Laura's work and social media can be found at her website laurasimons.com.

LEE F PATRICK *(The Defender)* lives and writes in Calgary Alberta, writing science fiction, fantasy and mixed genres. Five novels (soon to be more) and over twenty short stories and poems have been published. Over a dozen shorts are currently out looking for publication opportunities. In 2018, Lee was nominated for the Prix Aurora Award in Poetry. Lee lives with a Linux guru/writer and several distracting kittehs. Check Lee's Facebook page for upcoming events, publications and other news.

MARA LYNN JOHNSTONE *(The Bone Fairies)* grew up in a house on a hill, of which the top floor was built first. She split her time between climbing trees, drawing fantastical things, reading books, and writing her own. Always interested in fiction, she went on to get a master's degree in creative writing, and to acquire a husband, son, and three cats. She has published several books and many short stories. She writes, draws, reads, and enjoys climbing things. She can be found up trees, in bookstores, lost in thought, and at: MaraLynnJohnstone.com twitter.com/MarlynnOfMany MarlynnOfMany.tumblr.com facebook.com/AuthorMara.

NAOMI ESELOJOR *(Krest)* is a speculative fiction writer from Nigeria. Her works are in and forthcoming at 365 tomorrow's, tree and stone magazine, Omenana magazine, Hexagon magazine and Improbable press. You can find her on Twitter as NEselojor or Instagram as naomieselojor.

PATRICK HURLEY *(Sung Heroes)* has had fiction published in Factor Four, Galaxy's Edge, New Myths, and Abyss & Apex. He's a graduate of the 2017 Taos Toolbox Writer's Workshop and a member of Codex, SFWA, and the Dreamcrashers. Find out more about his work at patrickhurleywrites.com.

SARAH TOLLOK *(Flower)* Multi-genre writer Sarah Tollok lives in the beautiful Shenandoah Valley of Virginia. When she isn't writing about cryptids, she can be found in her garden or watching her offspring play basketball. Her biggest lament in life is that she will never be able to read *all* the books. Sarah thanks her husband for his unwavering support of her writing. Her debut book, *Bookstories,* will be published in 2024 with Balance of Seven. You can find Sarah on twitter and Goodreads by name, on Instagram as @Sarah_Tollok_author_reader, and at SarahTollok.com.

STACY NOE *(The Creeping Horror)* lives in the foothills of the mountains and enjoys writing cozy, modern fantasy extolling how magical it is. They have fiction in The 100 Word Project, Worm Moon Archive, and the 2022 Queer SciFi anthology 'Clarity.' You can find them at StacyNoe.com and on Twitter @proseyposey.

SUMMER AUSTIN *(The Sparkhunter)* is a professional daydreamer, constantly concocting epic adventures and jotting down new ideas for stories, compliments of her overactive imagination. She spends the majority of her time chasing two young offspring on daily real-life adventures, so her time to write is currently limited. However, she loves writing so much that she squeezes it into her schedule every chance she gets. She has a bachelor's in Writing Studies and has published various short pieces with several novels currently in the works, plus a serialized fantasy called Dance With Death premiering on Kindle Vella in October 2022.

THOMAS BADLAN *(Taniwha)* has wanted to be a writer for as long as he can remember. He studied Creative Writing at the University of Derby and currently works as a literacy teaching assistant in a Manchester High School. He is a long-standing member of the Manchester's Monday Night Writers group. He has had five previous stories published with World Weaver Press, Future Fiction, Eibonvale Press and Brain Mill Press.

VĚRA BENEDEKOVÁ *(The Ripening)* writes horror, sci-fi and fantasy. Though writing is her one great passion in life, she also enjoys drawing, embroidery, photography, and tilling the land of her plot near the forests of beautiful northern Bohemia. She also works as a caretaker of her nine gorgeous cats.

Dark Cheer: Cryptids Emerging (Volume Blue)
Tales for those who never outgrew goosebumps

Here are stories for lovers of chupacabras and hulders,
griffins and gargoyles.
Here be darkly cheery tales of ancient creatures
beneath still waters, in the attic,
or the shadows right by the bed.

Herein an autistic hiker meets a cryptid
who wants her camera;
a Japanese tanuki seeks his fox daughter;
and two women fall in love, never
mind one's a swamp monster.

Here be stories of changelings, nix, and
demons adopted, of hungry kraken
and cryptids we'd see if only, if *only*
we looked into treetops, behind doors, or in
our own back gardens.

Here there be monsters.
Thank all the gods.

Dark Cheer: Cryptids Emerging (Volume Silver)
For the lovers of things that go bump in the night

Here be stories of South African grootslang
and bayou grundylow,
tales of elementals, jackelopes,
and flying motels.

Within you'll find tiny leviathans and rock whales,
cambion and kelpie,
a girl between time,
and a man who saves a gun's life.

These are stories of cryptids who sing or swim or
save us, living side-by-side so often unseen
…and then seen.

So very much seen.
When we look.

**Get These and More Great Stories
at
ImprobablePress.com**

From ancient gods rising, to road trips on the trail of cryptids, from romance to mystery to adventure,

Improbable Press specialises in sharing the voices and tall tales of women, LGBTQIA, disabled, BIPOC, and neurodiverse people.
Come along for the ride.

Sign up for our newsletter *Spark*
at Improbablepress.com
Find us on Twitter @so_improbable
Instagram @improbablepress

Improbable
PRESS

www.ingramcontent.com/pod-product-compliance
Lightning Source LLC
Chambersburg PA
CBHW021946010726
47493CB00016B/1855